SWAMP GAS

SWAMP GAS

Nicole Paolini

THOMAS
DUNNE
BOOKS

St. Martin's Press
New York

THOMAS DUNNE BOOKS.
An imprint of St. Martin's Press.

www.stmartins.com

Design by Heidi L. F. Eriksen

Library of Congress Cataloging-in-Publication Data

Paolini, Nicole.
    Swamp gas / Nicole Paolini.—1st ed.
        p. cm.
    ISBN 0-312-26235-3
    1. New Orleans (La.)—Fiction. 2. Polish Americans—Fiction. 3. Women
lawyers—Fiction. 4. Elections—Fiction. I. Title.
PS3566.A5945 S9 2000
813'.6—dc21   00-024866

First Edition: June 2000
10 9 8 7 6 5 4 3 2 1

SWAMP GAS

Prologue

The New Orleans branch of the Polish-American Small Businessmen's Association was holding its monthly meeting in the back room of Franky and Johnny's Restaurant. The eatery was a few blocks from the Mississippi River, in a slightly run-down frame building that shared its corner on Tchopitoulas Street with a rutted, clamshell-paved parking lot. The floors were scarred black-and-white tile the coin-operated bowling machine operated sporadically, but the food was some of the best in town.

"Let me ask y'all this. Who is the most famous Polish-American you can think of from New Orleans?" David Souchecki looked expectantly across a tableful of sucked-dry crawfish heads, brimming ashtrays, and empty beer bottles at the Association members. His question was met with silence.

A waitress leaned in to place another tray of crawfish on the table. "That's easy," she said. "Stanley Kowalski."

"Yeah, Stanley Kowalski," chorused several voices. *"A Streetcar Named Desire."*

"Unfortunately," Souchecki pointed out, "Stanley Kowalski is fictional."

Souchecki had recently been elected president of the group and was determined to transform it from a social club to an organization of influence. As he watched a member hang a crab claw from his earlobe, Souchecki realized the group had a long way to go, but a man had to have his dreams.

"The problem is," said the proprietor of an Uptown video store, "there aren't too many of us in this city. Hell, there aren't too many of us in the whole state. The Cajuns, the Italians, even the Irish get more press than we do." He sucked sadly on a crawfish. "We're invisible."

"Exactly," said Souchecki, pulling the head off a particularly large and juicy prawn. "That's why I want to do something a little ambitious. I suggest that we sponsor a candidate in one of the elections this fall." He began stripping the shrimp of its little pink legs, wiping them from his thick fingertips onto the paper napkin stuck in his collar. "It's a great way to get publicity."

"But who?" asked another member. "No one knows any of us. Not even you, David. The only people we could get to vote for us would be our wives. Jesus, Eddie couldn't even get that."

Eddie tossed a wadded napkin at the speaker.

"That's why we need someone with at least some name recognition," Souchecki continued. "I've done some research. In an independent campaign, most of the budget is used to inform the voters that the candidate *exists*. If we get someone who's at least a little recognizable, not only will we save some money, we won't be the only ones voting for him."

"We should get somebody that doesn't just appeal to the Polish, too," offered Eddie. "Maybe a woman. Then you've got a lot of built-in votes from the ladies."

"Good point," said Souchecki. "Anybody got any ideas?"

"*Mrs.* Stanley Kowalski," suggested one of the men.

"Wait. I've got someone," piped up a barber from Midtown. "What about that lawyer? The one with the billboard on I-Ten."

"Lana somebody, right?" asked Souchecki, incredulous. "Isn't she an ambulance chaser?"

"Lana Pulaski. No, she's not that bad. She was my next-door neighbor's lawyer when he had some trouble with one of his suppliers. She got him a good settlement."

"She's in my wife's volunteer group," said Eddie. "I think she's in a lot of those networking organizations. And she is well known. I've seen her ads in the *Times-Picayune*."

"Lawyers always make good candidates, right?" said the barber. "And how many other Polish-American, New Orleans women lawyers can you name off the top of your head? Besides, she's lived here all her life. She's Joe Pulaski's kid. Do you guys remember Joe?"

"That's right," said an upholsterer. "He owned a tavern down by the warehouses. He was a good guy. Liked the horses. I think he lives in Florida now. His daughter's office is down on Magazine Street."

"Okay," sighed Souchecki. "I guess that we can talk to her."

"What's she going to run for anyway?" Eddie asked.

"Something local, obviously," said Souchecki. "Maybe city council. Nothing too big."

Seventy-five miles west of New Orleans, Ronnie Prejean was striding nervously across the western edge of Mr. Hebert's cane fields, out where they abutted the Boudreauxs' land. A large roll of bills in Ronnie's pocket pressed into the skin of his thigh, a persistent reminder that he had to stash the money, and fast. Thank God he'd finished the morning's chores and could now hide the cash. He didn't think he could have stood the stress much longer.

He hadn't seen anyone all morning; he did the farm work by himself because Mr. Hebert was too old to get around much anymore. Still, he looked over his shoulder several times as he walked toward the old, half-collapsed storage shed. No one had used the shed for years, and Ronnie figured it would be a safe place to secret the money from his wife. The woman's addiction to the home shopping channel had reached gargantuan proportions. If he hadn't been holding back some of his pay and hiding it in the empty Community Coffee can under the sink . . . Ronnie shuddered. A week before, he'd awoken to hear his wife's voice echoing out of the TV. Trudy Spice, the home shopping pitchwoman, was actually interviewing Wanda on the air about an Extendo-Mop that she'd purchased for the unprecedented low price of $29.95. Then last night, he had come home to a twenty-piece set of Heroes of Nashville commemorative plates stacked on the kitchen table. Hank Williams, Jr., had grinned at him from the porcelain, in mute mockery of Ronnie's dwindling finances. What are we going to do for money when I retire? he'd asked Wanda. We'll make a fortune on this stuff, she insisted, shocked that he would even ask such a question. The plates are collector's items, she told him. They said so on the TV.

Ronnie knew then that the coffee can was no longer secure.

He'd brought a crowbar out with him, and he used it to pry open the splintering wooden door of the shed. To his surprise, he managed to inch it open in one piece. Although sunlight filtered through the cracks in the board walls, it took Ronnie's eyes a minute to adjust to the dimness of the shed. While he waited, he thought nervously about a lab-created emerald tennis bracelet that Mrs. Prejean had been babbling about several days ago. Had she ordered it? She didn't even play tennis!

Ronnie glanced around. Most of the old tools in the shed were so rusted that it was almost impossible to tell what they had been. But in the corner was an old, covered aluminum seed bin, still in pretty good shape. That would be a safe place for the money. It would be protected from the elements. Ronnie pulled the wad from his pocket. The bills were packed in a Zip-Lock bag. He caressed the roll of twenties through the plastic and breathed a sigh of relief. On a good day, without her arthritis acting up and slowing down her touch-tone finger, Wanda could go through that cash in a single afternoon. Ronnie slid his fingertips under the lid of the bin and threw it open.

The smell of decay wafted from the bin. A raccoon must have gotten trapped inside and died. Now where was he going to put the money? Maybe once he cleaned out the carcass, the bin would still be okay. After all, the money was hermetically sealed in plastic. Probably wouldn't soak up the smell too badly. Ronnie peered in the bin. He instantly wished he hadn't.

The skeleton stared up at him from empty eye sockets. No flesh remained on the bones, but a diamond embedded in one of the long, white incisors glinted at him in the fractured light. A heavy gold ring dangled impossibly from a finger bone. Ronnie backed frantically out of the doorway and almost fell down in the mud outside the shed. As he ran in the direction of the road, a truly frightening thought pierced his brain. What if they had tooth diamonds on the shopping channel?

One

The Law Offices of Lana Pulaski and Associates, though plural in title, were singular in reality. Wedged in between a Payless and a five-and-dime, the Offices contained only Lana and her secretary within their walls of imitation wood paneling, and smelled of stale cigarette smoke and routine. Decorating scheme: black vinyl leatherette and drop ceilings. A glance around the waiting room revealed that the Offices were never thoroughly cleaned. A paste of greasy black dust and stray hair filled the crevices where the asbestos tile floor met the paneling. The ashtrays always held a liberal assortment of lipstick-stained cigarette butts. The overall look was deliberate—Lana kept the Offices shabby on purpose, having found that her clients felt at home with its pre–urban renewal atmosphere and six-month-old *People* magazines.

It was a Tuesday in April, and Lana sat at her desk attired in a leopard print dress, the buttons of which strained bravely to contain her. This was a difficult task, for Lana was the sort of person whose entire being—not just her physical self—seemed ready to erupt like a Texas oil gusher that even Red Adair couldn't cap and bring under control. Her fuel reserves did not pass unnoticed by the small woman sitting across from her. Mrs. Hebert was nervous and fretful. She'd related to Lana how her husband had been indicted by a grand jury and taken away by the police that very morning, several weeks after a worker on the couple's farm had stumbled upon human remains in an old shed.

As Lana read through the indictment, she could see the woman observing her covertly, obviously impressed. And, in fact, the woman couldn't help but be awed. Lana's face—round as the full moon and almost as luminescent under a thick layer of orange makeup—glowed from across the desk. The pattern of her dress strobed. Long red nails flashed as she flipped through the documents. The total effect was just short of hypnotic, and probably capable of inducing seizures in high-risk epileptics.

In this workaday uniform—suitable, Lana believed, for the Offices, court, or any occasion—her sturdy frame easily topped six feet, although a percentage of the height was composed of spike heels and hair. The heels, the hair, the tight clothing (underneath, to be consistent, Lana wore garters and a push-up bra) insured that Lana received attention wherever she went. But it was the hair, the four-inch-high–by–foot-wide hair that pulled the look together. Dyed a dubious shade of red and teased into a flip, the ends of which bravely cantilevered above her shoulders at such an angle that it appeared to have an internal structure of rebar, the hair crowned her Lana: Queen of Plaintiffs' Attorneys.

Lana finished her perusal of the warrant and looked up. The woman was now staring at her openly, rapt. Lana raised her right eyebrow (a Greta Garbo eyebrow, so sharply arched, so perfect—just the way that Lana had drawn it on that morning, right above where she'd shaved off the original). The woman's gaze did not waver. Lana let a beat pass. Predictably, the woman became uncomfortable and shifted her gaze to the Loyola University law degree hanging in an ornate gilt frame on the wall behind Lana. She began nervously twisting the strap of the handbag she held in her lap. Satisfied, Lana leaned back in her chair.

"You came here all the way from Thibodaux? That's a long way from New Orleans, Mrs. Hebert. How did you get my name?"

"I saw your ad on the back cover of the Yellow Pages. We got a New Orleans phone book at our house."

Lana smiled, pleased at the new client base being generated by the ad. Now she even had a client from the Cajun parishes, a good hour and a half west of New Orleans. Remarkable. No doubt a TV spot would send hordes of the injured and compromised to her portals. Confident that Mrs. Hebert couldn't read upside-down, Lana picked up a needle-sharp pencil from the jar on her desk and made a quick jot on a Post-it pad: "TV ads." She stuck the pencil into her hair and scratched her scalp with the point.

"Has there been an arraignment, Mrs. Hebert?"

"What's that?"

Lana sighed. The ignorance of the masses—her clients in particular—never ceased to amaze her. "Has your husband been before the magistrate?"

"No, not yet. I came here as soon as they took him away. He's in the parish prison. Can you help us?"

Lana surveyed the woman's plastic rain scarf, her powder-blue polyester overcoat, and the shabby, pilled sweater underneath. "A murder defense can be extraordinarily expensive, Mrs. Hebert. My fees are one-fifty an hour, and two-twenty-five for court time. There's research, legwork, filings . . . A simple murder defense will cost you at least twenty-five or thirty thousand dollars. And that's at the lowest end. If the facts get complicated, there's no telling how much it could cost."

"Like O.J."

Lana groaned inwardly, though at the same time she was reassured of the power of the airwaves. "Probably not that complex, but you've got the idea." TV ads, definitely. Probably during the morning

9

talk shows. Perhaps she should get an 800 number. Something catchy and easy to remember. Like 1-800-BIG-BUCKS. No, too many numbers. 1-800-BIG-BUCK. No, sounded like a gay phone sex number. Lana was lost in numeric reverie when she remembered that Mrs. Hebert was awaiting her advice.

"I don't know about your situation, Mrs. Hebert, but many people finance a defense by taking out a mortgage on their house."

"I don't think we'll have to do that. Years back, they found oil under Dennis's daddy's *vacherie*. He leased to Standard Oil when the market was high. Dennis got it all when his daddy passed."

"I'm sure that was quite lucrative." Lana made a mental checkmark. More important than the innocence of her client (which was frequently and easily enhanced through a little coaching) was his liquidity. The charm bracelets on Lana's wrist jangled cheerfully as she began to take notes.

"Have they identified the victim?"

"They're pretty sure it's Thierry Boudreaux. He disappeared back in . . . had to be almost twenty years ago. We was all at a *fais-do-do*, dancing and all. I can't remember the band. Anyway, Thierry left early and no one ever saw him again. I figured he'd run off with some girl. He had him a diamond set in his tooth, right here." Mrs. Hebert pointed to one of her coffee-stained canines. "There was oil under his place, too, you know. The skeleton had a diamond in the same tooth. There aren't too many people so showy in the parish. It's gotta be Thierry's bones."

"Twenty years ago. I don't think I've ever heard of a murder so old being prosecuted. I'm surprised a grand jury would indict, with the inherent evidence problems."

"I guess they really think it was Dennis. But he's innocent, Miss Pulaski. I swear he had nothin' to do with this."

"What was your husband's relationship to Mr. Boudreaux?"

"He was our neighbor. A bad neighbor. Dennis and Thierry didn't get along. They had a big fallin' out over Thierry's oyster leases. Thierry saw Dennis out on Mink Bayou one day, said he was trollin' for shrimp on his oyster leases, and took a shot at the boat. Almost hit Dennis. But the real fight was after they found the oil. Thierry started arguing that we were sitting on some of his land. It's not true. We had that land surveyed. It's always been in Dennis's family. Then Thierry started sayin' that it had become his property because his cattle had been grazin' on it for years."

"Acquisistive prescription," Lana stated. She would have done the same thing if there were oil under that cow-chip-covered piece of swamp.

"Huh?"

"It's a legal concept. Basically, Mr. Boudreaux was saying that the land had become his through open, uninterrupted use of the property. Were there any court proceedings over the land?"

"Yeah. He sued us a few months before he disappeared."

Lana rolled her eyes toward the yellowing ceiling tiles and thanked the God of Billable Hours that she collected whether she won or lost.

Lana finished with the morning's clients by eleven thirty. Two divorces, a drunk driver, and a will—or "estate planning" as she euphemistically and more profitably called it. Most of her clients' estates were limited to a naugahyde couch and a '76 Dodge Dart, but they all wanted that will. It made them feel like Donald Trump.

Lana needed to get on the road if she was going to meet with Dennis Hebert before his arraignment. She pushed a button on the intercom and a buzzer could be heard in the waiting room outside her office. A good fifteen or twenty seconds passed before Carl answered. He was her secretary and a smart-ass, but had the singularly admirable quality of not breaking into tears when Lana screamed at him, which was often. In fact, her harangues seemed to amuse him more than anything. Sometimes Lana suspected that he was baiting her. Carl could afford to annoy Lana. As the son of Marshall Hope, Lana's mentor, Carl knew he would never be fired. Not for his insubordination, not for his Queer Nation T-shirt, not for the time he put her home phone number in a classified ad for dominatrix services in the *Times-Picayune*. Since Lana was sure Carl could not keep a job anywhere else, she was forced to employ him for Hope's sake. His sarcastic mouth and frequent incompetence only secured his position more firmly.

"No one is left out here," Carl reported. "This will please you, though. The guys are here with the sign."

"Good. I'll be right out."

Lana hurried into the waiting room, where a large, wooden sign was clearly visible through the fingerprint smudges on the plate glass window.

The sign was at least six feet wide and painted on both sides. It was white with a border of blue stars surrounding a gold eagle. Superimposed over the eagle in red letters were the words *Lana Pulaski—Attorney General*. Two men in coveralls, one on a ladder and one standing on the sidewalk, were trying to level the sign. It hung crookedly under the moldy eaves of the wrought-iron balcony that ran across the front of Lana's building. "Lift up the right side about half a foot," the man on the sidewalk bellowed, as if to someone very far away. The man on the ladder shortened the chain attached to the left side of the sign.

Lana rapped her knuckles against the inside of the front window. "What are you doing?" she yelled. "You're not supposed to hang it up. I haven't even announced my candidacy yet!"

This comment seemed to induce a measure of confusion in both men, who looked in the window at her, then at the sign, then at each other. They shrugged. Carl grinned.

"Why on earth didn't you stop them?" Lana fumed.

"I thought you might be anxious to see your name up in lights."

Actually, she was. Lana had been contemplating public office since her teens; being a lawyer was too small-time for a woman of her intelligence and vision. The overture from David Souchecki and his Polish-American Small Businessmen's Association came just as she had been gearing up to enter the political arena on her own. Lana liked to think that she'd been spurred into action by the corruption and scandal that had resulted from the legalization of gambling in the state.

As a child, Lana had watched her father, a tavern owner, struggle with an addiction to the racetrack. Time and money that could have been put into his business were siphoned off for the ponies. His losses drove his volatile wife to epic fits of screaming and violence that remained the most unpleasant of Lana's childhood memories. Around Lana's tenth birthday, Joe Pulaski suffered a particularly large setback. Acting on a tip from a racetrack buddy, he put the week's receipts down on a nag that not only failed to win, place, or show—the horse actually stumbled out of the gate, broke a leg, and had to be shot right on the track. When Mrs. Pulaski found out, she broke several barstools, put her fist through the wall, then packed her bags and left her husband and daughter for good. Joe never made another bet. But Lana was left with a lifelong aversion to gambling. When the state legalized casinos, she was angry. When the former governor was indicted for accepting four hundred thousand dollars to pave the way for a crony's riverboat gaming license, she was livid. Louisiana's politicians often profited off the citizenry, but seldom had they so blatantly exploited their constituents' weaknesses. The state needed strong leadership to lead them out of this morass of corruption and vice. Lana knew that she was equal to the task.

Her opposition to gambling justified her campaign, but it was merely the tip of Lana's motivation iceberg. Lurking underneath the waters of her consciousness was the ugly bulk of her desire: She wanted to prove something to the establishment that had ignored and belittled her.

Lana had been at the top of her law school class at Loyola and had expected to secure a prestigious associate position at a premier law firm. All of her fellow law review members found lucrative jobs at the large New Orleans firms by the beginning of their third year. Lana, however, never got beyond a first interview. Taught to dress by her Aunt Flo (who supplied the girls to her father's tavern) and with a working-class New Orleans accent as harsh as any from New Jersey, Lana was rebuffed by every silk-stocking firm in the city. When graduation rolled around, the only offer she had was from Carl's father, for whom she'd been working since high school. Even though she'd gone on to be successful as a plaintiffs' attorney, this rejection had gnawed at her for years. Lana knew that she was better than her peers, and being elected to statewide office would be an effective way of proving it.

Seeing the sign hanging there stirred up pleasant feelings of righteousness and revenge. "What do you think of it?" she asked Carl.

"Very tasteful. But what else would one expect?"

She was tempted to respond that a thirty-five-year-old man with a green buzz cut and a matching emerald ear stud was no arbiter of good taste, but she knew that Carl would just one-up her on the insult. Ignoring his comment, she said, "I'm going out to the parishes. I won't be back for the rest of the day."

Carl smirked. *"Bon voyage, cher."*

Two

Scarlett L'Enfant leaned closer to the bathroom mirror and peered carefully at her reflection, inspecting for blemishes, embarrassing facial hair, wrinkles, or any other insults to her physical, and by extension mental, image. At twenty-four, Scarlett was still at the age where she was insecure and yet acutely narcissistic. Both traits fed off each other and grew more and more robust, until Scarlett felt that they constituted the sum total of her psyche. That is, when she wasn't merely clueless. She had always believed that she would someday develop a delightful and interesting personality, the kind that *ping*ed as sweetly as when you flicked a champagne glass with one manicured fingernail. So far she had not, so she'd decided that she had better *look* interesting instead. To this end, she opened a jar of ivory makeup and smoothed it on her face, achieving a consumptive complexion. For contrast, she added a thick coat of deep maroon lipstick. On the other hand, who was there to impress? About the only person she ever saw was the Judge, a man who was at the age (he was eighty-four) where he was captivated by the raisins in his morning oatmeal. Scarlett blotted her lips with a wadded Kleenex. Life was not turning out as she had expected—being stuck out in the L'Enfants' dilapidated eighteenth-century plantation home in rural St. James Parish was not the Audrey Hepburn–esque existence for which she had always hoped.

She could hear the Judge calling her from downstairs, but she continued the ministrations to her lips until guilt won out. She made one last pucker at the mirror, turned off the bathroom light, and went down the stairs to the sitting room at the bottom of the steps. The Judge liked to sit on the chaise under the chandelier and read his morning paper in this room. It was a pretty room if you didn't look too closely, large with a high ceiling and a chandelier the size of a small treetop suspended from a carved plaster medallion. But the system of cracks and crevices in the walls was so extensive that it resembled a map of the tributaries of the Mississippi. Old framed prints were hung to disguise some of the more offensive and possibly structural fissures. Water damage had left brown stains on the ceiling and several of the panes in the tall French windows were held in place precariously by Scotch tape. Scarlett peered in, but the Judge's chaise was empty. She was about to check the kitchen when she heard a crash from the dining room, across the hall and at the back of the house. Oh God, had he fallen over again? She raced down the hall.

The Judge stood in the dining room next to an overturned Chippendale dining chair. He held a large silver serving fork in one fist, tines pointed straight down. His eyes were fixed on the threadbare Aubusson rug. "Watch out, sweetheart." He had the reedy but resonant voice of the very old. "There's a huge roach in here. Quite a nasty fellow. Aha!" The tines of the fork headed toward the rug, as if the Judge was going to spear a fish. His attack, however, played out in something slower than real time. Halfway down, his back locked. "Oof."

Scarlett darted across the room and eased him over to an upright chair. "Are you okay, Grandfather?"

"Watch out, he's still around here somewhere."

Scarlett took the serving fork out of the old man's hand. "This is the good silver. Next time, just use a rolled-up magazine like everyone else."

"Filthy creatures. I can't stand them. Can you get an exterminator in here?"

"I'll call someone. You're late for work."

"Let's get going, then. I don't want to give them another reason to retire me." Local reporter Bolton Hultgrew, having recently lost a lawsuit before the Judge, had developed a vendetta for the old man. He'd pointed out in print that the Judge was far past the state's constitutionally mandated retirement age. He'd even gone so far as to write an article alleging that on several occasions, clerks and other workers had witnessed the Judge wandering confused in the courthouse, unable to find his courtroom. So far, public opinion was with the Judge and no action had been taken by the judiciary commission. In the sixties and seventies, he'd encouraged several large chemical companies to locate in the surrounding parishes, bringing a good number of jobs to the region. In recent years, he'd become a kind of local institution since he could always be counted on to speak at a high school graduation or to show up for the opening of a new grocery store. Lately, though, his public appearances had become less frequent and he had begun to worry about his political vulnerability.

"I'll get your jacket." Scarlett ran up the grand stairway, which creaked threateningly at the third and eleventh steps, and into the Judge's room. The Judge always kept the heavy beige brocade draperies shut and the room was airless and close. The jacket was lying in a heap, tangled in the bedclothes. Scarlett picked it up and shook it but it retained a rumpled appearance. She reminded herself to take some of the Judge's suits to the cleaners. She had just been so preoccupied. She clambered down the stairs.

The Judge was still sitting in the dining chair, but his eyes moved back and forth across the carpet. The older he got, the more the Judge seemed to fixate on things, as if his brain could only hold one thought at a time. Scarlett could see that this morning that single thought had become "roach," a roach of epic proportions, a Trojan roach filled with six-legged troops that scrambled and crawled among the neurons in the Judge's memory bank. He would be able to think of little else for the rest of the morning, including his cases. Several weeks ago, he had become obsessed over a *Times-Picayune* article about tainted oysters. "They're particularly dangerous for the elderly and invalids," he had informed her repeatedly. For several days he had closely examined every bite of food that went into his mouth, extensively questioning Scarlett about the possible presence of any bivalves in the recipe. Scarlett shuddered. She feared the day when his obsessions became vertebrate.

Three

"I didn't kill the bastard."

"Uh-huh," Jimmy Crouton mumbled automatically. He hadn't heard anything Hebert had said for the last twenty minutes. He was too busy trying to come up with his *own* alibi to listen to Hebert's attempts. The old guy was obviously guilty . . . why was he raising such a fuss? Besides, a man his age? He'd be out in a year or two. Especially for a murder that old. They weren't going to let *granpere* croak behind bars. Now he, Crouton, was a different story. The cops would love to see him rot. Twenty-seven years old, a long list of priors, eighteen months for B&E . . . Crouton sighed. He'd been behind the eight ball since the day he was torn from his mama's womb and slapped with the surname of his no-good, runaway father. Crouton. A child should not be named for salad fixings. Jimmy didn't know a lot, but he knew that his name had gotten the shit kicked out of him from his first day of school until the day he'd finally dropped out in the tenth grade. It was no wonder he'd turned to crime.

This time, the infraction that had landed him behind the peeling institutional-green cinder block walls of the LaFourche Parish Prison was a robbery. Crouton had been drinking malt liquor in a dark corner of the parking lot outside the local Wal-Mart when he'd spotted a shriveled old broad walking to her car. Around her neck was an obviously expensive necklace. Crouton had jumped out of his old pickup, hit the woman upside the head with a foot-long steak sandwich he'd just purchased down the street at Subway, and snatched the chain. The cops stopped him a half-mile down the road. Crouton felt that he might have talked his way out of the arrest had the pigs not found the widow's monogrammed gold locket hidden under the Houston Astros cap on Crouton's greasy blond head. He was presently trying to formulate a defense (I was just going to get the thing polished!) when Hebert's voice grew louder, snapping the fraying, gossamer-thin thread of Crouton's thought.

"So what if we was in the same place the night he disappeared? Everyone was at the *fais-do-do*. The whole goddamn town. I don't see the rest of them in this cell with me."

"Listen, old man—" Crouton began.

A heavyset guard appeared outside the bars. "Hebert, you're being arraigned. Your lawyer is here."

"Thank God!" shouted Hebert.

"Thank God," thought Crouton.

His docket was supposed to be assigned at random by the filing clerks, but the Judge felt that, over the last few years and by no accident, the better cases were going to the district's younger judges. His cases seemed either smaller, more boring, less legally significant, or a combination of the three. In just the past year, he had heard four dog-bite suits. That could not be the luck (or unluck) of the draw. This morning, he was actually filling in for a magistrate with the flu, arraigning prisoners. What was next? Traffic court?

He knew that the other judges thought that he was senile. That he was aware of this fact was clear evidence to him that he still had

his faculties. He wasn't surprised at their belief of his mental inca-
pacity, though. He was old and frail and halfway deaf and blind. He
was dependent. These infirmities naturally prevented complete
social interaction. Even Scarlett thought he was senile. She followed him around the house, a scrawny, washed-out nag, picking
his clothes up behind him, grabbing him by the elbow at his slightest misstep, cutting his meat at dinner. Sometimes he would wake
from a nap and catch her staring, watching his breathing for shal-
lowness and irregularity. At first he had taken her attentions as
plain familial love and concern. Now he was pretty sure that she
thought that there might be some financial payoff in doting over him
in his final years, and that she was just watching his breathing to
see if he were dead yet.

In the end he'd decided that it didn't matter if they thought he
was senile. It gave him a sly advantage. Sometimes, he even faked a
bit of confusion. It was easier to get people to do what he wanted if
they weren't threatened by him. It also allowed him to be cranky as
hell—a small but not-to-be-underestimated pleasure. Ah, if he had
only been so cranky when he was young, the things he could have
accomplished, the heads that would have rolled. His courtroom
would have looked like a bowling alley, with the ugly, balding pates
of the attorneys tumbling down the aisles.

The Judge shook off his daydream and surveyed his docket
sheet through the smudged reading glasses pinching the end of his
long nose. What luck, he thought, seeing the name of the first pris-
oner. "Hebert, Dennis," he announced.

But the Judge's attention was suddenly diverted as old Hebert
was shuffling to his feet. What caught his eye was the most perfect
example of womanhood that a man could ever hope to view.
Resplendent in her animal print dress, the defendant's attorney
shimmied to a standing position. The bright red color of her jauntily
bobbed hair pulsated pleasantly on the Judge's retinas.

"Lana Pulaski," she spoke confidently, "representing Mr.
Hebert."

The Judge smiled. The vision smiled back. The Judge continued to smile. So did the woman. The Judge suddenly couldn't remember his next line. He glanced meaningfully at his law clerk, who hissed to him, "Charges!"

"Mr. Hebert"—the Judge felt like an inept summer stock actor—"you are charged with first degree murder in the death of Thierry Boudreaux. How do you plead?"

"Not guilty, your honor."

"Good." Ack. He hadn't meant to say that out loud. He was just so pleased that he'd be seeing this woman around the courthouse during Hebert's trial.

"Bail," the clerk shot at the Judge.

"I know," the Judge snapped loudly. There were some titters from the motley assortment of defendants and counsel.

"Does the state have a bail recommendation?"

"Well, your honor . . ." The district attorney looked harried. "The charges are very serious. Ordinarily, we would ask that bail be denied. But given the defendant's advanced age . . ." The D.A. was afraid of a lawsuit if Hebert expired behind bars awaiting trial. ". . . the state recommends that bail be set at $100,000."

"He's younger than me," the Judge pointed out sadistically.

"Uh . . . excuse me, your honor."

The Judge softened his glare and turned to Hebert's attorney. "Miss Pulaski?"

"Your honor, Mr. Hebert is a respected member of the community. We request that bail be set at $10,000."

"Agreed," said the Judge. It was best that Hebert got out of jail as soon as possible; the longer he spent behind bars, the more he might be inclined to start talking. If, in fact, he knew anything. "I'm setting the trial for June 23, with Judge McAllister." Under the Speedy Trial Act, he couldn't put it off much longer than that.

Glancing back over the courtroom, the Judge noticed a well-groomed, elderly man in the back row. Hebert's arrest had obviously popped up on Stanley Leighton's radar. The two of them would have to talk.

By the time Scarlett had dropped the Judge off at the courthouse and done the grocery shopping, it was almost noon. She was glad to steer the Judge's old Lincoln toward River Road, back to Shady Oaks.

The flat, winding stretch of River Road between New Orleans and Baton Rouge was known as Cancer Alley in homage to the glut of petrochemical plants and storage facilities lining the banks of the Mississippi between the two cities. These river parishes west of New Orleans were where the state's semi-tropical Cajun Country began. Scarlett always felt claustrophobic driving River Road, hemmed in on one side by the thirty-foot-high grassy levee that blocked any view of the river. The other side of the road fronted expanses of cane field, sporadically interrupted by a succession of small river towns, all of which had seen more prosperous days. Most were only a block or so deep, as if they were trying to cozy up to the Mississippi like hungry puppies to their mother's teats. Nearly all of the wood-frame buildings were one-story. Their paint was flaking—at best. At worst, there were large holes in the siding through which one could see weathered tar paper. In between the towns and the fields were the petrochemical plants and refineries, so tightly packed with smokestacks, tanks, pipes, and buildings that when Scarlett passed by at forty miles an hour, they appeared to be the spewing innards of some monstrous transistor radio. These plants made Louisiana (despite its relatively small population) the second largest toxic polluter in the nation. Any leftover land was swamp and rapidly disappearing wetlands.

Scarlett passed Consolidated Chemical, which had been built on Shady Oaks' former cane fields. The huge plant produced base chemicals, solvents, and resins. Today it was producing its usual orange haze, which hung over Shady Oaks, stripped the paint off the cypress siding, and made Scarlett's eyes water. She stopped at the mouth of the driveway, where two iron gates had to be opened to admit the car. After driving through the gates, she stepped out of the car again and shut them before proceeding further. If she forgot, the goats and cows milling about in the deep front yard of the house would be out on River Road in minutes. There they'd wreak havoc with the plantation-bound tourists who sped around River Road's hairpin bends at ill-advised speeds, often still under the influence of their previous night's revelry on Bourbon Street. Scarlett had to tow at least two or three out of the borrow pits along the side of the levee each Mardi Gras. The Lincoln, with its huge old V-8 engine, was particularly well suited to such work. Sometimes the tourists would offer her money for pulling their cars out. Scarlett always took it. Once she'd gotten a twenty.

Set back a quarter mile from River Road, Shady Oaks had been built by the L'Enfant family in the late 1700s. The style was characteristically Creole. The large symmetrical house was raised off the ground on brick piers and topped by a hipped roof. A broad gallery extended along the front and back of the house. The walls were of bousillage construction—the studs were held together with wooden pegs, packed with a cement-like concoction of mud and moss, and finished with cypress clapboards.

Scarlett climbed the steps to the gallery and went in the front door. Inside, she changed from the clean clothes that she wore in public into an old torn sweatshirt and a pair of cutoffs. She pulled on her high-tops and pinned her long curly hair into a knot on top of her head. She was about to go out the door when she remembered the Judge's roach.

While obsessing over her lack of personality recently, Scarlett had realized that she had more than a few annoying character traits. This would be fine if they were interesting or even tragic idiosyncrasies—perhaps a gambling problem, heroin addiction, drinking in secret, that sort of thing. It seemed inconceivable that someone from an old Southern family could escape a tragic character flaw. Didn't God read Faulkner? Disappointingly, though, Scarlett's chief vice was procrastination. An unmentionably common and boring defect. Accordingly, she had decided to eradicate this weakness with all due prejudice. The roach was a fine place to start, as it was easily and quickly correctable by someone else and involved no heavy lifting. In this spirit, Scarlett found the phone book and looked up "exterminators."

She ran her finger, with its well-gnawed fingernail, down the column of listings. Her eye fell on an ad with a drawing of a cape-wearing superhero. On his chest was a large, red *B*. The ad copy read: "Terrorized by pests? Call BUGMAN! Satisfaction guaranteed." Something about the picture appealed to Scarlett. She picked up the phone, dialed the number, and arranged with a secretary for the exterminator to come out that weekend. Feeling inordinately proud of herself for having accomplished the task of arranging for pest control, she skipped out the back door and down the steps.

A gravel path went from the back steps to a barn about a hundred yards from the house. The path used to be lined with a variety of flowers, but it was now overgrown with crabgrass that tickled around Scarlett's bare shins as she walked toward the barn.

She was sweating in the early spring Louisiana heat when she reached the barn and tugged on one of the doors. The rusty hinges protested, screeching as the door swung open. Dust swirled around her in the streaming sunlight. About ten feet from the door, an easel and stool stood. Several canvases lay on the floor around the easel. Paint brushes and sponges soaked in linseed oil in an old coffee can. Sticky cans and tubes of paint sat everywhere—in piles next to the stool, in the corner by the door, on some metal shelves that Scarlett had bought at the hardware store in the ultimately futile hope of getting organized (disorganization being a second dull and annoying flaw).

Scarlett rubbed her hands together and cracked her knuckles. "Okay. Let's go," she said to herself under her breath. Nothing happened. She sat down on the stool for a second, then popped up and began lining the canvases up against the wall where she could see them while she worked. Some of the canvases were complete, but most were half-finished. Getting started was almost as hard as finishing. When she walked down the path from the house to the barn she was always brimming with ideas and promise, but the minute she sat at the easel the ideas evaporated, having become unachievable, unoriginal, or just plain no good in the presence of the intimidating white rectangle of canvas. Scarlett sat back down and stared at her latest, barely begun work for a couple of minutes. "I need some inspiration," she said finally.

She went to the door of the barn and whistled through her teeth. Within moments, several small gray goats appeared at the door. Excitedly, they began nudging at her with their noses. Scarlett rummaged in the pocket of her cutoffs and came up with half a lint-covered Milk Bone biscuit, which she brushed off and offered to the most persistent of the goats. She pulled it into the barn by the collar around its neck, and shut the door on the others, who bleated unhappily before wandering away. "C'mon, boy," she urged the masticating animal. It followed her obediently.

Scarlett picked up a canvas and laid it next to the goat, then began to search through several cans of paint, deciding on a deep green. She found a screwdriver on the floor and pried the lid off. Taking a clean sponge from a package next to the coffee can, she dipped it in the paint and went over to the goat. She wiped the sponge across the bottom of one of the goat's hooves and slid the canvas under its feet. The goat did a little dance trying to get back on level ground, leaving several green smears on the canvas. Scarlett daubed some of the paint on the goat's ear, picked up the work-in-progress, and pressed the canvas against the ear. She then stepped back and took a long look. "Great." She took another sponge from the package, poured some oil from a bottle of Crisco sitting on the floor, and carefully wiped the goat's hoof and ear until only a slight tinge of pigment remained on the animal's hair.

Satisfied, she led the goat back out of the barn, where it trotted off to join the other goats, some of which wore various shades of reds, blues, and yellows on their coats. Scarlett went back into the barn and turned on a large boombox that was sitting in the corner. She placed the canvas back on the easel and squeezed an assortment of paint blobs onto a palette. Picking up a brush from the coffee can, Scarlett began to paint around the images left by the goat. First she painted some buttocks in one corner of the canvas, then a breast, using one of the goat prints as the nipple. She drew some lips so that they looked as if they were being trodden on by one of the goat's hoofprints. She turned up the boombox and began jumping around the canvas to the beat of the music. Scarlett whirled and threw some orange paint at the picture, careful not to obscure the goat's stylings, which were the centerpiece of this work. By accident, she spun herself into one of the heavy wooden posts. Bouncing and slamming against the post, she flung more paint at the canvas. After an hour or so of gyrating about the canvas, Scarlett stepped back for a look. It wasn't Georgia O'Keeffe, but she was satisfied that she'd achieved the same idea—human anatomy found within other images from nature.

She had turned to painting several years ago, through process of elimination. She had no other marketable skills (although she was only irregularly and fleetingly convinced that her painting was marketable), and since she had dropped out of LSU, she couldn't even simulate skills by flashing a degree. So the art was part of a last-ditch plan to escape from Shady Oaks. She couldn't wait until her show, scheduled for July in Baton Rouge. Scarlett cautiously fingered several small bruises left on her arms from her dance with the post. She could feel that something big was about to happen.

Crouton was lying back on his narrow bunk counting his toes from left to right, then back again (the number was the same almost every time), when he noticed an elderly man watching him through the bars. The man, despite his age, was tall with a poker-straight posture. His thick, snowy hair was neatly combed back from the his tanned face. With his elegant features, the man reminded Crouton of one of the actors on the soap operas his mother used to watch in the afternoon. This man could have played the role of the surgeon. Or the captain of industry character. Crouton was sure the guy was carrying a wad on him, and grew excited. Unfortunately, he couldn't think of a way to liberate the man of his wealth while incarcerated.

"I need to ask you a couple of questions, son."

"Who the fuck are you?"

"My name is Stanley."

The way the old man said it, even his name sounded rich. "Big fuckin' deal," Crouton replied, to hide the fact that he was impressed.

"It may be a big fucking deal for you." The old man's tone, though smooth and modulated, was vaguely threatening. He had a faint smile on his lips, through which Crouton caught a glimpse of a full set of pearly whites. As a group, Crouton's extended family did not possess a complete set of thirty-two teeth. The clan's greatest talent was their ability to spit a plug of tobacco even with jaws clenched shut. His great aunt was noted for the distance and arcing trajectory she could get on an olive-sized glob of Red Man, which she would expel from the gap where her front teeth and right incisor had formerly and briefly been.

"You a lawyer? I ain't got no money for a lawyer."

"Just answer some questions for me, and maybe I'll talk to your judge and get you out of here." The man clucked his tongue. "Clocking old widows with a twelve-inch Italian sub . . . that's not going to get you too much sympathy."

Crouton considered. The people of the State of Louisiana truly had him by the short hairs. Best to play whatever cards he might have. "What do you need to know?"

"Did Mr. Hebert tell you anything about the murder?"

After the arraignment, Lana stopped for lunch at a shabby roadside tavern. Walking in the door, she noted with approval the chipped Formica tables and the flypaper hanging over the cash register.

Having grown up over her father's tavern, she was always comfortable in these places. She sat at the bar and ordered some boudin and rice and a glass of iced tea.

Meeting with Hebert before the arraignment had been unproductive. He had asserted his innocence, which wasn't a surprise. Lana had believed him, which was. She'd grilled him about the events leading up to the lawsuit. Hebert's story differed little from his wife's, though he added that several members of Boudreaux's family were notoriously lawless and that Lana might look at relatives who'd received a windfall at Boudreaux's death.

"Why would I kill the bastard? He had no case, my lawyer said so. Even if he was going to win, I wouldn'ta killed him. I'm no animal."

She had asked him a few more questions about the lawsuit, but it was clear that Hebert hadn't been worried that his land was at risk. From Lana's perspective, one motive had evaporated.

"What about the shot he took at you?"

"I wasn't actually too mad about that. I used to troll on his oyster leases pretty often."

Was he serious, or was he just trying to convince her that he hadn't been angry at Boudreaux?

"Come on," Lana protested. "If someone shot at me, I'd be pretty enraged."

Hebert only chuckled. "He was just givin' me a warnin'. I can't say that I wouldn't have done the same. Things work a little different out here than in New Orleans, Miss Pulaski. Or they used to."

Lana had ended her interview with Hebert convinced of his innocence.

The pudgy middle-aged bartender served her boudin and Lana dug in with gusto. When she'd finished her lunch, Lana asked him for directions to the coroner's office in Gonzales.

"Honey, I ain't got no idea. Haven't had to patronize him yet," he laughed.

Lana fixed him with a cold stare.

"Uh, there's a phone book right here behind the bar. I'll look it up for you."

"Thank you," Lana answered curtly. The empty-headed humor of most of the people she encountered was one of the more grating annoyances she faced each day.

By the time she was a teenager, Lana had decided that she was smarter than anyone at her school, even the nuns, and especially the priests. This realization had given Lana an aloof air that mixed badly with her bulk, at least in the opinion of the other high school girls. By the age of thirteen, she had understood that if she wanted something from the world outside of her father's bar, she was going to have to scratch and claw for it.

She didn't mind the rejection she faced at school—in fact she encouraged it. Most people were really boring. Why waste any time with them? Better to be left alone.

Lana had developed two lines of defense to control her peers. She thought of them as Level One and Red Alert. Level One was an arch glare. She had always been able to raise her right eyebrow independently of and an inch above the left one. She would fix this glare on the offending schoolgirl and hold it for five seconds. The glare cowed at least seventy percent of the girls who were disrespectful of Lana. Red Alert was the nail file. On those few occasions requiring it, she had pulled the pointed metal file out of the pocket of her jumper and suggestively picked her nails with it, eyes held menacingly on the offending schoolgirl. She got this maneuver from a detective movie that Joe had taken her to see one afternoon. In the movie, the weapon of choice was a switchblade, but the nail file seemed to have the desired effect on her inferiors. Besides, it was more easily explained to an inquisitive nun. Red Alert had worked so well that even Lana was surprised the day that she was forced to find a more effective method.

The unprecedented escalation of arms was instigated by Eileen McPherson, a blustery girl almost Lana's size. Unlike Lana, Eileen was popular with the other girls at school because she wore a back brace to remedy her scoliosis. The brace, which started at her hips and came all the way up under her chin, made Eileen an object of envy—an exotic, carefully tended creature. Eileen could talk endlessly about her brace, about her orthopedist (the "most well-respected in the South")—and by extension, she was seen by the other girls as an expert on all matters physical.

One day Eileen leaned over to Lana in study hall (when Eileen leaned, her whole braced body tilted as one fixed unit, not unlike the tower in Pisa) and hazarded the opinion that the size of Lana's growing breasts would turn her into a hunchback by the age of twenty. "My doctor says it happens to overdeveloped girls all the time." The girls surrounding Lana and Eileen began to giggle and passed the information around to the rest of the room.

Lana raised her right eyebrow almost up into her hairline. Instantly, the other girls fell silent.

"Of course, it's probably too late to do anything now. Your parents should have taken you to see someone years ago."

Brow still hoisted, Lana withdrew the nail file. She held it up and examined the point, turning it slowly so that the fluorescent lights in the ceiling glinted off its steel shaft. Unfortunately, she hadn't taken into account that her opponent was protected by a surgical steel and plastic breastplate, impenetrable by even the most advanced military artillery, and was therefore fearless of physical reprisal.

"But, maybe not," Eileen continued. "My brace was very expensive. I don't know if a tavern keeper could even afford something like this." She sighed theatrically. "Poor, hunchbacked Lana." Seeing that Eileen wasn't afraid, the other girls recommenced to giggle, until they were shushed by Sister Angela.

Lana planned her revenge carefully.

The next day she came to school with a small vial that had been provided to her by one of the sailors, a regular at the bar whom Lana had gotten to know pretty well. Inside was a gray powder that the sailor had called "Spanish fly." Influenced by the flourishing Cold War, Lana had taken to thinking of it as "uranium powder."

"I wish I'da never heard a this stuff," the sailor had told her morosely, and went on to describe the itching and the blisters. "And I only used a pinch of it. It was supposed to help me with the ladies, but the only ladies I saw was the sisters in a clinic in Caracas where I ended up with my dick next to falling off. Oh," he said, embarrassed, " 'scuse me."

"Don't worry about it," Lana assured him.

"It's not deadly or nuthin', but it will make you wish you was dead. That's why I held onta it. Thought it'd come in handy someday."

"Thanks," Lana told him. "I really appreciate it," she had added, sincerely.

Suppurating lesions sounded just about right for Eileen.

In chapel the next morning, Lana had positioned herself on the aisle, several rows in front of Eileen. She waited patiently through the sermon. The priest was a young, superstitious man who'd been sent back to Italy by his immigrant parents to study with the Cappuccini monks. He insisted on saying the mass, including the sermon, in Latin. Several of the girls around Lana were nodding off, but Lana was alert and acutely aware of the feather weight of the vial in the breast pocket of her blouse. Then it was time for communion. Lana had followed the line of girls to the front of the church, taken communion, and had returned to her pew when Eileen started up the aisle. Holding her rosary beads and praying silently to herself ("Dear God, let Eileen have sensitive skin."), Lana watched as Eileen walked in line up to the front of the church, as she knelt stiffly at the bar, as she took the communion wafer. Still holding the beads, Lana extracted the vial from underneath her jumper. Winding her rosary beads around the vial to disguise it, she carefully withdrew the cork. She eyed the girls around her. They had their heads down and were whispering among themselves about the altar boy—he was the only high school boy in the diocese with a motorcycle, and therefore was quite popular. Lana glanced down over her nose at the vial's contents. There was so little and it looked so innocuous.

With the rosary entwined in Lana's hand, it was almost impossible to see the vial. As Eileen approached, head down in feigned prayer but with a smirk on her face, Lana made the sign of the cross. In the name of the Father, the Son (Eileen was even with Lana now), and the Holy Spirit. On "spirit," Lana let her hand slide from her shoulder and quickly tossed the meager, but potent, contents of the vial between the back of Eileen's exposed neck and the brace.

The sailor had told her that the powder would start to itch after just a few minutes. But just as Lana had managed to slip the vial back into her bra, she heard a scream. At the front of the church, the surprised altar boy dropped the gold communion paten, which hit the marble floors with a clank that shook the stained glass in the windows.

"Something's burning me," shrieked Eileen. The whole church, including Lana, spun around to see Eileen flailing helplessly at her back. Encased in the heavy brace, she was helpless to scratch at herself. Limbs windmilling, she was as impotent as a turtle flipped on its shell. She began to writhe and slam her back against the pew in front of her, trying in vain to put out the fire on her skin. The girls around her tried to grab her and subdue her, but were shaken off by Eileen's seemingly superhuman force.

Suddenly, the priest came running down the aisle, a large crucifix raised in front of him like a battle shield. "Get thee behind me, Satan," he yelled, as he approached the demonically possessed girl.

They never did find out what caused the vicious, weeping rash on Eileen's back, but no one bothered Lana after that.

The bartender sent Lana on the road with an elaborate map drawn on the back of one of the paper menus. "You can't miss it," he assured her repeatedly, eager to find his way back into her good graces. Lana left him an ample tip, which somehow made him feel even worse.

four

Lana pushed open the glass door and immediately wrinkled her
nose. The smell of decay permeated the dreary brick building that
housed the coroner's office. She put her hand over her nose and
mouth and peered at the directory that was posted on a chrome
stand next to the entry. The office was at the end of the hall, and by
the time she reached it she was queasy and regretting the boudin
she'd just eaten.

The door to the small reception area was open. Christmas tree
air fresheners—the kind found in taxicabs—dangled from the
lamps, the coat rack, and the ficus in the corner. They did little to
mask the stench. Lana gave the secretary her name and, after several stinky minutes, was ushered in to see the coroner.

Not wanting to linger, she introduced herself, shook the man's
hand, then cut right to the chase. "Can you tell me how Thierry
Boudreaux died?"

The coroner was a balding man of about fifty. His hair was
parted near the nape of his neck, combed forward to cover his bald
spot, and terminated in a perfect pomade-cemented point between

his bushy black brows. Lana rarely found herself riveted by any-one's physical characteristics besides her own, but this tonsorial flight of fancy had her full attention. Did he comb it into the same shape every morning? Was Wednesday a swirl, and Thursday a fringe? Did he do it himself, or did his wife help?

"He was apparently killed by a heavy blow to the skull with a blunt object."

Maybe the coroner was trying to hide a similar unsightly defect with his cranium cover. Lana straightened up in her chair, arching her neck in an effort to spot some sort of skull deformity.

"He was hit from behind. Could have been a rifle butt."

Lana could see nothing. Disappointed, she slid back down into her seat. "But you're not sure what he was hit with."

"No, I can't tell for sure. There isn't too much to work with after so many years, especially in these parts. With the heat and the humidity, it only takes a few weeks for a body to decompose. If there was any foreign material from the weapon left in the wound, like splinters or paint chips, it decomposed with the body. But we were still lucky with Mr. Boudreaux. Being stuffed into that bin like he was slowed down the decomposition process. If he'd been out in the elements, the only thing left would be the diamond from his tooth."

"Was he murdered where the body was found?"

"Again, we don't have a lot to go on, but I'd say not. I gotta ask myself why someone holdin' a rifle would hit him instead of shoot him. The only reason I can think of is noise. But noise wouldn't have been a factor way back in the fields where that shed is. Back then, there was nothing but cows and sugarcane for miles. So Mr. Boudreaux was probably killed in a more public place. But there's no way of knowing for sure."

Lana sighed. "I thought pathology was a more exact science."

"After twenty years, there isn't too much science to it at all. The Psychic Friends Network could probably help you more than I can."

Lana was frustrated. But she wasn't about to leave without finding out something important. "Can I ask you a question?"

"Ask away."

"It's about your hair."

five

Back in the Offices the next morning, Lana was antsy. She was working on a complaint for a manicurist who'd slipped and fallen in a Winn-Dixie in the Ninth Ward, but the import of her client's injuries paled in comparison to Lana's nascent campaign. She suspected that her client had intentionally broken the jar of spaghetti sauce in which she'd slipped, anyway. Lana made several more onslaughts on the pleading, but spent most of the morning staring at her watch. Finally, it was almost noon.

She pressed the button on the intercom. "I'm going to lunch with my campaign manager and my publicity chairman," she barked at Carl. Lana liked the way the titles sounded coming off her tongue. She could just as well be running for the U.S. Senate. "We'll be at Antoine's. I'll be back before one-thirty. If there are any appointments before then, push them back."

"Your devotion to the huddled masses is touching."

"Just deal with them." Lana strutted out from her office to the coat rack by the door and chose a wide-brimmed straw hat. She clamped it down on the stiff red hair, which crackled audibly as it yielded to the shape of the hat. She blew through the door, stiletto heels clicking on the sidewalk, and walked up to the throng waiting for the bus in front of the Offices (through some networking, she had made sure that the city put a bus stop in front of her door; like beauty salons and shoe repair stores, some of her best business came from walk-ins). Lana stuck out her hand to a startled man reading the newspaper. "I'm Lana Pulaski," she told him. "How do you feel about your elected officials?"

Since 1840, Antoine's Restaurant had been in business on St. Louis Street, in the heart of the French Quarter. Marked by a small black and white sign hanging under the elaborate ironwork of its second-floor balcony, Antoine's was one of the most famous restaurants in New Orleans. Its noisy, tile-floored main dining room was always filled to capacity with tourists looking for traditional Creole cuisine. Its back rooms were filled with locals actually *getting* traditional Creole cuisine. Lana entered the restaurant, waved off the maitre d', and bulldozed her way to one of the upstairs dining rooms. Tippy Sheridan, her publicity chairperson, was seated in the shadows in the left rear corner of the room where she could observe all of the comings and goings of the clientele.

Tippy was from a New Orleans family so old that they could, with a collectively straight face, nickname their daughter with a moniker more befitting a chihuahua than a person. As it turned out, her nickname fit her precisely. Tippy was petite and high-strung, with disquietingly bulbous eyes. Besides, her Christian name was Cornelia, which was equally awful from Lana's perspective. Aside from her job in public relations, at which she was not particularly artful (though she knew everyone and was in that way very valuable), Tippy's main claim to fame was chairing a committee dedicated to preserving Spanish moss, which was disappearing at a rate startling to Tippy and her well-bred friends. On the weekends, Tippy and her committee traveled about the state climbing and shrouding shamefully naked live oaks with farm-grown moss.

As Lana drew up to the table, she saw that Tippy was clenching a cellular phone with one perfectly manicured, clawlike hand, carrying on an animated conversation with the person or persons on the other end. Tippy flashed a wide expanse of expensive dental bonding in acknowledgment of Lana's arrival. In her too-rich, too-thin face, the smile looked like the exposed toothy grimace of a skull. Tippy crooked the index finger of her free hand and a waiter appeared in a silent cloud of obsequiousness by the side of the table.

"I'll have a Bloody Mary," Lana told him, "and bring the bread now." The waiter made a shallow bow and left. Lana leaned back in her chair and looked at Tippy, who turned slightly into the corner, as if this would prevent Lana from hearing her conversation.

Lana was bored and began to rummage through her purse. She pulled out a compact and a flame-orange lipstick that she had purchased at the five-and-dime for ninety-nine cents. She flipped up the cover on the compact, pulled her lips tight against her teeth, and began dragging the lipstick in a circle around her lips. Tippy clapped her hand across the mouthpiece of the phone, leaned over the table, and said in a whisper, "I prefer Chanel. Better texture." She smiled, gave Lana a small, satisfied nod, and returned to the phone.

Souchecki showed up and slid into the chair next to Tippy. He and Lana nodded at each other in greeting.

The waiter arrived with the Bloody Mary and a basket of French bread. Lana took a gulp of the drink, poking herself in the eye with the celery stalk garnish. Her lipstick left a flame-orange half-moon on the outside of the glass that would still be there after the glass was run through the dishwasher.

She and Souchecki began liberally buttering hunks of the bread. They looked at each other uncomfortably. Without Tippy as social grease, their conversation was always awkward. At their first meeting, Lana had detected a steady drip of disapproval seeping from the tight and conservative Souchecki. Fortunately, Tippy quickly clicked off the telephone and slipped it into the tan Hermès bag that hung from the back of her chair. She brushed an errant lock of hair back behind her ear. "I'm terribly sorry," she said to them in a voice that oozed with the assurance that she was forgiven even if she really wasn't. "A woman's work is never done, as they say. And you would know about that as well as anyone, Lana. Well, maybe we should order."

Lana and Souchecki had, by this time, emptied the breadbasket and Lana's hunger was temporarily sated. "Do you have the results of the telephone poll?"

"Yes, I do," said Tippy. "But let's get some lunch first. We have plenty of time to talk about that. Andre tells me that the trout is very fresh today. Amandine or meuniere?"

"Meuniere."

"That sounds good," Souchecki agreed.

Tippy raised her hand, and the waiter again materialized instantly by her side. Tippy was a notorious overtipper. "Three meunieres, Andre. And I'll have a glass of the fume blanc."

"Bring me another Bloody Mary." Lana had found that lunch with Tippy required lubrication.

Souchecki cleared his throat. "Just an iced tea, please."

Tippy's eyes followed the waiter from the table. Lana had noticed that Tippy liked to watch the proletariat toiling for her.

"Well," Tippy announced in a let's-get-back-to-business voice. "Last time we talked about the broad parameters of your campaign. Which office you wished to run for, etc."

Originally, Lana had wanted to run for governor. Why not start at the top? But Tippy and Souchecki had convinced her that such a campaign was premature at this point in Lana's political career. Tippy had proposed a campaign for Clerk of Court, Souchecki for City Council. After Lana had pointed out that the Polish-Americans had only come up with three thousand dollars in support and, that she would be using her own money to open the campaign headquarters, hire her staff, and begin the campaign, the three had settled on Attorney General. The Attorney General's office oversaw gaming and was sufficiently high profile. Lana could still accomplish her goals.

"Now we need to work on personalizing your campaign. You know, possible material for the campaign ads. Tell me about your background. How you got to be where you are."

"Haven't we gone over that?"

"Not in detail. And not the way we want you to tell the voters about it. There is more than one side to the truth, you know. Now. Begin."

"I'm a plaintiffs' attorney. I also do some criminal defense work."

"No, start at the beginning. Growing up. Let us hear the human interest stuff. We can always use human interest in the campaign."

"My father raised me. My mother left when I was ten."

"Good. Sympathy." Tippy nodded vigorously.

"My father owned a bar," she continued aloud. "On the corner of Tchopitoulas and Calliope. We lived over it. I worked there on the weekends, waiting tables, serving drinks. . . ." Lana had driven past the spot, now an on-ramp to Highway 90, on the way to the restaurant.

"Hmm. I don't know about that." Tippy's tone clearly indicated that she would prefer that Lana somehow retroactively alter that aspect of her past. "How is it that you came to be a lawyer?"

"My father wanted me to be one."

He had insisted, in fact, after Lana had told one of the nuns at her school that she wanted to be a bartender when she grew up. It was a scandal that had rocked Sacred Heart for weeks. Actually, Joe Pulaski had given her a choice—lawyer or nun. But Lana had seen enough of nuns to know that there was no future in it. The wardrobe alone was enough to depress a cheerleader.

"He helped me get started after I graduated."

Having failed to garner any lucrative job offers during law school (except from Marshall Hope, whose practice wasn't large enough to support an attorney with Lana's aspirations), Lana decided to hang out her shingle.

Joe, a businessman far more creative than his modest tavern suggested, thought to have cocktail napkins printed up with Lana's name and phone number in red ink. In bold type was written, "INJURED? YOU NEED AN ATTORNEY. PROTECT YOUR RIGHTS AND YOUR WALLET." A napkin went under every drink, in the basket with every order of fried oysters. Customers wiped their lips with them, blew their noses into them. They also read them and took note.

The bar was next to the warehouses on the river and proved to be a fertile source of stevedores and longshoremen with wrenched backs, lost limbs, and other personal injury bonanzas. Not to mention their domestic problems. Within five years, Lana had retired her father to Fort Lauderdale with an old-age nest egg that included a half million in no-load mutual funds and tax-free bonds, and then she'd bought the building on Magazine Street.

"Well, maybe we can work with that for the TV ads. A working-class background is very hot in politics right now. You couldn't buy the credibility it gives you."

The entrées came. Tippy took a small, delicate bite of her trout.

"Wonderful. Speaking of the TV ads, we have to do something about the way that you come across visually." She frowned at Lana's pink stretch-velvet suit. Souchecki looked away uneasily.

Lana knew that Tippy, in her tailored suits from Saks on Canal Street, could never understand the power of spandex and cleavage. From the way Souchecki was staring at the ceiling, she also sensed that Tippy and her campaign manager had already discussed this issue. She decided to change the subject.

"Right now, I'm more concerned about the telephone poll."

"Okay," said Tippy, reluctant. "We'll have to come back to image. . . . Well, I have good news and bad news about the poll. As you know, its purpose was to measure your name recognition and public opinion of you. The good news is that you are solid in New Orleans. At least with the lower middle class and below. The people know you already. It must be those TV ads for your firm. And the ad on the back of the phone book, that was a terrific move for someone with your practice, especially since your clients don't have to be able to alphabetize to find you. Who thought of that? Brilliant."

"That was my idea. But I believe that most of my clients know the alphabet."

"Hmm . . ." said Tippy, dubious.

"What about the rest of the state?"

"Well, it's too early to tell about Shreveport and the cities up north, but if you go with the anti-corruption and gambling stance that we've talked about, I think you'll do well enough. They're all Baptist up there. They hate the casinos. And Taylor was fired from the D.A.'s office years ago. I haven't found out why, but we can intimate that some sort of corruption was involved. Taylor will still get the good ol' boy vote, but those God-fearing churchgoers are going to vote for you."

"What's the bad news, then?"

"The bad news is in the southwestern part of the state. There are almost a million Cajuns in the twenty-two southern parishes. They're going to be the swing vote in this race, and they're in Taylor's corner right now. Not only are they an independent bunch, they're Catholic. They think God forgives everything and you know how the Catholics like to gamble—those people just *love* bingo. So your platform doesn't mean much to them."

Lana decided to let Tippy's sociological observations go uncommented on.

"Besides," Tippy chattered on, "how much corruption can there be out in the bayou?"

"I'm sure that they have lots of other legitimate concerns. Unemployment is low right now because of the oil boom, but what about environmental problems? Toxic waste, Superfund sites, saltwater incursion . . ."

"Those things aren't really an attorney general's concerns. Let the governor worry about that."

"I disagree. As attorney general, I would be responsible for keeping industry in line. Policing dumping, that sort of thing."

"Okay, I'll look into those issues. But we don't want to harp on how hopeless a situation they're in. You want to make them feel good. Remember 'Morning in America' and 'a thousand points of light.' The point is, Bobby Taylor was raised in Iberville Parish, and from the way he talks, you would think he made his living trapping 'gators before he got into politics. He milks that accent for all it's worth. I've even heard him call TV interviewers *'cher.'* I mean, come on. On top of which, he's already a state representative and he's a local boy. They've got plenty of reasons to vote for him, and precious few to vote for you. If we don't work on this, you'll be back in civil district court representing some shopper who slipped and fell in the Winn-Dixie."

Lana winced. "You know, I got a Cajun client this week."

"Well, that's one vote out of a million. If you win the case."

Lana could feel herself growing testy. "Do either of you have a plan?" She drank the last of the Bloody Mary and began sucking on the ice cubes, digging in the nooks and crannies with her tongue in search of any last drops of vodka.

"Making a plan is my job," said Souchecki. "But it doesn't happen overnight."

"Well, I can start with a little networking. I met an old judge out in the parishes yesterday. I'll get in touch with him." Anyone that old had to have a lot of contacts. The Judge's attraction to her had been obvious. Lana decided that she would ask him on a date. That would get his attention.

"It's a start. But we need to position you as one of them," Tippy declared. "Do you hunt or fish? I hear that the Cajuns are very big on hunting and fishing. 'Sportsmans' Paradise' and all."

Lana leaned back in her chair and began drumming the table with her Poppy Splash acrylic nails. She gave Tippy what she thought to be a wilting stare, but Tippy remained irritatingly erect in her suit. Finally, Lana moaned. "Good God. Is that the best that you can do?"

"You can always marry in and become beloved by the people. It worked for Imelda Marcos."

"She was exiled."

"True. But she's made an inspiring comeback. And those shoes!"

The Judge was sitting behind his desk, staring at a photograph in a pewter frame on his bookshelves. The picture was a black and white one, turned black and yellow over the years. It was of a delicate, pretty woman—Odile, the Judge's late wife. She'd died some twenty-five years before of pneumonia. In the middle of the hot Louisiana summer. Only the pathologically vulnerable Odile could have died in such an unlikely way, the Judge mused. Odile had been no more fun alive than she was dead. She was weak-willed and easily manipulated. More a girl than a woman, even in her late fifties. The Judge had always felt that Odile actually enjoyed her frailties, indulging in them the way that a hobbyist might indulge in stamp collecting or model trains. He wadded up a piece of memo paper and tossed it at the frame. It missed. Guiltily, he toddled over to where it lay on the floor and kicked it under the bookcase, out of sight.

Just then the clerk entered the room, carrying a vase crowded with yellow roses. "Good God," croaked the Judge. "Where did those come from?"

"I don't know. The florist just delivered them. Read the card." The clerk set the vase down on the desk and waited.

"I can read without your help," the Judge said, making a shushing motion with one arm. The clerk scurried out, shutting the door behind him. The Judge reached into the flowers and plucked a small envelope off a plastic spike in the middle of the stems. He carefully tore it open. Holding the card at arm's length, he read slowly: "I admire your judicial talents. Meet me at the Hilton dining room at nine for dinner. L. Pulaski."

He smiled. "How nice." A delicious memory of Lana's assets

floated through his mind, then he realized, chagrined, that he had committed to officiate at a bake-off at the local church. Well, he'd just call her and reschedule. Besides, it would be a good idea to find out if Hebert had told her anything. He doubted that Hebert knew about the Judge's involvement with Boudreaux, but better to err on the side of caution.

Scarlett would arrive any minute to take him home. The Judge stood and began to pull his robe over his head, but became tangled and confused in the dark folds. Struggling made it worse. The fabric bound around his bony elbows and shoulders. A snarl of black polyester and limbs, the Judge bumped into the desk, then took several steps and walked into the bookcase. The framed portrait of Odile fell over and he heard the glass shatter. "My God," the Judge cried weakly through the cloth, "help!"

Six

Crouton couldn't believe that he'd been released from jail on his own recognizance. That old fart must have had some pull, Crouton mused as he ambled in his loose-jointed fashion down St. Mary Street. Too bad he hadn't gotten the geezer to get his truck out of impound—on top of arresting him, the pigs had discovered over four hundred dollars of unpaid parking tickets. Crouton had never in his life had that much money at one time.

He reached into the pocket of his jeans to see what kind of cash he did have. Two dollars in damp dimes and nickels that he had fished out of the fountain at the mall before being chased off by some bitch from Mrs. Field's. Damn. His meager resources made Crouton realize that he was hungry. Prison food never stuck with him.

He briefly thought about showing up at his mama's, but she'd refused to bail him out this time, and probably wasn't in the mood to feed him. He'd have to find another option. Crouton looked around and spotted a Pizza Hut up the street. That would be good for a free meal, so long as the waitresses were slow bussing the tables. Salivating slightly, Crouton picked up his pace. He entered the restaurant and hovered by the video games in the corner. The staff would think he was waiting for take-out; nobody would bother him for five or ten minutes. Crouton leaned against Mortal Kombat and scanned the restaurant. By the window, a couple was sliding out of a booth. At least a third of their large pepperoni remained uneaten. The couple passed Crouton on their way out the door.

"How ya' doin'?" Crouton nodded at them.

As soon as the door shut, Crouton stepped quickly across the floor to the booth. It was his lucky day. Not only had they left food, they'd left a tip. In a single smooth motion, Crouton doubled his net worth by sweeping the two dollars from the table into his pocket. He reached for the pizza. It was stuffed crust!

"What the fuck do you think you're doing?"

Crouton looked up into the angry eyes of the squat, sixteen-year-old waitress.

"I'm just finishin' my dinner."

"Security!"

Out of the corner of his eye, Crouton saw one of Thibodaux's finest bearing down on him. Shit! How could he not have spotted the off-duty cop?

He was back in the same cell within half a day of leaving it. A new record. But he was not worried. He'd used his phone call to summon his new benefactor.

Stanley Leighton was smugly amused. The recidivist's rapid return to the Parish Prison had validated all of his dearly held notions about the poor and uneducated, which boiled down to this: They deserved what they got. If there was anything that he enjoyed, it was being proved correct. It was his due.

Leighton sat in the booth in the prison visiting room and watched the guard set Crouton down on the other side of the smudged, spittle-flecked pane of glass. He took a linen handkerchief out of his pocket and used it to pick up the black receiver that hung in front of him.

"Mr. Crouton," he said, his mouth several safe inches from the undoubtedly infectious mouthpiece, "I was hoping that we wouldn't have to meet under such circumstances again."

"Yeah, I'm havin' a streak of bad luck," Crouton admitted through the phone on his side of the glass.

"That's a shame, but why did you call me?"

"I think you can get me out of here again."

"Why would I do such a thing?"

" 'Cause if you don't, I might be tempted to call the newspapers and tell them that you was sniffin' around for inside information on poor old Mr. Hebert. I been in prison a number of times, and ain't no rich fairy godmother ever showed up before to spring me. That ain't standard procedure. Makes me think you got a personal interest."

Leighton considered. Ordinarily, he wouldn't care if Crouton had taken out a full-page ad in the *Acadian Star* with his half-baked allegations. But with the pressure that reporter had been putting on the Judge, it might be wise not to stir up any trouble. Maybe the convict could even be of some use. He was familiar with Hebert. The irascible old Cajun might try something stupid like going to the press, and Crouton could easily be induced to keep an eye on him. Leighton was getting too old for the legwork. Best to seize this opportunity—it wasn't often he ran across a useful petty criminal at the country club or a Republican fundraiser. Not that Leighton's acquaintances were strangers to illegal acts. But these tended to be on a grander, socially acceptable scale. Embezzlement, toxic dumping, that sort of thing. Besides, he was busy getting his golf game in shape for the annual tournament at the club. He didn't have *time* to deal with Hebert right now.

"Okay, Mr. Crouton. Let's see about setting you free. I think that there is something you can do for me."

Seven

Lana sat at a table in the dining room of the Hilton, waiting. It was nine thirty. She considered leaving, but then formed a mental picture of the Judge driving toward the hotel. He was wearing a hat, the fedora kind that was popular in the forties. The crown of the hat was all that was visible over the steering wheel except for the pair of gnarled, white-knuckled hands that clutched the wheel itself. He was moving very slowly and a long line of traffic had built up behind his automobile, which floated slowly from side to side as it traveled, banging up against the painted lines on the road like a car in a video game. She decided to give him until nine forty-five. She sipped slowly at her martini. Where was he? She had been sure that the flower thing would work. Maybe she had sent the wrong kind. Was there a specific floral arrangement suited to elderly men? She should have asked Carl. Those boys knew all about flowers. When the Judge hadn't arrived within his allotted period, she threw a five on the table and went into the bar.

Hotel bars always depressed her. They were generally dark, plastic places—actually, their atmosphere rather resembled that of the Offices. That might be the problem. A bad top-forties band was on the small stage playing an old Whitney Houston song. The singer was slightly off-key and had comically buck teeth that prevented her from pronouncing her *M*s. Lana puzzled over this. One would think that a woman in the entertainment business would spend a little money and get those teeth tethered into place. After all, appearance was everything. It might even be deductible as a business expense, mused Lana, though she had little interest in or use for tax law. Most of her clients got by every April with the EZ form.

The only other patron in the lounge was a fortyish man at one end of the bar. She sized him up. Not a businessman. No suit or tie. Nor did he have that peculiar sallow businessman skin, cured daily under fluorescent tube lights and dried in climate-controlled air. He was wearing wire-rimmed glasses. Professor? Lana wondered. Architect? He was not unattractive. She crossed the maroon carpet, tucking her bra straps back inside the shoulders of her sweater as she walked, and sat down next to the man. He was drinking what appeared to be scotch and was sneaking olives out of the well of fruit that sat on the other side of the bar with the cocktail stirrers and napkins. The bartender was watching a basketball game on TV, the sound drowned out by the band, and was ignoring or was oblivious to his clientele. Lana leaned over and put her mouth next to the man's ear, noticing a small and intriguing scar above his left eyebrow. "Hungry?" she asked.

The man turned, startled. Lana watched his eyes move from the orange flip to the snug fuschia sweater and down to the black leather skirt. "Are you . . . working?" he asked carefully.

Lana had had this reaction before. "No, hon'. I'm relaxing after a hard week in and out of the courtroom."

"What were you charged with?"

Lana decided to take this as an attempt at humor. "I'm a lawyer."

The man's consonants were liquidy and slurred by three double Johnny Walker Blacks. "You don't look anything like my lawyer," he said happily. "His name is Howard and he wears seersucker suits." He reached over the bar, picked up another olive, and held it in front of Lana's mouth. "Let me buy you dinner," he said, popping it between her lips.

The food in the Hilton dining room was as mediocre as she'd expected it would be. Lana chewed unhappily on her flavorless salmon. She reached across the table for the pepper shaker and felt her companion's hand sliding up her thigh. What was his name again? She hadn't a clue. She examined him in a detached fashion. The scar above his eyebrow had grown brighter and brighter pink with each of the several glasses of scotch he'd tossed back. During the appetizers, Lana had been indulging in the fantasy that he'd been injured during some sort of daring adventure. Tagging black rhinos in Zimbabwe, maybe. Racing his Ducati in Monaco. As dinner progressed, she got to know him better and had been forced to curtail her imagination. Pushing her plate away to peruse the dessert menu, she arrived at a more probable scenario: Her dining partner had stumbled inebriated into the restroom of some singles bar, bent to fumble with his zipper, and cracked open his skull on the urinal.

Which made him no less suave than most of the other men she slept with.

Having passed most of her youth in a tavern filled with longshoremen, stevedores, and her Aunt Flo's girls, Lana was left with no illusions about men. In fact, she felt the same about them as they, in her experience, felt about women. They were only good for one thing. That was why she'd never been married, never even had a relationship lasting more than several months. Once she had seen all of a man's tricks, she found no reason to stick around. Lana tried to look interested as her mystery date plodded pointlessly through an anecdote about his fraternity days.

". . . and when I woke up the next morning, I was in the middle of a cow pasture, wearing a pair of panties on my head."

After cracking open his skull on the porcelain, she decided, he'd probably vomited on his shoes. "Why don't we go up to my room?" Lana proposed. At least it would get him to shut up.

By the time the elevator doors opened, Lana's companion had his left arm and his entire head up her sweater and was grappling with one breast while he slurped noisily at the other. She felt as if she were nursing a voracious hundred-and-seventy-five-pound infant. Lana backed into the hall, and the suckling man stumbled along with her, caught under the sweater and trying desperately to maintain his grip. God, but he was artless. Was this even going to be worth the effort? Lana placed an exploratory hand on his fly. Okay, maybe it was. She reached into her purse for her keys, unlocked the door, and dragged him into the room after her. The toe of his left shoe got caught in the carpet and he stumbled, causing him to bite down on her breast.

Lana didn't see him trip and assumed that he was the kind who liked it rough. She could do it that way. She pulled him from under her sweater and tossed him onto the bed. She fell on top of him and grabbed the skin of his neck in her teeth.

"AAH-AAH!"

She had no way of knowing that the scar she'd been contemplating was the result of a traumatizing dog bite incident and that her nibbling was plunging her lover into the throes of a terrifying flashback. Lana mistook the man's noises for pleasure, and bit down a little harder.

"AAAAHHHHGGGHH!" There was no mistaking this strangled sound for enjoyment. The man's right hand flew to the scar on his forehead, which was now pulsing bright red. With his left arm, he shoved Lana from on top of him and scrambled from the bed. Startled, Lana rose on her elbows and watched him flee the room, slamming the door behind him and leaving her puzzled and alone.

After the incident with Eileen and the Spanish Fly, the only real problem with being left alone, as far as Lana could see, was the surplus of free time. She had been anxious to get away, start college, go to law school—this made the extra hours seem even longer. But what can you do when you're sixteen? Nothing. Then one day, she'd had an idea.

Since she didn't work in the bar during the week (Joe believed, naively, that she needed the time for schoolwork), she decided to go to the courthouse after school to watch the proceedings. It was only a short trip on the streetcar.

She was surprised to find the courtrooms always nearly empty. Shouldn't the public be more interested in their judicial system? But after several weeks of observation, she had understood why. Most of the actions concerned petty matters. Squabbles between business partners, minor property disputes; the people in the court-room reminded her of her bitter and provincial mother. Their world the size of the Leonardo da Vinci sketch—the diameter only the length of their arms' reach. Lana decided then that the practice of law would only be a means to a much grander end.

One day during a recess, a man approached her. He was stocky, with thick blond hair going to gray. He looked as if he'd been born in his seersucker suit and white bucks. She recognized him as one of the attorneys that she had seen often in various courtrooms.

"Excuse me, miss," he'd said, "but I see you here almost every day. Are you a law student?"

Lana had looked down, incredulous, at her school uniform— plaid jumper, white Peter Pan collar blouse, and blue knee socks. "You're kidding, right? You think I chose these clothes?"

"It's just that you seem so much older than a schoolgirl."

Lana had noticed that many of the girls her age treated adults with respect and awe. She didn't. She'd been working in the bar long enough to know that most of them were no better than her peers. Just older. Adults were less self-confident than she was, and almost all of them were less intelligent. Why should she give them deference that they didn't deserve?

"Back off, mister. I'm sixteen. You'd be in jail in about three minutes."

"I'm sorry, but I think you've misunderstood."

"I think *you've* misunderstood. I'm not an idiot."

"No, I can see that." He held out his hand. "I'm Marshall Hope. I have a solo practice on Camp Street."

"Yeah, I've seen you here." Lana did not offer her hand. She was still suspicious. She'd seen it all at the bar. Hope held his hand toward her for another second, then shrugged and put it in his pocket. He jangled his change idly.

"I notice that you take a lot of notes."

"I like to understand what's going on."

"You want to be a lawyer?"

"For a while."

"For a while?"

"I have other ambitions."

Hope had smiled, a bit condescendingly, Lana noted. "Well, that's good. It's good to be ambitious. Besides, who wants to do this? I know I don't, but I've got a kid and a mortgage and a wife who wants a new kitchen. That's why I'm talking to you."

"Are you looking for a babysitter or something? I don't like kids."

"Miss, you are probably the last girl I would hire to watch my kid. We've got enough problems with him as it is."

"Yeah?" Although his patrician accent had initially put her off, Lana had begun to warm to Hope. At least he seemed honest.

"What I need is someone to help me out around the office. Someone smart to do the boring work—file things, type pleadings, things like that. You're obviously an intelligent girl. I assume you would also work cheaply."

"Oh, okay. I understand. Yeah, I would work cheaply. I'm sitting here for free, right?" Hell, she didn't have anything better to do. Might as well pick up a little money for law school.

"How fast do you type?"

"Fast enough." Typing was required of all the girls at school. Just went to show how little the nuns expected of them.

58

"Can you work three afternoons a week?"

"Yeah, I guess so. I get off school at three."

"Okay." Hope pulled out a business card. "Here's the address. How is Monday, Wednesday, and Friday?"

"Why not?"

"I'll see you Friday, then."

Sixteen years old, and she was already a lawyer.

Lana examined her stretched and misshapen sweater under the hotel room's fluorescent vanity light. Ruined. And for what? She still didn't understand what had happened. Oh well, no use dwelling on it. She tossed the sweater in the trash can and turned her thoughts to the Judge. He was a little decrepit, that was obvious, but she'd asked around and found out that he was well known in the region. With his backing, she could amass quite a bit of support. Lana walked over to the rumpled bed, picked up the pillows, and carried them over to the room's other bed, which was unused. She piled the pillows against the headboard, threw back the bedspread, and settled herself in. She turned out the light and clicked on the TV with the remote control. The day after tomorrow was Saturday. She'd take the mountains to Muhammad.

Eight

"You're going to want to use your wedge in the sand, there, Louis."

The Judge looked down at the putter in his hand. He was sure he'd chosen the wedge. Time for a new pair of glasses. Did they come any thicker? The Judge was not sure that his neck could support a stronger prescription. "You missed your calling, Stanley. You should have been a caddy."

Stanley laughed. "No profit margin in it. Besides, I would have missed all the fun we've had." Leighton had been the president of Consolidated Chemical until ten years ago. During their heyday, he and the Judge had been involved in some business deals and had become friends. Since his retirement, Leighton had been doing little but golfing. He and his wife had even bought a condo in one of those golf course developments. The Judge knew Stanley, though. As much as Leighton loved golf, the sport could never replace the world of corporate wheeling and dealing.

"I don't think either of us has had fun for awhile," said the Judge.

"I'm out of the game, Louis. But that's all right. There comes a time in every man's life when he has to step aside and let the young blood take over."

The Judge wondered if Leighton had read Hultgrew's articles and was diplomatically trying to tell him to retire. Perturbed, he pulled the wedge out of the bag, snagging the five iron and one of the woods. The clubs clattered onto the ground next to the golf cart. "Oh, damn it," mumbled the Judge, stooping slowly to pick up the mess. Leighton leapt to his assistance, bending down and gathering up the clubs.

"So, Louis," Leighton said with a forced casualness, "I went and spoke to Hebert's cellmate."

"I figured that you would."

"He says that Hebert didn't say anything about Boudreaux except that he was innocent."

The Judge tottered back into the sand trap. "I told you that I don't think he knows anything. Why didn't you worry about this back in '77?"

"I did. I'm afraid that I acted a bit hastily."

That was putting it mildly. The Judge made a couple of practice passes with the wedge, brought it back over his shoulder, took a deep breath, and took a swing at the ball. The head of the wedge sailed over the top of the ball, clearing it by a full inch.

"Nice form, though," Leighton comforted. As the Judge took position again (Leighton had hit onto the green from the tee), Leighton asked, "But what if he does know something?"

"Stanley, it's been twenty years. Don't you think he'd have said something by now?"

"He was never indicted for murder before. Never had a reason to say anything. I have someone keeping an eye on him so that we can take some preemptive action if necessary."

The Judge grimaced and whacked the ball with a force he had imagined he no longer possessed. Leighton's preemptive action was what had gotten them in trouble in the first place.

Nine

Crouton jumped out of the bed of the pickup truck. He was at the intersection of Route 308 and a narrow dirt road that ran straight down the middle of a huge sugar cane field and disappeared into the darkness.

"You sure you know where you're goin'?" the driver called out his window.

"Yeah, this is it. I just have to walk a little."

The driver shrugged, put the truck in gear, and left Crouton standing in the damp, dark heat. Crouton watched the truck's taillights disappear, then turned and started back up the road in the direction from which they'd come. He was feeling quite smug. A less professional criminal would have had the driver leave him right at Hebert's road. But Crouton had bluffed him, sending him a half-mile past.

Although Leighton had merely told him to follow Hebert to see if he went to the papers or to his attorney, Crouton could read between the lines. Leighton wanted him to take Hebert out. Of course he couldn't come out and say so—what if Crouton had been wearing a wire? But that was obviously why he'd hired a man of Crouton's caliber. This promotion from petty criminal to assassin was bound to carry with it a corresponding raise in compensation and the attention of the kind of women you only saw on TV. Crouton was ready for the good life.

It took him a good fifteen minutes to walk back toward Hebert's farm. In that time, only one car passed. Jesus, the old geezer lived out in the middle of nowhere. Must be boring as hell to live in the country like this, Crouton thought. He turned up Hebert's unpaved lane. It was another ten-minute walk before he saw the lights of Hebert's house winking through the cane, and by then Crouton was out of breath. He'd been hitting the crack pipe pretty frequently in the last twenty-four hours—after being sprung from jail, Crouton had set himself up in a cheap roadside motel and had quickly and efficiently located the in-house dealer. Crouton bent over, put his hands on his knees, and panted. If he was going to be a world-class assassin, he'd have to get in better physical shape. He made a resolution. No more drugs, except when he needed them.

His dealer had been good for more than drugs, however. He had also sold Crouton a .22-caliber pistol. "It's the kind the Mafia uses," he'd told Crouton. "You get right up against the dude's skull and, *pop.* The bullet doesn't have enough power to come out the other side of his head, so it ricochets around the asshole's brain and turns it to pizza."

The night was so quiet that Crouton could hear Hebert's TV two hundred yards away. Either Hebert was deaf, or he had his windows open. Crouton decided to take no chances; he would approach under cover, as stealthily as death himself. Pulling his gun out from the waistband of his jeans, Crouton tiptoed off the road into the cane. He had taken only two or three stealthy steps when he tumbled into a drainage ditch, twisting his ankle. He landed painfully in the mud, and heard his .22 go off with a most unstealthy crack. The noise from the pistol was followed by the barking of dogs. Crouton tried to get to his feet, but the sharp pain from his ankle sent him back to the ground, where he curled into a fetal position. Before he could attempt to stand again, the dogs were sniffing at him, trailed in short order by Hebert, who was carrying a rifle.

Crouton rolled onto his back and stuck his legs up protectively, waving them like an overturned beetle. He pointed his .22 through his flailing limbs at Hebert. Hebert started to laugh.

"Am I supposed to be afraid of that thing?"

"I'll kill you, old man."

"Not with a .22. Not unless you're within six inches of me. Besides, your barrel is full of mud. You sure that thing will even go off? Now this," Hebert stroked his obviously well-cared-for rifle, "is a weapon. You try to shoot me, and I'll put a hole in you so big you'll be more hole than asshole."

"You all right, Dennis?"

Mrs. Hebert had appeared behind her husband. She, too, was armed. Crouton had the fleeting thought that they made a nice old couple.

"I'm fine. Honey, this is Mr. Crouton. He and I shared a cell at the parish prison. He wasn't too friendly then, but I never thought he'd show up at our house carrying a gun."

Crouton knew when he was outnumbered. He tossed the .22 at Hebert's feet. "Don't shoot me," he whined.

"What are you doin' here, boy?"

"Hunting. I'm sorry, I didn't mean to trespass."

Hebert and his wife both threw their heads back and laughed.

"With a .22? What are you huntin'—chipmunks?"

Crouton was silent. He couldn't think of a better excuse.

"You ain't doin' no huntin'," reasoned Hebert. "I think you must have been comin' out to burglarize us."

Crouton considered for a moment. If he confessed to burglary, Hebert would call the cops, and he'd find himself right back in jail. If he told Hebert the truth, he would feel the proud glory of announcing himself a professional assassin for about two seconds before Hebert shot him in the cane like a rat. Wincing at the pain from his swelling ankle, Crouton looked up into the barrel of Hebert's rifle. Suddenly, the prison seemed a safe, comfortable place, a refuge where an injured man could get free pain medication.

"You're right, sir. I was tryin' to burglarize your home. I'm very sorry."

To his surprise, Hebert said, "I should call the cops, but after what they done to me . . . just get the hell outta here. I don't expect to see you around again. If I do, I'm shootin' first and asking questions later."

Crouton scrambled painfully onto his feet. "Thank you, Mr. Hebert. I sure appreciate it." He limped out of the cane and onto the drive, then remembered something and turned. "Hey, could I get my gun back?"

Crouton felt the breeze as the bullet from Hebert's rifle whizzed six inches over his head. Suddenly oblivious to the pain in his ankle, he took off flying toward the main road.

Several hours later, the last of his money in the hands of his dealer, the vials of crack that Crouton had been smoking since his return from Hebert's farm began to have the desired effect. He found that he had totally lost his fear of Hebert. Conversely, he had developed an overwhelming terror of not being able to buy any more crack. This divergence drove Crouton's next decision—he'd return to Hebert's farm and finish the job.

Crouton lit the remnants of his last rock and took a final drag off his pipe. When he'd smoked the bowl empty, he leaned back against the headboard of the unmade bed. He was in his dealer's motel room. The blackout curtains were drawn in the window, and Crouton's bloodshot eyes could barely make out the long dark hair and tattooed arms of his supplier through the gloom and smoke. "Hey, man, you got a car?" Crouton asked.

"I look like fuckin' Hertz to you?"

"Come on, man, I gotta do this job. Who's your best customer?" Crouton wheedled.

"Just what I need. Some crackhead to wreck my car and rat on me to the police. No way, you drugged-ass fucker. You want a car, go steal you a car like any other self-respectin' addict."

"I don't know how," mumbled Crouton. "Can you show me?"

"Jesus Christ, you pitiful fuck. I gotta take you by the hand like a baby?"

Crouton threw in his only bargaining chip. "No car, no more money."

Ten minutes later, he was driving down 308. If he'd known the hot-wiring thing was so easy, he would have been stealing cars years before. There were so many opportunities out there, Crouton thought, spirits buoyed by his last rock of crack. The dealer had even lent him another gun and a pair of leather gloves to hide his prints. This time Crouton was armed with a sawed-off shotgun. So the Heberts didn't stand a chance when the chemically emboldened Crouton drove right onto their front yard, kicked open the door, and blasted the old couple before they even had the time to get out of bed. Almost as an afterthought, he went through the nightstand and took some jewelry and a wallet. He'd need some money to tide him over.

Ten

Saturday morning, around eleven, Scarlett was mending one of the Judge's socks when the doorbell rang. She turned to the Judge, who was sitting on the chaise trying to read the morning paper without his glasses. "That must be the exterminator."

"Mmph," said the Judge, who seemed to have forgotten all about the roach.

Scarlett went to the door and opened it. On the gallery was what appeared to be a man in particularly unflattering drag. "Are you the exterminator?" she asked doubtfully, trying to peer around the strange visitor's ample hips to see if there was a truck in the drive.

The visitor seemed surprised to see Scarlett, and after a long pause finally said, "I'm here to see Judge L'Enfant. My name is Lana Pulaski."

Scarlett looked a little closer. It was a woman. "Just a minute," she said hesitantly. She closed the screen door on Lana and walked into the sitting room. "Grandfather, there's a strange woman on the porch. She says her name is Lana something. Something with a *P*."

"Oh?" the Judge asked. He seemed pleased. He fingered the

yellow rose he had slipped into the lapel of his bathrobe as a bou-
tonniere. "Bring her in." The Judge cupped his hand over his
mouth and nose and blew some air out, checking his breath. Satisfied, he closed the paper and leaned back into the chaise. It was the
first time Scarlett had noticed any particular interest on his part in
oral hygiene. Pondering this new development, she went back to the
front door. Lana had not moved a muscle and Scarlett, though not
particularly clairvoyant, could sense concentric circles of determi-
nation broadcasting from her like microwaves from a radio tower.
She opened the door and Lana strode past her, straight into the sitting room.

"Judge L'Enfant, what a beautiful home you have," Lana boomed.

"Miss Pulaski. What a surprise," the Judge answered. Scarlett
thought she detected a trace of ersatz Cary Grant in his delivery.
The Judge made the introductions.

"Nice to meet you," Lana said to Scarlett, without turning her
attention from the Judge. Scarlett took this as affirmation of her
basic nonexistence. She probed her cheek with her fingertips to
make sure there was solid flesh and bone under the Kabuki makeup.

"If you have the time," Lana was saying to the Judge, "I'd like
to discuss something with you, your honor."

"You don't need to call me 'your honor' outside of the court,"
the Judge chuckled debonairly. "We're old friends by now. I'll call
you Lana."

"I have some work to do outside," Scarlett interjected. "Nice to
meet you, Miss Pulaski." She backed out of the sitting room and
scurried out the back door.

What could this woman want with the Judge? A worrisome
thought began to form in Scarlett's brain. What if she was somehow
associated with the reporter who had blown the whistle on the
Judge's failing faculties? Scarlett shuddered at the thought of the
Judge with no courtroom to go to every day, following her around
Shady Oaks, unfocused and unhappy, small and demanding. Every
moment would be spent tending to the Judge. Cooking for him,

cleaning for him, making sure he didn't leave the gas on or forget to turn off the bathroom tap. Scarlett began to gnaw on a fingernail. She wouldn't be able to paint. Then she'd really be trapped. On the other hand, he was so old. How much longer would she have to care for him? At this thought her panic transmuted into guilt. She began to picture the roaring hellfires that most certainly waited for a person who cared for an aging relative with the expectation of receiving a sizable inheritance.

A roar out front brought Scarlett to attention and she ran around the corner of the house. A motorcycle was coming up the gravel driveway, a cloud of dust billowing in its wake. The rider rocketed the black Harley up behind the lawyer's Buick and cut the motor. Scarlett walked over to the bike. The sidecar held a pair of metal tanks that sprouted various rubber hoses. Painted on the sidecar were an assortment of roaches, ants, and other vermin, all with large red Xs through them. The license plate read BUGMAN1.

The rider pulled off his helmet. A mane of smooth black hair tumbled into his eyes. He shook his head and the hair parted for a moment. Scarlett caught a glimpse of deep brown, almond-shaped eyes before the curtains fell back into place above the rider's straight nose and square, clean-shaven jaw. She felt a tingling that started in her chest and quickly spread to the tips of her fingers and toes. "Hi," the rider said. "I'm the Bugman. Do you live here?"

Scarlett answered with a sneeze. The dust had worked its way into her sinuses. Mortified, she rubbed at her nose with one knuckle. She sniffled. "I'm Scarlett. I called."

The Bugman looked back and forth between Scarlett and the large, pillared house. "No shit? Your name is Scarlett?" Scarlett nodded, mutely. The Bugman laughed. "That's pretty funny. Your mom must have seen *Gone with the Wind* about a hundred times, huh?" The Bugman held out his hand. He had large hands with long slender fingers. Scarlett shook, uncomfortably aware that she had just wiped her nose with the hand. He didn't seem to notice or care. "My name is Daniel."

"It's not really Bugman?" Scarlett began to giggle nervously.

"No, that's just my stage name. Um, what did you need me for?"

That was a trick question. Better answer carefully. Scarlett started to formulate a response, but heard a loud clatter of heels behind her. She turned to see Lana striding down the steps, trailed by the hunched figure of the Judge. He looked like a little dinghy bringing up the rear behind a coal barge. He had gotten dressed, and Scarlett noticed that his pants were too long and he was treading on the cuffs with his heels.

"Wow," whispered the Bugman, "is that your mom?"

"My mother died twenty years ago."

"Oh, that's good. I mean, that that isn't your mom."

"Yeah," Scarlett breathed, struck by the absolute and incontrovertible truth of the statement.

"Hey," the Bugman whispered, "did you ever wonder what it would be like to be, like, really fat? I mean, not just fat like her," he motioned with his head toward Lana, "but so huge that you were just immobile. Someone would have to bring you food, change the channel on the TV for you, change your clothes for you. It would be like you were one of those big queen termites being serviced by the worker drones. You'd just be sitting there, pulsing and laying eggs."

Scarlett opened her mouth to answer that she *had* thought about it, though not specifically in a *termite* sense, but was interrupted.

"Excuse me," Lana called authoritatively, "you'll have to move that motorcycle. We're leaving to go to lunch."

"What?" Scarlett asked the Judge.

"Miss Pulaski has asked for my advice on her campaign for attorney general," he explained.

"This," whispered the Bugman, "is why I never vote."

Shady Oaks was raised a good five feet off the swampy Louisiana soil on its brick piers. Underneath the house was darkness, piles of old leaves and various pieces of broken and rusted farm machinery.

Scarlett peered into the gloom, where she could see only the yellow circle of the Bugman's flashlight. God, thought Scarlett, just let me have this one thing. She began to picture herself painting the Bugman, rather, smearing paint *onto* the Bugman. In this mental movie, the Bugman had his shirt off and she was spreading cadmium red on his chest. She pressed him up against a canvas, leaving a perfect chest imprint, then up against her. . . .

It had been several years since she'd had a boyfriend. There had been the occasional date, usually arranged by her god-mother, Inez. The boys were always handsome, steady, dependable. They were definitely someone's type, Inez's maybe. Unfortunately, they were not Scarlett's, and usually only lasted for a date or two.

Scarlett could feel herself falling in love with the Bugman, with the palpable certainty possessed only by the very lonely.

The circle of light came toward her, and she backed away from the house, flushed. The Bugman stepped out into the sun and Scarlett felt the numbness spread through her limbs again.

"How bad is it?" she asked.

"It's not good." He put his hand on his hip. Scarlett became fixated on his biceps. They were well defined, but not bulky. He was lean. That was it. Lean. She wanted to paint his arm, too. Cobalt blue. The Bugman continued, oblivious. "You definitely have roaches. You also have termites. See." He walked over to one of the brick pillars, bent down and pointed. "This little mud tunnel going up the brick, the termites made that. They crawl up through it and get into the wood. You have a movable feast of insect life here." He shook his head. "An old house like this, you have to watch it."

"Can you do something?"

"Yeah. It's just bugs. The house isn't going to fall down or any-thing. At least not in the near future. I'll spray for the termites today. It's getting late. I'll have to come back for the roaches. We have to use something special for them. These guys aren't wimpy northern roaches like in New York or Chicago. These are big, strong

Louisiana roaches. They laugh at normal bug spray. You practically have to take them out with an AK-47."

"Wow. You sure know a lot about bugs."

"It's an ugly job, but someone's gotta do it. I'll go get the spray."

Scarlett tagged after him. "How did you get to be the Bugman?" she burst out, desperately trying to think of a way to continue the conversation.

He did not seem to notice anything awkward about the question, and answered without missing a beat. "Well, my father was a bugman, and his father before him. It's kind of a family tradition."

"Really?"

"Nah. I was taking some time off from school, and my uncle had a crop-dusting business. I started working for him, flying a little, then I started doing this. It's not, like, a calling or anything."

"I don't think that I have a calling."

"You should get one. Focus is important."

"What's your focus, then? I mean, if it's not roaches."

"Maybe I'll show you sometime." The Bugman reached into the sidecar and pulled out one of the tanks, a pair of heavy work gloves and a mask. "You might want to go somewhere while I do this." He nodded at Consolidated. "Looks like you get enough toxic waste around here. I'm surprised you have any bugs at all."

"I'll be in the barn." Scarlett waved in its general direction. "Just come get me when you're done."

"Sure." He pulled on the gloves. Scarlett started thinking about his hands in the gloves. Her face went red with embarrassment and she wheeled about and hurried off down the path.

The Judge sat across the table from Lana, gnawing his fried chicken and staring openly down the front of Lana's ruffled electric-yellow blouse. Hell, he was old. He could do whatever he wanted to do. One of the benefits, the only benefit, of getting old, was that people let you get away with so much more because they felt sorry for you.

Although this woman did not appear to feel sorry for him—she clearly wanted something from him. The Judge was not so old that he could not recognize opportunism. The question was what *he* would get out of the deal. Distracted by the intriguing possibilities, he picked up his napkin, wiped his oily lips on it, then realized it was the tablecloth.

"Judge L'Enfant," Lana said loudly. She so startled the Judge that he yanked at the tablecloth still wadded in his fist, causing the water to slosh out of the glasses on the table. Lana continued, apparently unshaken. "You see my predicament."

"Oh yes." What had she been talking about? Whatever it was, it had made her breasts heave attractively under the blouse. The Judge decided to fake it, in hopes of having her continue. "Your . . . dilemma."

"Yes, my lack of name recognition and support in the Cajun parishes."

Good, it had worked. You had to listen so carefully these days to follow what people were saying. People used to be clear and to the point. These days they mumbled circuitously. The Judge found himself wishing that he could go back a few decades. Wheeling and dealing, living in prosperity, the life of the party. He had pull then. Nowadays, he just felt pushed. Or, rather, kicked from behind by a very large and thick-soled boot. He wondered what Hebert had told this woman. There was no reason that Hebert should know anything about the Judge's dealings with Leighton, unless Boudreaux had said something. Unfortunately, the Judge could easily imagine Boudreaux bragging to Hebert that he had the case won. But Boudreaux wouldn't have stopped there. He would have to rub it in, really let Hebert know that he had no chance despite what the law said. And the most satisfying way for Boudreaux to have done that would have been to describe to Hebert just what kind of dirt he had on Judge L'Enfant. The Judge felt a tightness in his chest.

Suddenly the Judge remembered Lana. "You were saying . . ." he sputtered.

"I feel that if I have an endorsement from someone well-respected in the area, someone that everyone trusts, it will go a long way toward helping my campaign."

"I'm certain that it will," the Judge agreed, nodding. He took a roll out of the breadbasket and tried biting into it, but succeeded only in flaking some crumbs off it with his dentures. He held the roll out in front of him and regarded it unhappily. "I think that these are stale." He didn't feel like eating it anyway. He was beginning to get nauseous.

He started to place the roll back in the breadbasket, but Lana quickly detained his liver-spotted hand with her smooth, plump white palm. The Judge was reminded of a particularly juicy chicken breast. "Judge L'Enfant, it's your support I need," Lana declared firmly. "I think that with your connections, I can really accomplish something for this state. We've had the old boys in power too long." Lana's voice rose. She pounded the table with the fist clenching the Judge's. "The state's image is tarnished. There's corruption. We need fresh blood. New ideas. I believe that I'm the best person for the job." She paused, but the Judge did not answer. He had fallen face forward into the dinner rolls.

Eleven

Lana stood in the waiting room of the coronary intensive care unit. She held a small, damp, napkin-wrapped parcel with her fingertips. It was the Judge's dentures, which the EMT had removed while administering CPR. Lana sighed. This day had certainly been a waste of time in an already too-short campaign. The Judge would probably die, and how much could he help her dead? She was contemplating this predicament when Scarlett stumbled in, her hair tangled and in her face. The motorcyclist was with her, holding a pair of helmets and looking uncomfortable. Lana noticed that he was very attractive and appealingly too young for her. She smiled at him, over the top of Scarlett's head. She saw his eyes grow wide under his jet bangs.

"How is he?" Scarlett gasped.

Lana began to answer, then remembered the dentures. "Here." Lana handed the lump of napkin to Scarlett.

Scarlett unfolded the napkin, exposing the teeth. "Oh God, no," she breathed. The teeth clattered to the floor.

"My God, he's not dead," Lana answered wearily. "Not last I saw of him anyway. They won't tell me how he is. I'm not a relative."

"Oh." Embarrassed, Scarlett picked up the dentures and wiped them on her pant leg. Lana winced.

"Why don't you ask at the nurse's station?" the young man suggested quietly.

"That's a good idea," Lana agreed, hoping to get rid of the shaken Scarlett, if only for several minutes.

Scarlett turned to the young man. "You don't have to stay. I really appreciate you bringing me here. I don't think I could have driven."

"Oh sure. No problem. I'll be out Monday to finish up."

"Good." Scarlett smiled softly.

"Unless, well, maybe you should call me when you want me to come back, I mean with your grandfather here and all."

Oh good God, thought Lana. He's the sensitive type.

"Okay. Thanks."

Scarlett stumbled to the nurses' desk and the young man walked off toward the elevators. Lana sat down in one of the waiting room chairs and began to search through her purse for a Wash-n-Dry to remove the memory of the dentures from her hands. She wondered how bad the heart attack had been. With someone as old as the Judge, it just took a little palpitation to put them into the ground. She daubed at her hands with the towelette, picturing the funeral. It would probably draw a big crowd of mourners—lawyers, other judges, local politicos. It wouldn't be a bad idea for her to attend. She might be able to do some networking. She saw herself standing by the casket, resplendent in a beaded black sheath. Beautiful—with the right accessories, of course.

Scarlett walked back over. "The doctor thinks he's going to be okay. They're going to let me see him in a little while. Thanks for calling me." She slunk back to the nurses' station.

"No problem," Lana said to the girl's retreating back. Well, there was no point in staying. Lana picked up her purse and headed toward the elevators, her mind on strategy. Maybe the old guy could be of some use to her after all. At the same time, she felt a little disappointed over the dress. But how long could he really last? Maybe not long enough to pull strings or do her any good. Lana went back to the funeral, seeing herself the center of attention, and suddenly the answer was clear. The Judge could be of great use to her dead, long after his funeral even, if she were the grieving widow.

Marriage to the Judge would give her connections and political legitimacy. And he wouldn't be that bad a companion. He was obviously an intelligent man. His courtly, respectful attitude appealed to her. He'd certainly be more pleasant company than, say, the mammary mauler from the Hilton. Lana imagined herself ensconced in the capacious, shabbily opulent rooms of Shady Oaks. The house (despite its need of renovation—or maybe because of it) exuded history and power. History and power, Lana knew, were her destiny. But the old man was decrepit and her window of opportunity was small. She would have to work fast.

The waiting room was dimly lit, with a fuzzy TV set flickering at one end. Scarlett twisted uncomfortably in a chair in front of the set, trying to fit her entire body into the chair somehow so that she could get some sleep. The doctor had said that she could see the Judge soon, but it had been almost six hours. Several other similarly gloomy persons were interspersed about the waiting room, none sitting too close to the others, all staring morosely at the TV.

Scarlett wadded her denim jacket behind her neck and closed her eyes. She felt unexpectedly grim. The Judge was a pain, a chore, and she had her eye on inheriting his estate—but she loved him. He was both a father and a mother since her own had died when she was so little. She didn't even remember her parents, not clearly anyway. One evening they left her with her babysitter to go to a party, and then they didn't return. Her father, blind drunk, had collided head-on with an eighteen-wheeler. The next day, Scarlett was with the Judge, his Haitian cook, and his maid. Inez, her god-mother, her *marrain*, came by every weekend. Scarlett was the center of attention. After the loss of his son, the Judge had directed his affection toward Scarlett. He had coddled her, indulging her every whim. He spent his free time taking her fishing, playing with her on the floor of the sitting room, buying her toys. She barely noticed that her parents weren't there. At least, not until now. Now, she was afraid that the Judge would disappear, too, leaving her by herself, a small barnacle broken off from the boat, floating helplessly and without direction. Who would be there to care about her? Suddenly the inheritance and the escape seemed less important (though not totally forgotten). Scarlett scrunched up inside herself, a heap of self-pity, and sniffled.

She was wiping her damp cheeks when a nurse came into the waiting room and called out her name. Scarlett felt a jet of fear tear through her. She uncrumpled herself from the chair and followed the nurse out of the waiting room and down the hall.

The CICU was made up of a series of glass cubicles encircling the nurses' station, each cubicle filled with a chair, a bed, machines, and a patient attached to the machines by a network of wires and tubing. The nurse led Scarlett past three or four of these cubicles, giving Scarlett plenty of time to develop a feeling of real dread before getting to the Judge. She gasped when she saw him. He appeared tiny and gray against the white hospital sheets. His skin was a sheet of cellophane stretched across barely functioning veins and organs. He looked profoundly ill.

The nurse called to him loudly. The Judge opened his eyes halfway and saw Scarlett. He motioned to her, weakly, with a hand impaled by an IV tube. Scarlett walked closer to the bed and leaned down to him. "Scarlett." He reached out and gripped her collar. "Where is Miss Pulaski?"

Twelve

Several days after the Judge's nosedive at lunch, Lana tried to visit him in the hospital. She wasn't able to talk to him—they'd only let her peer into his glass cubicle. He'd looked better than the last time they'd been together—less blue. Seeing him as helpless as an infant, Lana had the irrational urge to grab him up and press him to her breast. She'd been unexpectedly relieved when the nurse said that the Judge would be released any day.

As long as she was out in the parishes, Lana decided to go to the clerk's office in the Thibodaux courthouse to review the *Boudreaux v. Hebert* acquisitive prescription case. Lana gave the clerk the name and approximate date of the case. The woman disappeared into a storeroom and was gone a good twenty minutes. When she finally returned, she presented the file to Lana with such a triumphant air that she might have been handing over treasure from King Tut's tomb. Instead, Lana received a stack of papers that was old, yellow, and distinctly musty in odor. The pleadings were typed on onionskin, and the impressions from the typewriter keys felt like Braille under Lana's fingers. She began to read through the file, faintly amused by the archaic language and facts.

It was clear from the pleadings that Boudreaux had no case. But Lana was not surprised that the man's attorney had filed it. He must have smelled the money on Boudreaux the minute the diamond-toothed Cajun had walked through the door. There couldn't have been too many paying clients out here twenty years ago. Probably still weren't.

Then something caught Lana's eye—the name of the Judge. That was a strange coincidence. Did it mean anything? Probably not. How many judges could have been in this district back then? Two? Three? She'd ask him about it, though. He might have some insight on what had happened.

"Can I get this file copied?" Lana asked the clerk.

"Sure thing, hon. It's twenty-five cents a page."

"No problem." Lana noticed the clerk's name on a plaque on the counter. Boudreaux. Another coincidence. "Look at that." Lana showed the woman the name on the pleadings.

"Oh yeah," said the clerk. "Thierry was my uncle."

"Really?"

"Yeah. I remember when this case was filed. My mama was clerk then."

"Really?" repeated Lana. Her cell phone rang before she could question the woman further.

"Bad news, boss," Carl announced. "Your newest client and his wife were just found shot to death in their bed."

"You've really made a mess, haven't you, son?"

Leighton's voice was colder than Crouton remembered it. The addict's eyes darted nervously around the neglected, weed-choked little playground where the two sat back-to-back on benches. No one was around, the swings and rusted merry-go-round were empty, but Leighton had told him that if he even acknowledged his presence, any deal was off.

"I got rid of your problem, that's all that matters," Crouton mumbled through tight lips. His fingertips nervously traced and retraced the graffiti carved into the splintery bench. He hadn't had any crack for more than twenty-four hours (there had only been two twenties in Hebert's wallet and the dealer wouldn't give him anything for the jewelry he'd taken from the Heberts' bedside table) and he was feeling jittery. He just wanted his money so that he could go back to his hotel and erase the bloody incident with a puff of bitter smoke.

"I never told you to kill Mr. Hebert and his wife. I just asked you to keep an eye on him and tell me what he did."

"Yeah, well, you wanted him killed, didn't you?"

"That's neither here nor there, is it?"

"Just give me my fuckin' money."

"What is the going rate for a sloppy shotgun murder? Not very much, I'd assume. What did you do with the gun?"

"I threw it in the bayou," Crouton lied. Actually, he'd conscientiously returned it to his dealer—he didn't want the guy pissed off when he came to him for more drugs.

"But now that Mr. Hebert is dead, we don't know what he may have told his lawyer. If she knows something, she may make trouble."

"That's your problem."

"No, I'm afraid that's *your* problem, Mr. Crouton. Now you're going to have to finish this job." Faking a yawn, Leighton stretched his arms out and dropped a folded piece of paper over the back of the bench. "That's the lawyer's name and address."

Crouton slid the paper over to his thigh and unfolded it with shaky fingers. "This is in New Orleans. How am I gonna get there?"

"I'm going to leave five hundred dollars under a newspaper on my bench. Wait a couple of minutes until I'm out of sight, then come over, pick up the paper, and read for a few more minutes. You can read, can't you?"

"Yeah, I can read." What an asshole, thought Crouton.

"After a few minutes, take the money and leave. If you do a good job, there will be another forty-five hundred for you. If you do a bad job, you get nothing. So don't fuck this up, Mr. Crouton. Be a little more deliberate this time. No more shotguns, do you hear?"

"Yeah, no more shotguns," Crouton repeated mechanically. Just give me the money, the money, the money, he thought to himself. Five hundred dollars would definitely buy him enough of a stash for the bus ride to New Orleans.

Thirteen

Lana looked over the Heberts' tidy front yard. The flower beds in front of the white frame house were well-groomed. In the middle of a cluster of peonies was a wooden cutout of a woman with polka-dot knickers bending over to garden. A plaster deer stood at attention next to the azaleas. The domesticity of the setting made the electric-yellow police tape even more incongruous.

"We don't usually do this," Officer Aucoin said, unlocking the front door and lifting the tape aside so that Lana could enter.

In her years of practice, Lana had found that there was almost always a way to get people to do things that they didn't usually do. In Officer Aucoin's case, Lana had merely purchased twenty-five dollars worth of the Amway products that were prominently displayed on the officer's desk, expressing particular interest in the "environmentally friendly" window cleaner. Soon thereafter, she and the bony, hatchet-faced officer were in a squad car driving through tall green fields of sugar cane toward the Heberts' house.

The Heberts' living room was neat and undisturbed, giving Lana the feeling that what was to come couldn't possibly be too bad.

She took in the furniture—reproduction colonial, intermingled with some genuine antiques, all waxed to a high gloss. There was an almost-new TV and VCR, a collection of crystal figurines in a breakfront, and an old upright piano. It was the house of a comfortable but frugal elderly couple. She followed Aucoin down a hall lined with framed photographs of children and grandchildren. "It was the daughter that found them," Aucoin told her. "She hadn't heard from her mama for a few days and she was worried. So she came by the house, and . . ." Aucoin stopped and motioned into a bedroom door. Lana peered in.

It *was* bad. Blackened, dried blood made two huge spots on the bedding and splattered the headboard. Even from across the room, Lana could make out bits of skull and gray hair stuck to a lampshade. The drawers of the bedside tables were ajar, their contents, brown with dried blood, littered the floor. "Jesus," she said, sickened.

"Not pretty, is it?" Neither Aucoin's voice nor sharp features displayed any emotion.

It was strange. Hebert and his wife had seemed so alive and vital, despite their ages. Now all that remained of the old couple were remnants of meat and bone. Lana thought about how she'd feel if she went to visit Joe and happened upon a similar scene. She felt herself growing angry. Very angry.

"What do you think happened?"

"I think some son of a bitch took them out to make the burglary easier."

Lana shook her head. "It doesn't make sense. Once they were dead, he could take what he wanted at leisure. Why didn't he take the TV and VCR? You said you found tire tracks on the lawn, so the killer had a car. He could have easily carried away a lot more than just a wallet and some jewelry."

"Maybe someone spooked him."

"I doubt it. It's pretty isolated out here. Besides, if anyone else had shown up, he could have shot them, too."

"There's no making sense of these animals anymore. Most of them are high and they're not thinking straight. If there's one thing I've learned from this job, it's that most criminals aren't logical."

Apparently, the police weren't either.

fourteen

Bolton Hultgrew shuffled through the papers on his desk. It was chaos; he could never find anything. He had to have his article written in an hour if it was going to go in the morning edition of the *Acadian Star*. All around him, fingers clacked productively on the keys of word processors; the staccato noises echoed and bounced off the tile floors and high ceiling of the old newsroom. Hultgrew hummed tunelessly in an effort to block out the disturbing sound of others' accomplishments. After going through the mess for the third time, he wrapped his arms around the heaps of paper, magazines, old matchbooks, pens, and paperclips and gathered it all into a pile in the center of the desk, hoping that the clipping he was searching for would slide down the side of the mound and into his lap, like sand off a sand pile. All that fell off were some old eraser crumbs and a sticky and ancient half-eaten Little Debbie cake. He peeled off the shredded cellophane, brought the cake up to his nose and smelled it, trying to remember how long it had been on the desk. It seemed okay. He shrugged. Junk food had a half-life. Better living through chemistry. He took a bite out of it and swallowed gratefully. He had missed lunch. He bent over and began to dig through the trashcan with his unoccupied hand. Long, slender calves suddenly appeared before his eyes.

"Hey, Bolt," said the owner of the legs.

Hultgrew straightened up reluctantly, having enjoyed the view twelve inches above ground level. His wire-rimmed glasses had slid to the tip of his nose, and he pushed them back into place and peered at Cami Gooch, star of the *Star* and proprietor of the legs. "Hey, Cami. Where ya' been all my life?"

"I've been where the action is, Bolt. Didn't see you there." This was true. Cami had an unerring instinct for finding herself in the middle of a bank robbery or a five-car pileup. Right now she was investigating the robbery and shotgun murder of an old couple out on their farm. The photos Cami took at the crime scene had been spread across the front page of the paper for two days. Hultgrew usually found himself covering the local Kiwanis banquet, and Cami didn't let him forget it. She curled her lip at him. "You have cream filling on your chin."

Hultgrew wiped it off with his thumb, annoyed at Cami. She always caught him at his least debonair, which, to be fair, was most of the time. "What do you want?"

"I just got a call from my source at General. Your favorite judge was brought into the CICU a few days ago with a heart attack. I thought you might want to know, maybe send flowers or something."

Hultgrew could feel the scar above his eyebrow pulsing and red. He wasn't sure if it was from bending over or from hearing about the Judge, but he suspected the latter. "That senile fuck better not die until I have a chance to pin him to the wall."

"Bolt, you are a gentleman and a scholar." Cami turned and headed back toward her desk.

Hultgrew watched her go, then picked a phone book off the floor and found the number for Bayou General. He dialed and asked to be connected to the CICU. He identified himself to the nurse on the other end of the line. "I'm calling about Judge Louis L'Enfant. What can you tell me about his condition?"

"He's in serious condition, but the doctor expects him to recover."

There was still opportunity. Hultgrew hung up, flushed with a manic glee. He was going to get L'Enfant this time. He didn't know how, or with what, but there had to be some dirt on the old man somewhere. The heart attack had to be a good omen. It gave him hope.

The memory of the Judge dismissing his dog bite case was still strong. "What's the matter with you, teasing that beautiful dog?" the Judge had admonished him. "You deserve whatever you got, you chicken-livered bully. It's a shame that the dog aimed for your head— it's obviously your least used appendage. You're lucky I don't throw the book at you." Hultgrew had suspected at the time that the Judge had been paid off by the dog's owners. Otherwise, why would he have decided against Hultgrew in a case where a dangerous animal was running loose off the leash? All Hultgrew had done was lure Fang to the front door with a frozen T-bone and then whap him in the head a couple of times with the rock-hard steak. Fang hadn't taken offense at the blows—he thought Hultgrew was playing. In the spirit of the game, he'd leapt at the reporter in an attempt to grab the steak. Hultgrew yanked the meat away at the last second, and one of Fang's long, lustrous teeth gashed Hultgrew's forehead. Hultgrew was still stunned that he hadn't been awarded at least ten grand in pain and anguish. His actions had clearly been reasonable; the dog had been shitting on his lawn. Instead, Fang's owners countersued, alleging that Hultgrew's cruelty to Fang had caused them tens of thousands of dollars of psychological trauma. As punishment, the Judge had saddled Hultgrew with a hundred hours of community service in the local animal shelter. To add insult to injury, the reporter had been assigned to clean cages, most of which were lined with old copies of the *Acadian Star*. It wasn't enough that Fang dumped on his lawn—the symbolism of scores of homeless kittens and puppies relieving themselves on his work product did not escape even Hultgrew's literal and lazy mind.

He descended in the elevator to the *Star*'s ground floor newspaper morgue. The doors opened on a kid with bad skin sitting behind a metal desk. He was wearing a heavy-metal T-shirt and reading a comic book. He ignored Hultgrew's approach. Hultgrew snatched the comic away. "This stuff will rot your head, kid."

"Yeah, so will this paper."

Hultgrew had to concede that this was probably true. "I need you to pull everything we've got on a Judge Louis L'Enfant. As far back as it goes."

The kid slid a slip of paper and a pencil across the desktop. "Write it down. Spell it right, too, or I won't be able to find anything."

Hultgrew sighed and printed the Judge's name in large, block letters. "Be thorough. This is important. And hurry up with it, I may not have that much time."

"No problem," the kid sneered. "I'm a professional."

Several hours later, having cleared his desk of its usual detritus by brushing it off onto the floor, Hultgrew sat behind a thick stack of yellowed newspaper clippings. Most were from the thirties and forties; there was a wedding announcement from 1935. After the forties, the clippings petered out. The last was five years old and detailed the opening of a new Winn-Dixie grocery store in Raceland. There was an out-of-focus picture of the Judge cutting a ribbon across the store doors with a giant pair of scissors. Something stirred in Hultgrew's brain. God, he had written the story. Even taken the photograph. Hultgrew realized that he hadn't advanced much further on the *Star* since covering shopping center openings. He felt a broiling dissatisfaction coming on, causing bile to rise into his throat. Then again, maybe it was just the Little Debbie cake. He tacked the supermarket story to the bulletin board behind his desk and drew a red *X* through the Judge with a felt-tipped pen. He massaged the throbbing scar with his forefinger and started reading. He was going to get that senile ass.

Fifteen

Scarlett pulled open the drapes, raised the window, and threw open the shutters. A cool, chemical breeze drifted into the Judge's room from the plant next door.

"Close that," moaned the Judge.

"You need some fresh air in here, Grandfather."

"I don't need to see Consolidated."

Scarlett sighed and shut the drapes. She crossed over to his bed and poured him a glass of water from the blue plastic hospital pitcher on the nightstand. The Judge had proven to be a difficult patient. It was as if he had to be obstinate to feel in control of the situation. Scarlett knew she should feel sorry for him, but he'd already winged the blood pressure cuff at her head once that morning. She was so harried after caring for him the past two weeks that she didn't even need her white makeup anymore. Her complexion had taken on a hue more sickly than the Judge's. "Are you hungry?" she asked, more out of duty than concern.

"I don't want anything to eat. When are you going to change my sheets? They changed them every day in the hospital. I like clean sheets. I have few enough pleasures lying here in this bed."

"The doctor said you could go back to work in another week. Can you just be a little patient?"

"I'm too old to be patient."

Scarlett gave up. "Okay. Let me help you over to the chair." She threw back the covers and took one thin, white, hairless arm.

"I can do it. I'm not an invalid."

"Good. Then you can change your sheets, too." Scarlett saw the Judge deflate under his baggy flannel pajamas. She felt the flames lick at her face. Hell. She was definitely going to hell. And down there would be thousands of sick, petulant Judges. For being such an ungrateful, bad person in life, she would be consigned to care for thousands of sick, petulant Judges for eternity. "I'm sorry, Grandfather," she said with a shudder. "The clean sheets are on the line. I'll go down and get them. Here." She handed him the morning papers. "Why don't you read while I take care of this?"

Halfway down the steps the doorbell rang. I can't get anything done, Scarlett thought. When she pulled open the door, Lana was standing on the gallery, wearing a chartreuse sweater with matching feather epaulets. She looked like a giant, overweight parrot. Where did she get that thing dry cleaned?

"How is the Judge?" Lana asked.

"He's doing all right." Scarlett noticed that Lana was carrying a box of chocolates and a bulky, gift-wrapped package.

"Can I see him?"

"He's kind of weak right now. . . ."

"Who is that?" the Judge screamed from his room.

Scarlett was amazed that he could hear the bell. The heart attack must have improved his nerve deafness. "It's Miss Pulaski," she yelled back.

"Have her come up," the Judge replied.

Reluctantly, Scarlett held open the screen door. "He can't have those chocolates. He's on a special diet."

"The chocolates are for you, sweetie," Lana said, a trace of smugness creeping into her voice. "I thought you might need a treat." She held out the box to Scarlett. It was Godiva. "This," she indicated the large package, "is an artificial sheepskin cover for his bed. Totally hypoallergenic. It prevents bedsores."

Scarlett cringed. "Thank you, that's really thoughtful." She led Lana up the stairs, which creaked under the woman's weight. The Judge's door was the first on the right. When he saw Lana, he hoisted himself out of the chair. The newspapers slipped from his lap.

"Miss Pulaski, I'm glad we meet under better circumstances."

"Judge, you're looking so well," Lana cooed.

"Well," Scarlett said uncomfortably, "I'll just go down and get the bedclothes." She paused. "Do you need anything, Miss Pulaski?"

"No, don't worry about me."

Too late for that, Scarlett thought as she started down the stairs. She knew that she didn't like Lana, a woman with an agenda as poorly hidden as her own. What Lana's agenda was, though, Scarlett was not yet sure. On the other hand, Lana was keeping the Judge occupied, if only for a little while. She could use the time to paint. Maybe she should be grateful.

But she couldn't shake the uneasiness out of her mind. Why would Lana want to spend time with the Judge? It wasn't like he was sparkling company. Good God, Scarlett was around him enough to realize that. Even his clerk hadn't been over to see him since the heart attack. It obviously wasn't physical attraction. This left Scarlett with one possibility, which terrified her. It had to be the money. Lana wanted Scarlett's inheritance.

Scarlett snatched the sheets off the line and raced through the house. She burst into the Judge's room, linen billowing behind her.

"Where's the fire?" asked the Judge. "I haven't seen you move that fast for me since I got home."

Scarlett didn't answer, she just stared. Lana had spread the sheepskin out over the bed and she and the Judge were both lying across it. Lana was running her palm over the fleece. "This really feels good. Why don't you try it?" Lana said innocently.

Scarlett recoiled and dropped the sheets in a pile at the foot of the bed. "I think you had better leave now. The Judge needs to take a nap."

"I don't know if I'm in the mood for a nap. Miss Pulaski's just told me some rather distressing news. I don't know if you've ever met the Heberts, but they were murdered a few days ago."

"I don't remember meeting them," Scarlett answered. "But that's an even better reason for you to try and relax. You can't be getting upset. You want to get back to work as soon as possible, don't you?"

"Maybe you're right." The Judge turned to Lana. "My dear, despite the news, you have been a godsend. I feel better already. I guess I'll see you Friday night, then."

"Friday night?" Scarlett squeaked.

"Miss Pulaski and I are going into New Orleans to the theater."

After Lana had gone, Scarlett ripped the sheepskin off the bed to change the sheets. She started sneezing uncontrollably as bits of chartreuse feather settled around her like polluted snow. Sniffing and wiping her nose on her sleeve, she went over to wake up the Judge. He was now sleeping soundly in his armchair, making little congested noises with each breath. Scarlett wondered if he were allergic to the feathers, too. She shook him gently.

The Judge stirred, then straightened up a little in the chair. "Where is Miss Pulaski?"

"She left," Scarlett answered breezily, hoping the Judge would soon forget that Lana had ever been there. "Don't you remember?"

"Oh yes. You made her leave." The Judge twisted his face into a mask of disapproval.

"You needed a rest," Scarlett protested. "Why don't you get back into bed now?"

96

"I might as well. There's nothing else for me to do. Besides, this news about the Heberts is very upsetting." The Judge rose from the chair, carefully and with great deliberation. Scarlett noticed that he had been almost as tall sitting as he was standing. "Will you find that old cane that's up in the attic?" he asked her. "I seem to be a little stiff."

When he had tottered to the bed she tried to tuck him in, but he pushed her hands away. He smoothed the covers over himself then rolled over with his back to her, becoming a small, accusatory lump under the quilt. She couldn't imagine why he was so upset about some couple he'd never even mentioned to her before. Scarlett stood for a moment by the bed, then shook her head and left the room to look for the cane.

As soon as he heard the door close behind Scarlett, the Judge shot up in bed. He had been faking sleep and confusion, of course. Still, it was somewhat disturbing how easily Scarlett bought his act.

That damned Leighton! Amazing that a psychotic like that had made such a success of himself. The Judge reflected for a moment. Actually, it was amazing that there weren't more like Leighton. He fumbled for the phone and dialed Stanley's number.

"Hello?" The voice on the other end sounded perfectly normal.

"What in God's name have you done?" hissed the Judge.

"It's nice to talk to you, too, Louis. How are you doing?"

"I was improving until I heard about your latest escapade."

"You know, you just can't get good help anymore."

"Stop trying to muddle this, Stanley. What are you going to do about the Heberts?"

"I'm not going to do anything about them. Nobody can trace this to us. Just pretend it never happened."

The Judge felt his stomach cramp up. A little corruption was one thing. He'd always felt that graft and bribery kept the wheels turning. Boosted the economy. Provided jobs. But the murder of two innocent people was more than the Judge could rationalize away.

"Don't you have a conscience, Stanley?"

"I do, and it tells me that I have to look out for myself. Hebert and his wife are already dead. Nothing can be done about it. Leave it alone, Louis. You didn't have anything to do with it anyway."

Didn't he?

Scarlett swung open the attic door. A wall of musty, warm air hit her in the face, smelling of old newspapers and sawdust. She paused for a moment, then started up the narrow staircase. She felt a little reflexive shiver as she reached the landing. Attics were always dangerous places in horror movies, weren't they? If she had been watching herself in the theater, she would be thinking, "Don't go up there, stupid." She shook the feeling off. This was real life, and she'd been up here lots of times before, although not in the last ten years or so.

At the top of the stairs was a series of connecting rooms. When Scarlett was little, one of the rooms had housed Marie, the Judge's maid, and the room behind had belonged to his cook. Originally, she guessed, the rooms had been used for the household slaves, but that seemed so far away and unreal that she wasn't really sure if it was true. And the idea of her family as slaveholders was too upsetting to think about anyway. She had enough to atone for without inviting her ancestors to the guilt party.

Scarlett reached for the wall and clicked the light switch, but the bulb was out. Then she saw an old candlestick sticking out of a box of ancient household knickknacks. She pulled it out and pawed through the box looking for something to light it with, finding an old silver lighter that had sifted to the bottom of the box. It had the Judge's initials engraved on it. Scarlett recalled how he used to smoke a pipe when she was a child. She had loved the spicy smell. Scarlett flipped back the lid of the lighter, and a little yellow flame popped up. She lit the candle and went into the first room, where the maid used to sleep.

There was a twin bed in the corner, under the eaves. It had been covered in plastic to keep the mattress clean. Next to the bed was a dormer window, which admitted almost no light, even though it was the middle of the afternoon. The window faced north and was blocked by the leafy branch of one of the large oaks. A film of brown soot from Consolidated formed a nearly opaque coating on the outside of the windowpanes. Scarlett wrinkled her nose. She looked around the room for the Judge's cane, but didn't see it anywhere. Scarlett decided to try the next room.

This room had been used by the cook, a kind Haitian woman named Lucie. Lucie had a lilting accent so beautiful that Scarlett was forever trying to imitate it as a child. Her attempts usually sent Lucie into peals of laughter. Lucie had used to give Scarlett big pieces of sugar cane to keep her occupied while dinner was being cooked. Scarlett had spent not a little time getting cavities filled when she was a child.

She looked around Lucie's room. There was an old steamer trunk sitting in the corner, the kind that people used to take with them on ocean liners. It was long enough to hold the cane. Scarlett sat the candlestick down on the floor next to the chest, jiggled the rusty lock, and it popped open. She raised the lid and began searching through the chest in the weak yellow light cast by the flame.

She had often explored this chest as a child—it had belonged to her grandmother Odile and was full of old photographs, costume jewelry, yellowed clothing, and bits of lace. The first thing she pulled from the chest was a silver toilet set—a hairbrush, comb, and mirror. The brush still had several long wavy dark hairs caught in its bristles. Scarlett pulled them out and drew them through her fingertips. She reached back into the chest and felt around among the old scarves. Her hand brushed against a picture frame, and she removed it from the chest. It was of Odile when she was very young, probably before she married the Judge. Scarlett held the picture under the candle flame for a better look. Jesus. She grabbed the silver mirror and piled her brown curls on top of her head. She glanced back and forth between the mirror and the photograph. She looked almost exactly like Odile, from the hair, to the eyes, to the pale delicate skin. She hadn't seen the resemblance before because she was so young the last time she had seen the photograph.

Scarlett began digging faster, deep into the recesses of the chest, looking for more photographs. She pulled out some flapper-type shoes that were several sizes too small, a couple of ancient books, their pages stuck together with mildew, and a pair of opera glasses. Something in the bottom of the chest punctured her finger. Cursing, she snatched her hand out. Her fingertip was bleeding. She stuck it in her mouth and sucked on it, and with the other hand she tipped the chest over, spilling out the bottommost contents. She sifted through them carefully, and came upon something wrapped in a monogrammed linen handkerchief. Scarlett folded the linen back. It was a small doll, impaled with several long hatpins, one of which had pricked her finger. She quickly spread the remaining contents around her on the attic floor. Among the flotsam and jetsam were a pair of chicken feet, shriveled and mummified, and a bracelet made of some kind of teeth. Scarlett drew a sharp breath. She had watched plenty of Sunday afternoon TV, and knew voodoo when she saw it.

She pulled a cracked alligator purse from the pile on the floor and stuffed it with the photograph, the mirror, and the voodoo accoutrements. Just as she was about to snap the clasp of the purse, the candle burned down and went out.

Scarlett felt her throat choke with fear. Jumping to her feet, purse still in hand, she began to navigate her way out of the room by the feeble light from the dormer window but bumped into the bed. Even in the dim light, she could see an army of roaches dislodge from the mattress and scurry about over the dusty bedclothes. Scarlett screamed and raced back through the rooms and down the stairs, slamming the door shut behind her. She ran into the bathroom, got a towel, and stuffed it into the crack between the door and the floor, then shoved a chair under the knob. When she finally caught her breath, she dialed the Bugman.

Sixteen

Lana combed through the Hebert file again. She had never had a client killed out from under her, much less murdered in bed next to his wife. The Heberts were good people, and their violent end offended Lana's sense of justice. It seemed obvious that the crime was tied to Boudreaux's death.

On the way to the Heberts', she had told Officer Aucoin all that she knew, but her words had fallen on deaf ears. The police were convinced that the murder was motivated by the robbery. Lana couldn't file away the Heberts' deaths that easily. She had made arrangements to see one of the Boudreauxs that afternoon. As she mulled over what her approach would be, Carl burst into the office and waved a pair of tickets in front of her nose. "Ah, the great white way," he crowed. "Memories . . ." he began to sing off-key.

Lana grabbed the tickets from him. "I thought you boys loved musicals."

"Do I look like I love musicals?" Carl pointed at his buzz cut, which was now dyed a vibrant purple. "Personally, I prefer Hüsker

Dü or Black Flag. You know me, I have issues. Anyway, I'd never go see some half-assed road company at the Saenger Theater."

Lana glanced down at the tickets. "It better not be half-assed for this price. And where's my change? I gave you seventy-five bucks."

"Service charge," he called over his shoulder as he closed the door behind him.

Holding the two orchestra seat tickets between her thumb and forefinger, Lana got up and paced the office. Thirty dollars apiece to see some second-rate road show. The movies were only eight-fifty. And you could eat while you watched them. That was the problem with theater. It was too expensive, and you couldn't chow down Milk Duds when the going got slow. Although, Lana recalled with some relief, you could drink wine. They sold it in the lobby in those little plastic cups. She put down the tickets and scrutinized her large palms. She could carry at least one plastic cup in each hand, possibly two. Maybe this would be bearable after all.

She pushed the button on the intercom. "Is anyone left out there?"

"Nah. Unless there's a bus accident with serious and disfiguring injuries right outside the door in the next ten minutes, I think it's safe to go."

Crouton stared out the window of the crowded bus at the bayous flashing by on I-10. What a dull ride. Nothing to see. He drummed his fingers nervously on his knees and hummed tunelessly. God, was he bored. He fidgeted a little in the seat, then began tapping his feet against the floor to disperse more of the energy that was threatening to burst out through the top of his skull. The young black woman in the seat next to him looked up from her magazine and glared at him. "Bitch," Crouton sang rhythmically under his breath. "Bitch, bitch, bitch . . ." By now he was a one-man band, all his limbs beating out the music, head jerking back and forth in time.

Without warning, his body twisted and leapt from the seat, and for the fourth time in the past twenty minutes he found himself stomping down the aisle to the little bathroom at the back of the bus. Once inside, Crouton quickly fumbled the lock shut and threw his weight against the door for good measure.

He was proud of himself. While scoring from his dealer, Crouton had realized that smoking would not be permitted on the bus, and had accordingly switched from crack to methamphetamine. A good assassin had to be adaptable to any situation. He dug in his pocket for the vial of white powder, poured some onto the back of his hand, and sucked it up his nostrils. His senses were so tweaked by the drugs already in his system that he could feel each individual razor-sharp crystal slicing through the already-inflamed membranes in his nasal passages. "Ouch, ouch, sweet Jesus!" Crouton slammed his head back against the door. Tears streamed from his pin-dot pupils and mucus dripped down his upper lip.

Crouton didn't bother to wipe his face when he left the bathroom. The black chick caught one glimpse of him, shot out of her seat, and ran up the aisle to stand next to the driver.

"More room for me, more room for me . . ." Crouton hummed. He slid back into his seat and recommenced his jerking, twitching symphony.

He fairly raced off the bus when it arrived at the New Orleans station, then came to a screeching halt inside the terminal. Where was he supposed to go? The address was on a piece of paper somewhere. Where? He began turning his pockets inside out. The vial of meth flew out of his jeans.

"Oh *fuck!*" Crouton screamed, watching in slow motion as the glass vial fell to the cement floor. Mercifully, it didn't break. Crouton scooped the vial up, noticing several heads turned in his direction. In his drug-induced paranoia, it seemed like *everyone* in the station was watching him. It would be just his luck if some cop had seen the vial. Crouton backed slowly toward the door of the terminal, then ran out into the bright New Orleans sunlight. A couple of blocks down the street, he realized that no one was following, and leaned against a streetlight to rest. Catching his breath, he looked around and then up, and there, atop a low-rise office building, was a huge billboard. Emblazoned across it was the name and face of the lawyer he had come to kill.

"Whoa!" said Crouton. Lana's image, with its electric-orange hair, turquoise eye shadow, and bright red lips, shimmered and rippled before his bloodshot eyes. He blinked a couple of times to clear his field of vision, then read the address.

"Hey." He grabbed the arm of a passing businessman. "How do I get to 1245 Magazine Street?"

"Magazine is about six blocks down that way." The man pointed. "Turn right, and it should be about a half mile up."

Crouton somehow managed several wrong turns. There were too many streets and people in the city. Too much input for his racing brain. Something would catch his eye—an attractive woman, a camera-laden tourist—and Crouton would find himself off track, trailing the stranger down one of the Central Business District's streets. The CBD's odd juxtaposition of modern office towers and nineteenth-century balconied buildings confused Crouton inordinately. After forty-five tense minutes of navigation he finally found himself before the Offices' doors. He decided to blend in with the people waiting at the bus stop out front and observe.

It was hot on the sidewalk. Banana trees sprouted in alleyways and swayed in the slight breeze. The faint smell of coffee wafted from the docks on the nearby Mississippi. It was damn tropical here, Crouton thought to himself. Like an African jungle. With meth-induced self-confidence, Crouton began to think of himself as a leonine assassin, lying in wait for his prey on the sere Kenyan plain.

"Grrr," he said under his breath. He rubbed his palms in his dirty blond hair until it stuck out in a manelike tangle. Then he took an experimental swipe at a couple of teenagers standing next to him. "Grrrr!"

"Fuckin' weirdo," one said as they backed away.

Several buses had come and gone when the front door to the Offices swung open and a large woman strutted out. It was the lawyer.

That's some big game, Crouton thought to himself. I should have asked for more money.

She turned into an alley next to the building. Crouton followed her, crouched on his haunches, imagining his huge feline head parting the savannah grass as frightened birds took to the air from nearby trees. The lawyer stopped at a Buick parked in the alleyway, and Crouton ducked behind a Dumpster. Peering out, he saw her get in the car. She started the engine, but left the door open to let the car cool until the air conditioner kicked in.

Crouton saw the attack in his head. He would spring from his hiding place, pull the prey from her car, and tear out her throat. To this end, he took the vial from his pocket, tipped it over his majestic muzzle, and took a huge snort.

The sharp crystals shredded through his mucus membranes like thousands of tiny knives. "Rarrrrhhhh!" he roared in pain, as he bounded from behind the Dumpster. He covered the few yards to the car in record speed. Unfortunately, his tear-filled eyes prevented him from seeing the lawyer grab the armrest to pull the door shut. As Crouton lunged for his quarry, his skull smacked painfully into the slamming door, and he crumpled helplessly to the pavement.

"What the hell?" he heard the lawyer say. The electric window rolled down with a whir, and she looked down at him. "Pervert!"

By the time Crouton's head cleared enough for him to note the can of pepper spray in her hand, it was too late. The aerosol hit him full-face, attacking his irritated eyes and raw nostrils with its searing heat. Crouton screamed. It was the piercing wail of a housecat, not a lion. He flayed helplessly at his face, rolling in agony on the hot cobblestones as the lawyer peeled safely away in her Buick. Whimpering, he dragged himself back behind the Dumpster to lick his wounds.

He was going to need an elephant gun to bring down this beast.

Lana puzzled over the Boudreauxs' large brick colonial, which looked out of place in its conspicuously downscale neighborhood. On the other hand, the rusting jalopies in the front yard and the old refrigerator on the porch were rotting with an ease and appropriateness. Lana took a couple of minutes to freshen her makeup after the long drive from New Orleans, then got out of the car, went up to the front door, and rang the Boudreauxs' doorbell. She was answered with a chorus of barking from deep within the house. A female voice cursed at the dogs, then the door was opened by an elderly woman in an electric-green satin shirt and tight Wrangler jeans. She looked Lana up and down and gave her a smile of affinity. "Are you Miss Pulaski?"

"Yes. Estelle Boudreaux?"

"That's what it says on my driver's license. Come on in."

Lana stepped past two German shepherds, and followed Estelle Boudreaux down the hall into the den. The largest TV that Lana had ever seen outside a bar was blaring a soap opera. Estelle motioned her toward an orange plaid couch. Lana settled herself into the cushions, and the dogs lay down across the room on the sculptured shag carpet, wary eyes fixed on Lana. Outside the sliding glass door, two stringy-haired teenage Boudreauxs were tinkering with an old Camaro that sat on the patio next to a large in-ground pool. Estelle picked up a remote control and muted the TV.

"Do you mind if I watch out of the corner of my eye? Birch is going to find out about the baby today."

"No, go ahead," said Lana, displeased.

"Can I get you some iced tea?"

"Yes, thanks." The humidity in the parishes seemed twice that of New Orleans, though Lana doubted that was meteorologically possible. While Estelle crashed about in the kitchen, Lana took a handkerchief out of her purse and patted at her forehead. As she bent her head down to blot the back of her neck, she noticed an old photo album on the coffeetable. Lana glanced in the kitchen. Estelle's back was to her, so she flipped through the first few pages. There was a young Estelle, barefoot, sullen, outside a wooden shack. The next couple of pages were similar. The people in the photos looked poverty-stricken and tired. Out of morbid curiosity, Lana continued to turn the pages. Halfway through the album, she came across a shot of a broadly smiling Estelle in a fancy dress and spike heels standing next to a man (apparently her husband) in front of a brand-new, late-seventies Cadillac. Something about the photo bothered Lana. She could hear Estelle still in the kitchen, stirring sugar into the tea. Lana slid the photo out of the album and into her purse. By the time Estelle returned and handed her the tea, Lana was watching the soap opera with convincing intensity.

Lana took several grateful gulps. "Mrs. Boudreaux, I represented Mr. Dennis Hebert. As I'm sure you know, he was charged with the murder of your brother-in-law."

"Yeah, I know. Poor Dennis. I was horrified when I heard what happened to him. Even though they said he murdered Thierry, I always thought he was a nice man. We don't often have that kind of crime out here, but I guess you're not safe anywhere anymore."

"You don't have to tell me that. Do you know that on the way over here a degenerate jumped out at me in the alley and tried to attack me?"

Estelle clucked her tongue sympathetically. "Thank God you're okay. You could have been raped."

"You know how it is. Those perverts see an attractive woman and they lose all control. Luckily, I had my pepper spray. I left the jerk lying in a heap in the street. I only wish Mr. and Mrs. Hebert had had my luck. That's why I want to talk to you," Lana explained. "I don't think Dennis Hebert murdered Thierry, so I was hoping that you might remember something about his disappearance that could help us find the real killer."

"That was so long ago."

"Did Thierry have any enemies?"

"Yeah, just about everyone in the parish. Thierry was a son of a bitch."

Lana sighed. "If you can remember anything at all, it would help. Even if it doesn't seem important."

"Well," Estelle's eyes were on the TV as she spoke, "the night before Thierry disappeared, he went into New Orleans to meet somebody. The reason I remember is that he made a big deal about it. I asked him to take me along, because my daughter's wedding was comin' up, and I wanted to go into the city and buy some lace. We didn't have a car back then. My husband wasn't working. We were havin' a hard time. . . ."

Until Thierry conveniently got murdered, thought Lana.

". . . Thierry wouldn't drive me, though. Said the meeting was top secret. He just didn't want to do anything nice for anyone. My husband passed last year. He could have told you more."

"Do you know who Thierry was meeting?"

"No. Hey, look at what Birch is doin'!" Estelle said hurriedly, pointing at the TV screen.

"What about the night he disappeared?"

"I don't really remember. We were all at a dance. I probably had too much to drink. See, Birch has just found out that Iris is carryin' that alien baby."

Lana made several valiant attempts to get more information out of Estelle, but learned little except for the strange cravings that one exhibited when carrying an alien child. During a commercial break, she let Estelle and the German shepherds show her to the door.

Estelle watched through the screen as Lana picked her way through some corroding transmission parts to the Buick. "Poor woman," she said to the dogs, "she has no idea."

Seventeen

Lana left the Boudreaux family manse and was soon headed down River Road in the direction of Shady Oaks to pick up the Judge for the play that evening. She needed to stop somewhere and change into her evening dress. She saw a small gas station up ahead. LIVE BATE AND CRAWFISH, read the hand-lettered sign out front. Lana parked the car at the pump, got out, and went around to the trunk, from which she pulled a dress that she'd just gotten back from the cleaners that morning.

When she had begun to compile her professional wardrobe, Lana had run into trouble finding a cleaner who could handle its unconventional fabrics and trimmings. The local chains just didn't know what to do with bugle beads. Eventually she had found a shop in New Orleans East staffed by an efficient Cambodian family, the members of which could be counted on to hand-polish the vinyl piping on her purple coatdress, among other tedious cleaning tasks. Not that such work came cheap. Lana was sure that she was financing the elder son's boarding school in Massachusetts (she had been sorry to see him go; he was the only one in the family who truly understood snakeskin). This suspicion had been confirmed when the father began showing her the boy's glowing report cards.

Leaving the dry-cleaning shop that morning, Lana had realized that the family might be valuable to her campaign. On the notepad suction-cupped to her dashboard, she'd written "L. P. making American Dream come true." As she strode into the gas station she pulled her cell phone from her purse and punched in Tippy's number.

"Hello?"

"It's Lana."

"How are you, dear?"

"Busy. Very busy. Tippy, do you have any idea how many immigrants are registered to vote in the state?"

"I wouldn't have the slightest idea, hon, but I'll look into it for you."

"Good. I think they could be an important group to target." Lana clicked off the phone. "Where's the bathroom?" she asked the kid at the counter.

He jabbed his thumb over his shoulder. "Out back."

Lana clattered out the back door. Under some oaks behind the main building was an old wooden outhouse.

"Oh, for Christ's sake."

She emerged through the wood-slat door several minutes later, tightly sheathed in a low-cut red suede corseted dress. The dress had matching lace sleeves, one of which snagged on an old nail protruding from the jamb.

"God, this day is going to kill me," she hissed to herself.

The clerk watched mutely as she walked back into the station and threw a ten on the counter. "Don't just stand there," she snapped. "Do I look like I'm dressed to pump gas?"

Lana was at Shady Oaks by six-thirty. The drive had been somewhat uncomfortable, since she had apparently gained several pounds since she had last worn her dress. The boning poked cruelly into the soft white skin around her midsection. She could feel the tip of each individual whalebone, and wondered if the dress could do permanent internal damage. She had had to lean the front seat back almost all the way to relieve some of the pressure while she drove. Lana prayed that suede possessed the tensile strength of steel cable.

The front door was answered by the motorcycle rider. Lana glanced at him approvingly, fairly sure by his expression that her glamour had overwhelmed his small-town mind. Assertively, she put one hand on her hip. "I'm here for Judge L'Enfant."

"Is that the old guy?" the rider asked.

"It's the elder gentleman," Lana corrected him.

"Oh right. C'mon in. I'll try to find him." He ambled off up the stairs. Lana wondered briefly where Scarlett was, but then the Judge was coming down the staircase. He took each stair one foot at a time, as if they were covered with ice. Lana ignored the urge to end the slow descent by racing up the remaining steps and picking him up under one arm like a rag doll. He finally reached the bottom.

"You look stunning, my dear." He had one arm behind his back, and now he brought it out, displaying a bottle of Margaux. "I thought we might have this later."

Lana peered at the bottle. "Why, Louis, this is a very good year." Lana was familiar with wine. She could easily afford the good stuff, so why not enjoy it?

"Yes, it is. I like to think of myself as a nonpracticing oenophile. I can't really drink, except on special occasions . . . like this."

He was actually rather charming. Perhaps this evening wouldn't be so bad. A perusal of the Judge's garb, however, dampened her pleasure. He was wearing a navy blazer with a pair of brown pants that clearly belonged to another suit. His tie was stained with something that appeared to be tomato soup. Lana sighed. Fortitude was required at times like this. One had to keep the goal in mind, and then the means to the end didn't seem so difficult. Idly (for the Judge seemed in no hurry, in fact he almost seemed to be asleep where he stood), she paused for a second to see if the motorcycle rider would come back down the stairs, but he seemed to have disappeared into the upper reaches of the house. Lana finally took the Judge by the elbow and steered him out onto the gallery.

"I think you'll enjoy this play, your honor. It's *Cats*."

"Oh my," the Judge replied worriedly, "I'm very allergic."

Scarlett stood in her usual position in front of the bathroom mirror, her lips pulled back from her teeth, which, she observed with dismay, looked unpleasantly large—almost like the cellophane-packaged wax teeth she used to get at the candy store as a child. She had never noticed it before, this horselike aspect to her face. She turned side to side, checking her nose, letting the light catch it at different angles. Secretariat. Definitely. Scarlett had spent a good deal of time in front of the mirror since the first appearance of the Bugman, much more time than she usually spent, and that was a lot. In fact, she had found a number of heretofore hidden flaws to add to an already long list of her apparent defects. God, how expensive would orthodontia be? The Judge would never give her the money. She'd have to wait until he died. There was a knock at the door. Scarlett let her lips clap back shut over the teeth.

"Yes?"

"It's Daniel. Can you show me where you found the roaches in the attic?"

"Um, can't you just spray the whole thing?" She was reluctant to go back to Zombieland.

"Well, yeah, I intend to. But I need to see if they're getting in somewhere."

"Okay, hold on." Scarlett reached into her shirt and pulled out several handfuls of Kleenex that she had experimentally stuffed into her bra. Before opening the door, she quietly swished a little Scope around her mouth.

"Mmm," said the Bugman as Scarlett stepped into the hall, "you smell good."

Scarlett inhaled, trying to remember what she had applied to herself that might have a scent. All she could smell was a slight chemical aroma that seemed to emanate from the Bugman himself. It sent her heart racing with desire.

"I don't think I've got any perfume on."

"It's the mouthwash. I love peppermint."

Scarlett felt her face grow hot and red, and hoped the Bugman did not attribute any ulterior motives to the Scope.

"Why is there a chair holding this door shut?" the Bugman asked, sliding it from under the knob of the attic door.

"Sometimes it won't stay closed," Scarlett answered quickly. "Just swings open in any little draft. Very annoying." The need to over-explain to disguise her actions continued unabated. "I've tried to fix it. I think it's the hinges. They're old. . . ."

The Bugman was attempting to open the door, but it was stuck on something. He tugged several times. Scarlett leaned down and snatched the towel from under the door. "I wonder how this got wedged in there?" She cavalierly tossed it over her shoulder, where it landed on top of a small hand-painted Limoges lamp, knocking it over onto the table on which it sat. She ignored the crash. The Bugman had switched on a flashlight and was starting up the stairs. Scarlett took a couple of deep breaths and started up behind him.

When they reached the top of the stairs, she pointed back toward the cook's bedroom. "They were in there. They were all over the mattress." She shivered involuntarily.

The Bugman walked into the room, using the flashlight to knock down some of the spiderwebs clinging to the doorframe. Scarlett stayed on the stairs, gripping the banister, poised to make a quick descent at the first sign of vermin. She could see the flashlight beam catching the room's clutter in its yellow circle. The Bugman reappeared in the doorway. "I don't see them anymore, although they did leave a lot of roach shit behind. Would you come up here and help me move the bed? The frame is pretty heavy."

Scarlett was momentarily struck by the fact that there was an activity involving the Bugman and a bed that she actually wanted no part of. Not wanting to look cowardly, though, she steeled herself and went into the room.

What little light had come through the windows during the day was now almost completely gone except for an inky purple tinge of twilight. Scarlett was a little disoriented, and jumped when the Bugman seemingly appeared out of nowhere to take her by the elbow. He led her over to a large dressing mirror that leaned up against the wall. He turned her to face the glass. She could barely make out her reflection in the dark, and could see almost nothing of his. He reached around from behind her. "Look." He clicked on the flashlight under her chin. The light reflected off the underside of her cheeks and brows. "Pretty creepy up here, huh?"

Scarlett felt uncomfortable looking at her reflection in front of the Bugman. She turned around, and came face to face with him. She hadn't realized that he was that close behind her and expected him to take a step back. She couldn't because her back had come up against the mirror. Instead, the Bugman leaned down and put the flashlight on the floor. He put his palms against the mirror at either side of her head. Scarlett felt like she should duck out from under one of his arms, but she stood where she was.

"You're not scared up here, are you?" His voice was low and muted. Or maybe it just seemed that way. Scarlett could barely hear through the rushing noise in her head. As he continued to stare at her, the noise grew louder and louder, and then there was a clatter.

He looked up. "What was that?"

Oh God, he could hear it, too? Suddenly, she heard the sound of running footsteps in the driveway below. The Bugman went to the window, opened it, and looked out.

"There's somebody running through your yard. I think he

knocked over the trash cans coming out through the window or something. He may have been in the house. You'd better call the police." He shook his head. "Crime. In our very midst."

The theater was sold out, and the crowd was noisy and excited. Lana and the Judge were seated in row D, waiting for the lights to go down. Lana had already drunk three plastic cupfuls of the over-priced white wine in the lobby, but the alcohol wasn't helping. She looked over at the Judge. He had the playbill open on his lap, but his jaw had dropped into his collar, and he was snoring softly. Lana was about to shake him awake (though she found him far better company asleep), when she heard her name being called from the aisle.

Tippy was leaning over the unfortunate man in seat 1, whose nose was being flagellated by the heavy strands of Chanel pearls hanging around her thin neck. The man was leaning as far back in the seat as he could, trying to get away from the lacerating costume jewelry, which swished and rattled like a beaded curtain being swept aside by an angry arm. Tippy was oblivious to his plight. "Darling, we need to get together soon. I've come up with some wonderful—" She suddenly noticed the Judge in the seat next to Lana. She cupped her left hand over the right, her bony right fore-finger pointing frantically at the Judge. This action served only to draw attention to her motions.

"Is that your date?"

"Yes. He's the judge I was telling you about."

"My God, you are more determined than I'd ever imagined."

Mauve and silver lily-print wallpaper. The Judge glanced around the living room of Lana's large Metarie condominium. It was deco-rated in an art deco theme, with black lacquer furniture. The Judge had had no use for art deco in its original incarnation, and he liked it even less now, poorly executed and some sixty years later. Spitefully, he tipped his glass of Margaux, so that several drops spilled onto the ugly peach couch. He heard Lana's footsteps coming back into the room and quickly set the wineglass down on the chrome and glass coffeetable, a little ashamed.

She carried with her a large platter covered with a selection of cheeses, three kinds of caviar, and crabmeat-stuffed mushrooms. It had obviously been purchased from a gourmet shop. The Judge was momentarily dismayed by this prefabrication, but carrying the foodstuffs, with her abundant white flesh pooling over the top of her dress, Lana appeared to him the picture of womanhood: mother earth, comforting, providing and warm, a human cornucopia spilling fruits and sustenance. The Judge was moved.

She sat down next to him. His end of the cushion lifted, seesaw-like. "So, Louis." She pronounced it with a hissing S sound.

"Lou-EE," he corrected her softly.

"Of course. Cajun."

The Judge was about to correct her again; he was Creole, not Cajun. The Cajuns were descendants of mostly poor French pioneers chased down in the 1700s from Nova Scotia to watery exile in Louisiana. The Judge's Creoles, on the other hand, were more prosperous settlers who came to Louisiana directly from France. An important distinction in the minds of both groups, but the Judge didn't want to embarrass Lana.

"Louis. Tell me about yourself, darlin'. Tell me about the L'Enfants."

The Judge was stumped. Tell her what? There was nothing to tell about him, unless she wanted to hear about the good old days. How he and Leighton had been so successful with the Consolidated Chemical deal that they had branched out—started a kind of corruption consulting service, facilitating industrial development in the area parishes and taking a piece of action as payment. He wondered how much Lana knew about his past dealings, if anything. He hadn't been able to explore the topic yet. Since the Hebert debacle, he'd actually been considering seeking her counsel on the problem. It might be time to come clean, before Stanley got them in any more hot water.

As for the L'Enfants . . . the Judge was aware that outsiders thought that anyone from an old Southern family was chock-full of anecdotes about family history, eccentric forebears, tragedy, and the like. The L'Enfants, though, were painfully ordinary. No mad aunts in the attic, no colorful civil war generals. The Judge came from a long line of farmers—*rich* farmers, but farmers nonetheless, and who wanted to hear stories about harvesting sugar cane? As for war heroes, the L'Enfants had a yellow streak a mile wide. Lana was such an attractive girl, though. The Judge wanted to accommodate her. There had to be some tragedy. He thought hard. "Well, the L'Enfants have always had a problem with their feet. Arches flat as an iron. Except for Scarlett. Where that girl got those feet, I don't know. It must have been from her mother's side. These L'Enfant feet kept me out of WWII." And thank God for that. The Judge struggled for a finish. "We call it the L'Enfant family curse." Well. That was a rather inspired tale. He had declined to mention to Lana that the L'Enfants *were* notorious liars. Pleased with himself, the Judge looked down at his big, black, orthopedic shoes and shook his head sadly.

"That certainly could be a problem," Lana agreed.

She was sympathetic, the Judge could tell.

"Louis, do you remember an old case involving my client Mr. Hebert? It was an acquisitive prescription case. About twenty years ago."

The Judge took as deep a breath as he could drag into his brittle lungs. Why was she asking? Out of curiosity, or out of suspicion? He wasn't ready to fess up until he knew that he could trust her.

"No, I don't think so."

Lana looked into his face for several seconds. Skillfully, the Judge held her gaze. He was relieved to find that mendacity was one activity he could still participate in successfully, even at his advanced age.

"So . . . what did you think of the play?" Lana asked.

The Judge hadn't thought much of it at all. A lot of people running around in silly costumes. What had happened to the days of Rodgers and Hammerstein, when humans played humans onstage? He decided to sidestep the issue by appearing to be confused. "Well," he answered carefully, "I've always preferred dogs to cats, myself. A dog will stick by you. They're real friends." The Judge smiled a little as he thought back to a particularly loyal Catahoula he had once owned. Then he noticed a look of mild exasperation on Lana's face. She either wasn't buying the act, or she had really wanted to hear his opinion. "I enjoyed it very much," he fibbed. "Especially the company." Actually, he thought, looking at the taut suede of Lana's dress, he really had enjoyed being with her.

"Yes," answered Lana, placing her hands on his, "I did, too, very much."

The Judge wondered how she could have enjoyed the company of someone who slept through the first act of the play. Too bad the show was so noisy—otherwise he could have snoozed through the whole thing. The chairs had been fairly comfortable, in fact. The Judge looked down at Lana's hands, warm and dry, engulfing his like two mounds of risen dough. Clearly she wanted something other than his company, which, the Judge had to be honest with himself, was less than enthralling. She had said it was his political support, but he couldn't remember the last time that Joey Guidry, the parish president, had taken him to the theater and held his hand in search of an endorsement.

The Judge noticed that Lana was swallowing nervously. This surprised him, because she had been so forthright all along. Out of curiosity, he decided to get the ball rolling. He patted her leg. "You're a wonderful girl," he told her. His hand stayed where it was. The leg was so soft, so plump and well fed. He began to stroke it, without really realizing what he was doing.

"Darlin'," Lana began, "I think that we're a good team. We

respect each other professionally, and we like to spend time with one another. We should take the next step."

The Judge felt the smooth, freckled knee under his fingertips. They had only had two dates, but things moved faster these days, didn't they? He liked these modern relationships. No beating around the bush. You could just reach out and take what you wanted—which had always been his practice whenever feasible. Enthusiastically, the Judge extended his other arm.

Lana intercepted his bony grasp. "I think, given our feelings for each other, that we need, that we *deserve* something more." She reached over to the tray, picked up a cube of smoked Gouda, and placed it in the Judge's mouth.

"Oh yes," he agreed happily through a mouthful of half-chewed cheese.

"Honey," Lana continued, after taking a healthy swig of the wine, "what I'm trying to say is that I think that we should get married." Lana took his face in her hands. The Judge sat quietly for a minute, masticating, his bulging cheeks contained firmly in Lana's fingers. Finally, he swallowed. "All right, my dear, if that is what you want." The Judge was overwhelmed. Never had he felt so safe, so secure, so . . . well nourished. He still didn't know what Lana was getting out of the deal, but at this point, he didn't care. She would be there with him, caring for him, feeding him, crushing him to her breast, guarding him from the hovering and mercenary Scarlett. It gave a man a reason to live.

Eighteen

Bolton Hultgrew pulled his Honda into his parking space and cut the engine. He was still panting, and he had a nasty bump on the back of his head where the window had dropped shut on it. A big old house like that, you would think they'd take better care of it. Hultgrew gingerly felt around the knot for blood or exposed bone. Fortunately, the injury seemed to be superficial, though you could never tell with these things. Head wounds were tricky. He could wake up with a fractured skull, dead.

Hultgrew had gone over to Shady Oaks as soon as darkness fell and waited outside in the bushes. His plan had been to get inside after the Judge went to bed, but then he saw him leave with a large woman. Hultgrew was nearsighted and had forgotten to bring his glasses with him, but even from his distant hiding place, there had been something familiar about the woman's walk that Hultgrew couldn't place. A sort of exaggerated swing of the hips, which, with hips of that magnitude, could be dangerous to anyone too near. Hultgrew had pushed that observation to the back of his head, concentrating on swiftly and quietly prying open the kitchen window once the car had pulled out of the drive. As he entered the house, he got a rush of adrenaline. *This* was investigative reporting.

Once inside, he didn't know where to begin to look, or even what he was looking for. He had rifled through the kitchen drawers, uncovering nothing but cooking utensils and the occasional bug scurrying from his flashlight. Then he had tiptoed out into the sitting room. There he had found a big old mahogany rolltop desk. He searched through the cubbyholes under the rolltop, then went into the drawers. In the bottom drawer, he came across a lockbox. He had been about to open it when he heard voices from upstairs. He had grabbed the lockbox, carried it into the kitchen, and was close to making a clean exit when the window dropped on his head, knocking him dizzy. Panicked, he had fallen out of the window headfirst, tumbling onto several overfull trashcans outside the kitchen window and getting covered with coffee grounds and wet newspaper.

But here he was, apparently safe and sound. And he still had the box. Hultgrew felt a swell of pride. Gooch would not have been capable of doing what he had done tonight. Oh, sure, she had a good nose for news (among other excellent anatomical features), but she didn't have the sheer guts that he had. Hultgrew felt, well, gonzo.

Hultgrew picked up the box and climbed out of the car, brushing some eggshell from his hair. He walked up the pathway to his apartment, which was one of a series of inexpensive connecting townhomes. While searching through his key ring for his front door key, he picked up an almost imperceptible rustle from the shadows in the neighbors' small front yard. Hultgrew began fumbling nervously with the key. He heard footfalls coming across the grass and jabbed the key toward the lock. He was just about to turn it when something landed against his back and he felt hot, fetid breath against his cheek. Hultgrew whirled around just in time to be knocked flat by Fang, the Doberman from two doors away, his attacker, his tormentor.

The dog stood on Hultgrew's chest, just staring. A little saliva dripped from the dog's lips and hit Hultgrew in his right eye. Frantic and now half-blind on the right, Hultgrew recalled that you were never supposed to try and stare down a hostile dog. He clamped both eyelids shut. But the dog did not move. Instead, it began to sniff about Hultgrew's face. Hultgrew could feel the soft brush of its damp black nose. The dog remembered him! It had tasted his flesh once already. Why go back to Alpo when it could have steak? Hultgrew screamed. The dog jumped back, confused. Hultgrew flipped onto his hands and knees, reached up and fumbled with the doorknob, and crawled into his apartment. He slammed the door behind him. His hand flew to the scar above his head. That animal had already proven to be dangerous. Maybe his neighbors had won in court, but out of plain human compassion, couldn't they keep that beast locked up? Hultgrew peered out the window. The dog was standing over the lockbox, which Hultgrew had dropped when Fang's front paws had connected with his chest. The impact had sprung the lid open. As Hultgrew watched, the dog lifted his leg and took a leisurely piss on the documents inside the box.

After dragging himself from the alley next to the lawyer's office several days before, Crouton had staggered blindly for blocks before happening across a flophouse off Lee Circle. The unkempt man at the front desk had asked no questions when Crouton, eyes streaming and nose bloody, tossed a hundred-dollar bill at him and demanded lodging. He hadn't left his dreary room since. Fortunately, his immobility had not impeded his ability to score mind-altering substances. He lay in a tranquilizer-induced haze on his bed, unfocused eyes aimed at the crummy black and white TV. A nature show on jellyfish blared at top volume. The sheets in which Crouton was wrapped were rank with sweat and worse, and the room was filled with greasy pizza boxes, empty beer cans, gun magazines, and other moldering trash. The maid refused to come in after Crouton's first night, when, coming off a marathon session on the crack pipe, he had chased her about the room making race-car noises. He couldn't quite remember why he'd done it, and he didn't really care. All he knew was that the money that Stanley had given him was running out.

He'd tried to call the old bastard several times about the hit, but Stanley had refused to talk to him. Probably worried about wire-taps. But Crouton knew he'd have to whack the lawyer soon—his habit demanded it. In a rare creative moment, he decided that he would present her ear to Stanley as proof of the killing. With such graphic evidence, he might get some extra dough out of the rich fucker. Crouton fingered the empty glass vials that littered the bed. He had one rock of crack left. He wondered how much credit he still had with his new dealer. The situation was desperate.

Nineteen

A few days after her engagement, Lana went to see an old friend of her father's. For forty years, Leon Price had been operating his mechanic's shop on Annunciation Street in a garage collapsing amidst overgrown banana trees and stacks of rotting tires. Price knew everything there was to know about automobiles. Lana showed him the photograph that she'd taken from Estelle Boudreaux's album.

"That's a seventy-eight."

"Are you sure?"

"Yeah, I can tell by the headlights," the mechanic said, prodding the photo with a greasy forefinger. "How's the Buick?"

"Running like a top." Lana gave him a ten, placed the photo carefully into an envelope and returned it to her purse. Her instincts had been correct.

With the Cadillac question answered, she felt free to turn herself to more pleasant pursuits. Her next stop was an antique store on Royal Street.

Lana had been debating whether her engagement ring should

be a large solitaire, or if she should dress it up with colored stones. Prince Charles (as she recalled from reading one of the *People* magazines in her waiting room on a slow day) had given Diana an engagement ring with emeralds. An irrefutable indication that colored stones were acceptable. Besides, she could afford a larger ring if she chose something besides just diamonds. Lana wanted the ring to make a statement, and that statement was: Read it and weep.

Parking was impossible in the Quarter. Lana drove around the block several times, snarling at the tourists. These were the people whose rental Geos and Neons took up every available space. Finally, she pulled the Buick into a loading zone. From under the seat, she took a laminated sign with the New Orleans Police Department crescent and star symbol, and clipped it to her visor. A policeman client of hers (nasty divorce) had given her the free parking card. Although it left a bad taste in her mouth, Lana found herself forced to use the card at least once a week. In New Orleans, moral purity was not compatible with day-to-day survival.

Lana entered the antique shop, one of several housed in the quaint block of brick, balconied edifices. The front half of the shop was filled with delicate and expensive European antiques. Lana barreled past divans and dining sets that looked like doll furniture next to her ample curves. In the back of the shop were several jewelry cases filled with elaborate estate jewelry. Lana hadn't been browsing the merchandise for more than thirty seconds when her eyes fixed on a ring with a grape-sized ruby. "Hey," Lana called out to the jeweler, who was waiting on a pair of Japanese tourists, "I want to see one of these rings." She added proudly, "The big one." Lana pressed a warm finger against the glass. "That one in the top row there, with the baguettes."

The jeweler whispered reassurances to the tourists, then glided over to Lana. Wordlessly, he took a small square of black velvet from behind the counter and spread it out on top of the case. Removing a set of keys from his pocket, he unlocked the case, took out the ring, and quickly relocked the door. Ceremoniously, he placed the bejeweled band in the center of the fabric. It glittered riotously against the velvet. Lana picked it up and tried to slip it over her finger, but it got stuck right below the top knuckle. She twisted it painfully, but it would go no farther.

"We can enlarge the ring to fit you," the jeweler offered.

"How much is that?"

"On a piece of that quality? No cost."

"Mmhmm." Lana grunted approvingly. She held her hand out before her, watching thoughtfully as the ring twinkled in the light. This engagement had been achieved with ease. She had expected some objection from the Judge, or at least a little befuddlement, but he had been right with her. It was almost as if the marriage had been preordained. Lana wasn't sure if that was a reassuring or a frightening thought.

"Is this the biggest ring that you have?"

"The biggest ladies' ring. It's a *very* nice piece. From the 1920s. Before the Crash, of course." The jeweler reached over and pointed at the setting. "This is handwork. You don't see that in the jewelry stores in the mall."

"How much?"

"Thirty-three thousand."

"Good God." Lana let her eyes get very narrow. "You don't see prices like that at the jewelry stores in the mall, either."

"We can hold the ring if you would like to bring your fiancée in to see it."

"I doubt it would go anywhere in the meantime." Lana tilted the ring back and forth again, catching her reflection in the large ruby in the center. She looked good. The ruby looked good. She bounced her hand up and down. The ring had heft to it. A discernible weight. Even if she were not looking at the ring, she would be aware that it was on her finger, if only because the ring was heavy enough to cause a smaller woman to list to the left. Better than that, the ring was an antique. Instant pedigree. If asked, Lana could claim it to be a L'Enfant family heirloom.

She had a sudden vision of her hand, adorned by the ring, at a victory celebration. Red, white, and blue confetti tumbling through the air, her supporters cheering, the ring glinting in the lights as Lana raised her hand in a victory salute. The vision mutated. Lana saw the ring on her hand as she danced at dawn through the streets of Paris, a bottle of Dom Perignon in one hand, a champagne glass in the other, the ring sparkling and glistening, reflecting in its facets the Eiffel Tower, the Arc de Triomphe. The ring on her hand . . . reaching into her wallet for her checkbook. Then she realized this last part wasn't a vision. She already had checkbook in hand, and the jeweler was offering her his expensive fountain pen with which to complete the check.

"Thirty-three even," she said firmly, "including the tax." The jeweler nodded in assent. Lana filled out the check slowly, thinking. She had the money for the ring. She knew what she wanted. If she were to have a ring at all, especially *this* ring, she would have to do it herself. Lana sighed. It seemed like she had to do everything herself. Propose, the ring, and, more mundanely, most of the paperwork around her office, sex . . . Was no one competent anymore? The Judge was certainly not capable of comparison shopping—God only knew what he would come up with if he were. She deserved the ring for her dedication to the mission, the goal of statewide public office. Okay, she was the primary beneficiary of the mission herself, but in this day and age, discipline itself deserved an award. And marrying the Judge certainly required discipline. Besides, she was so thrifty in the other areas of her life. She never ate out unless she could get someone else to pay for it, she always shopped at sales. That was where you found the best things anyway. These little economies alone had probably added up to thirty-three thousand over the past ten years. Lana signed her name to the check in a bold flourish of rationalization.

The jeweler held out a set of little silver rings. "Let's size that finger."

*　*　*

"I think Miss Pulaski and I are going to get married."

"What?" Scarlett wheezed at the Judge. The word barely made it out of her throat, which, along with every other muscle, was clenched as tight as a fist. They were in Shady Oaks' dining room, and Scarlett had just set the Judge's oatmeal in front of him. Morning light filtered through the dirty French windows and glinted off the Judge's wet dentures as he spoke.

"I think we're getting married."

"You're not sure?"

"Yes," the Judge stated more firmly. "I'm sure. Married."

"You're eighty-four years old."

"I know. She's a little young for me."

"She's *much* younger than you, Grandfather."

"*Everyone* is much younger than me."

"Grandfather." Scarlett pressed her hands against the sides of her head, trying to keep her brain tissue from exploding out of her ears. She had to be calm. Don't make a scene. Be supportive. "This all seems so sudden. Why do you think that she wants to marry you so soon?"

"Your guess is as good as mine, but at my age, you don't have time to waste figuring it out."

Scarlett collapsed into a dining chair and stared at the Judge. He had lost interest in her and was back to reading his morning paper. She watched his lips move slightly as he read. God, he was old. Liver spots covered almost every square inch of the exposed skin over his skull. His shiny, hairless head, with its network of blue veins and age spots and its layers of translucent skin, reminded Scarlett of a jellyfish she had once seen washed up on the beach in Pensacola. Actually, it was more horrible to look at. She suddenly remembered how long she had wanted to get out, out of Shady Oaks, out of St. James Parish, out of Louisiana, to where things were happening. Where was that? Somewhere exotic. Maybe

Tangier. She pictured herself in a courtyard, behind whitewashed walls, palms waving in the breeze and casting shadows across the blue tile floor and across her easel, where she painted while being fed figs by a beautiful Moroccan man . . . who, in this fantasy, resembled a browner version of the Bugman. Or Tahiti. She would be a modern-day female Gauguin. Scarlett saw herself tan and topless next to a turquoise sea, a pareo wrapped casually around her waist, daubing paint on her canvas while being fed breadfruit (or whatever it was that they ate on those islands) by a gorgeous Tahitian man, who resembled a South Pacific version of the Bugman. And these fantasies can come true, Scarlett thought, if Lana takes the Judge off of my hands. On the other hand, international travel was out of the question until she got her inheritance. And if Lana were in the picture, who knew if there would be an inheritance? The marriage had to be stopped. But the Judge could not know how she felt. She didn't want to turn him against her.

"Well, congratulations, Grandfather," Scarlett called to him.

"Thank you. I'm quite pleased. She's a lovely girl."

Scarlett would not herself describe Lana as a "girl," but she guessed that was all relative. She picked herself out of the chair. She had to get a plan.

Lana drove straight from the jeweler's to the Offices, parked in the alley, and turned the Buick's ignition off. It was only eleven A.M., but already a viscous, palpable humidity hung in the New Orleans air. It slapped her in the face as she stepped from the car's dry, air-conditioned interior, causing her thick makeup to become slick and fluid on her skin. She hurried through the door before the paint turned into a gelatinous mass.

The waiting room was empty. Carl's combat boot–clad feet were propped up on the desktop, cushioned by several files in Redwelds and keeping the beat to the crashing music coming from the boom-box on his desk. At Lana's approach, he had reflexively flinched, as if about to sweep his legs off the furniture and back onto the floor, but then he shrugged and changed his mind.

"What," Lana paused for emphasis, "are those shoes, and what are they doing on your desk?"

"They're pretty butch, huh? I've got my feet up because it's bad for your circulation to have them down under the desk all day. I don't want to get varicose veins. No one has been here all morning, anyway."

Lana reached over and clicked off the boombox. "Don't you think you're a little old to be listening to that music?"

"Don't you think you're a little old to be wearing Lycra?"

"My look is my trademark. It's good for business."

"Maybe if you're soliciting sailors. Oh, I forgot. That *is* how you built this business."

"You're just jealous because you don't have a sailor of your own."

"You know I love a man in a uniform." Carl grinned.

"Speaking of men, I suppose you should know that I'm getting married."

Lana was pleased to see Carl's eyes grow wide. "To whom?"

"To a Judge L'Enfant."

Carl composed himself. "Never heard of him."

"You would have if you lived in the river parishes, believe me." Lana puffed her chest out a little. "He's a very important man."

"Well, I hope you're not even considering wearing white."

Lana chose to ignore him. "In the meantime, I'm closing up shop for a while. I need to concentrate on my campaign. We're going to pack my files up and send them to Sam McHale. He's taking over my caseload."

After some haranguing, she stirred Carl into action. An hour later, they had just about finished packing the active files into boxes to be shipped to McHale. "I guess Sam is 'and Associates' now," Carl said.

"Don't tell him that."

The phone rang. To Lana's surprise, Carl actually answered it.

"It's the Thibodaux police," he said, eyebrows raised.

Lana took the receiver. "Lana Pulaski."

"This is Officer Aucoin over in Thibodaux."

"Nice to hear from you, Officer. What's going on?"

"A couple of days ago, we hauled in one of the local lowlifes. This guy was dealing out of the Silent Night Motel, and we picked him in a sweep. He had a whole arsenal of illegal weapons in his room, including a sawed-off shotgun. We did ballistics on it, and it turns out that it was the weapon used on Dennis Hebert and his wife."

"Do you have a confession?"

"No. His story is that he lent the weapon to someone. He may be telling the truth. The desk clerk says that he sent a call girl to this guy's room about the time the shooting occurred. Bastard's trying to cut a deal with the D.A. right now. I thought you'd want to know."

"Yes, thank you. When he gives his statement, could you give me a call?"

"It'll probably be a few days before the D.A. cuts the deal, he's pretty busy. If you want, I'll give you a call, and you can come by and hear the guy's story."

"I'll be there."

Lana hung up the phone, cheered by the break in the Hebert case. She told Carl the news, then sealed up the last box.

"We're all done here. I'm going to go meet your father at Napoleon House for a drink. Why don't you take the files over to McHale's?" Time to solicit Marshall Hope's support.

Crouton had stolen himself a set of wheels, an old Honda Accord that someone had been stupid enough to leave unlocked on lower Prytania. He hadn't wanted to approach the lawyer again on foot— Crouton's stash of drugs had run out, and with them his confidence. Now he was parked across the street from the Offices, simultaneously hoping for and dreading her appearance.

Crouton's meth-ravaged sinuses had been horribly damaged by the pepper spray. During his hibernation in the flophouse, his nose had swollen to double its normal size and it now oozed a foul fluid in a continuous drip. Crouton had treated this distressing symptom by packing his nostrils with pages torn from *Soldier of Fortune* magazine. He looked at himself in the rearview mirror. From his right nostril protruded a crumpled photo of an AK-47. From the left he could read several words from an ad for a sexual aid called Miracle Grow. That could come in handy when his assassin business really got rolling and he was scoring lots of chicks. Crouton tipped his head back and was trying to peer farther up his inflamed proboscis to read the rest of the ad copy when the lawyer walked out of her office.

He watched as she entered the alley. After a minute or two, her Buick pulled out onto Magazine Street. Crouton reached under the dash of the Accord and touched the ignition wires together. The engine turned over. Crouton eased in the clutch and put the car into gear. Unfortunately, he wasn't used to driving a stick shift and the Honda leapt forward and banged into the rear bumper of the car in front of him.

"Shit!"

The car stalled.

Crouton looked up anxiously. Fortunately, the lawyer was only a block ahead, waiting at a red light. Crouton grabbed at the ignition wires again. His eyes were fixed on the Buick, so he didn't notice that someone else had just left the Offices. Crouton got the Accord started again, revved the engine, and popped the car into reverse. This time he slammed into the front bumper of the car behind him.

"Hey!"

Crouton looked up into the face of an angry man with a turquoise crew cut and an earring. Pansy, thought Crouton.

"That's my car, buddy, and you just cracked the headlight."

"Yeah? What you going to do about it, fag?"

The next thing Crouton knew, the pansy had opened the car door and he was being hauled out by his filthy T-shirt.

"Please don't call me that."

"I'll kick your ass, pretty boy," Crouton threatened.

"Just give me twenty bucks for the headlight."

"I wouldn't give it to you if I had it." Unsuccessfully, Crouton tried to shake himself free. Damn, but the pansy was strong. In desperation, Crouton brought up one knee to jab him in the nuts. Weak from withdrawal, he was moving slowly, and his opponent saw it coming. He tossed Crouton onto the hood of the car, hauled back his right arm, and took a swing. The contact with Crouton's cheek sent him flying across the hood and into the gutter on the other side of the car. At this point, he decided that the better course of action was to remain where he was.

The victor got in his car, started the engine, and pulled away. "You should see me in the mosh pit!" he shouted out the window.

Napoleon House had originally been built to house the exiled ruler upon his departure from Elba. Unfortunately for him, Bonaparte never made it to New Orleans. Eventually, the house had been turned into a restaurant and bar. With French doors opening onto the sidewalk, ancient blistered walls, and a shady interior, Napoleon House was a quintessentially New Orleans place, popular with tourists and locals alike. Lana took a table in the courtyard under a large banana tree. Marshall hadn't yet arrived. As she sat waiting, Lana had one of her many strokes of brilliance. She pulled her cell phone out of her bag and punched in Tippy's number.

Lana could hear the wind blowing and the sound of traffic. Tippy was in her red Mercedes convertible.

"Tippy, I've had some more thoughts on the campaign."

"Good, good. We need to get together and swap ideas. It's time to pick up the pace. We need to formally announce your candidacy and plan some personal appearances."

"And I've got the perfect venue."

"Where's that?"

"A pirogue parade on the bayou."

"Excuse me?"

That was the problem with Tippy. No imagination.

Just then, Marshall Hope appeared. Lana told Tippy that she'd call her back, then turned to greet her mentor. He'd changed a bit in the years since he had hired Lana—he was a little more heavy-set, and there was a subtle thickening to his features that revealed his appreciation for drink—but he exuded the same air of casual prosperity. "Lana! You're looking good. We don't see each other enough. How's my good-for-nothing son?"

"I'll probably kill him one of these days."

"Good. It'll save me the effort." The waiter came for the drink order, and Hope asked for two Pimm's cups.

"So, the buzz says you're running for public office."

"How did you hear that?"

"Oh, around, around. People talk, especially the ones that I know."

"Here's something you can talk about. I'm getting married."

"Married! That's wonderful, Lana. Do I know him?"

"You may, you may. He's a judge," Lana said proudly.

"My goodness. Wait, let me guess who it is. I'm thinking on who's single. . . . No, no one is coming to mind. You're going to have to tell me."

"Judge Louis L'Enfant."

Hope gave a raucous belly laugh. "Come on. Who is it?" Lana was silent. After a moment, Hope said carefully, "That's just great, Lana. That's just—"

Lana cut him off. "I wanted to talk to you about my campaign, Marshall. I was hoping that I could count on your support. I thought you could talk to some people, use your influence—"

"Lana," Marshall broke in.

"Hmm?"

"I thought you knew this. I feel just awful, because under any other circumstances, I would be thrilled to help you out. . . ."

"What?" Lana knew that she was about to be screwed.

"I'm working with Taylor. He's an old friend of my wife's family. She's from Iberville Parish."

"I had no idea," mumbled Lana. There went the entire New Orleans business community. How many votes was that? She had been depending on Marshall to deliver the city's establishment, which she'd been opposing in court since she'd started her practice. Damn, how these things could come back to bite you in the ass.

"I really am sorry, Lana. I had no idea that you were running against him until recently. If you were aiming for city council or clerk of court, that'd be different. Hell, I'd be right in your corner."

No one was more thrilled about the impending nuptials than Bobby Taylor. He almost fell over himself thanking a puzzled Marshall Hope for passing on the news. How often did you get to bring down your political opponent and your oldest enemy in one fell swoop? Taylor picked up the phone and put in a call.

After seventeen years with the district attorney's office, Harry Carter was, with good reason, cynical. So he didn't raise a dandruff-filled eyebrow when word came down from the top that he was to investigate an elected official. In fact, he was relieved. Politicians were always the easiest cases. They left a trail so stinky that it could be followed by a three-legged bloodhound with sinusitis.

Twenty

Hultgrew was holding the telephone receiver up to his ear, pretending to listen. The loud brain-drilling buzz that alerts the customer that he has forgotten to hang up the phone was battering his eardrum, but he barely noticed. He was staring intently at Cami Gooch, waiting for her to get off of her phone, and was trying to look busy himself. Earlier in Cami's conversation, Hultgrew had actually gone over and stood by her desk, expecting her to hang up. She hadn't acknowledged his presence, didn't even nod at him or raise an eyebrow. She just kept taking notes and saying "Uh-huh." Once she had said "Gotcha," which had inspired a mixture of fear and jealousy in Hultgrew. "Gotcha" meant a hot lead, another prize-winning story of the kind that had gotten Cami a small picture of herself above her column. This photo, one-inch square in newsprint, loomed the size of a billboard in Hultgrew's mind. He was lucky to get a byline. Eventually, it had become too humiliating to stand next to her desk, ignored, like a servant boy or supplicant. Hultgrew had slunk back to his desk and pressed the phone against his ear. Finally, he saw Cami replace the receiver in the cradle and continue to make notes on her pad. Hultgrew jumped up, then gathered his composure and slowly shuffled across the floor toward Cami, stopping to take a drink at the water cooler, or feigning it, anyway. He didn't want to give her time to get back on the line. "What is it, Hultgrew?" she called out to him as he was wadding up the little pointed paper cup. It was still half-full of water, which slopped out over his fist. Hultgrew dropped the cup into the trash and nonchalantly wiped his hand against his trousers.

"I have something I want you to look at. I'm not sure what it is."

"I don't want to see your dick."

"Hah, hah," Hultgrew laughed snidely, "I know you could identify that, you've seen enough of them."

"I'm kind of busy, Hultgrew, show me what it is."

Hultgrew leaned over the desk and placed the rumpled brownish pages on Cami's desk. "It's some sort of legal document."

"I can see that. Jesus, these stink. What did you do, piss on these?"

Hultgrew groaned inwardly. He should have made Xeroxes. That Doberman was really a piece of work. He'd get Fang, right after he finished disemboweling the Judge. "Look, just tell me what they are."

Cami took an expensive pair of eyeglasses out of her top desk drawer. With them on, she looked even sexier, Hultgrew thought, like a dirty librarian or something. Cami began to read. After a minute, she motioned for Hultgrew to flip to the next page, which she obviously had no intention of touching herself. Finally, she looked up at him. "They're counter letters."

"What's a counter letter?"

"Well, it's kind of a sleazy thing. Say you're developing an office park, and you need my land, it's right in the center of the park. But you know that if I know it's you trying to buy it, I'll jack up the price because I know you need my parcel. So you have someone else buy it. At least, that's what the public records say. But between the two of you, there's a counter letter saying the land really belongs to you. You file a notice that the letter exists. But you don't file the actual letter. You're the one buying the land and no one knows."

"Is that legal?"

"Legal and binding in court. It looks like what happened here is that this company, Acadian Developing, bought this land and then sold it to Consolidated Chemical. But Acadian never really owned the land at all. Lafourche Land Exploration did both deals."

"Why would they have done it that way?"

"Hello, Hultgrew, that's your job, finding out things like that. I hope this isn't a news flash to you. What is this you're working on, anyway? I thought you were doing that piece on the new sewer."

"Fuck the sewer. This is something big. That's all I'm going to say."

Cami shrugged, her attention span visibly waning. "Whatever. Now get that stuff away from here. I don't want my desk smelling like a sewer." Hultgrew scooped up the offensive—and still slightly damp—documents and carried them back to his desk. He'd wait till they dried before copying them and showing them to his editor. He stuffed the pages back into the metal box. They really did stink. Hultgrew kicked the box under his desk and out of olfactory way. Then he picked up a pen and began writing down names— Consolidated Chemical, Lafourche Land Exploration, Acadian Developing. It was time to make some phone calls to the secretary of state in Baton Rouge to find out what was on file about these companies. He opened the bottom drawer of his desk and pulled out the Yellow Pages. No, these were the New Orleans Yellow Pages. Hultgrew dropped the book to the floor and was about to pull the Baton Rouge pages from the drawer when the back cover of the New Orleans phone book caught his eye. It was a woman lawyer in a blue suit wearing little black reading glasses, hair conservatively caught in a tight bun at the top of her head. She looked awfully familiar. Hultgrew thought for a moment, but couldn't place her. He opened the other phone book and picked up the receiver.

"Who is Lana Pulaski?"

Tippy and Souchecki were silent.

"Who is she?" Lana repeated more firmly, making it clear that she expected an answer.

Souchecki looked over at Tippy, and when no assistance was forthcoming, offered, "Our next attorney general?"

Lana smiled only slightly. The answer, while pleasing, was not helpful. "Every candidate needs an image. One that distinguishes her from and elevates her above her opponent. This image must be clear and consistent. It must be in my speeches and in any campaign literature. I shouldn't have to tell you this, Tippy," she scolded.

"Of course you don't. It's obvious. You are the people's candidate. You are the new regime, untouched by corruption. You are clean."

"Clean," said Lana. "That is the byword for this campaign. Clean." Of course, clean in itself was boring. Lana knew that she'd have to supply her own, personal brand of spice to catch the imagination of the voters. Tight dresses and big hair. It had worked for her law practice, and it would work with the electorate. There was nothing the voters loved more than sex. Look at Clinton. "Let me show you the brochure I've been working on," Lana suggested. She took a mock-up of a brochure from her desk and held it in front of them. Tippy drew in her breath. Souchecki blinked several times.

Lana was posed in profile. She was in full makeup, her cheekbone clearly delineated with a dark slash of rouge, her flip freshly tinted. She had her chin tilted in the air and her right hand raised as if she were taking an oath. Her breasts thrust out in front of her, and through the sheer fabric of her snug wrap dress, her nipples tickled the edge of the brochure.

"This," she said proudly, "is me. Fresh. Vital." She pointed to the upraised hand. "And honest."

"That picture doesn't really say 'clean' to me," Tippy opined. "Does it say 'clean' to you, David?"

"Let's not get too semantic, Tippy," chastened Lana.

"It's just that I was thinking more along the lines of this." Tippy pulled a brochure out of her briefcase and laid it on the desk. Souchecki nodded in approval.

"That is not me," said Lana.

"Of course it's you. I took the picture from your ad on the back of the Yellow Pages. It's a good photo. You look conservative and dependable. It's *your* ad."

"The typeface and colors you chose are fine, but I've never liked this picture," said Lana. "I had been planning to change it next year. Besides, I don't want to look conservative. We have to be consistent, remember? My image is as the clean, fresh, new candidate. My picture has to reflect that. I'm new blood. Someone with new ideas. Strong regulations on gambling, harsher policing of pollution, laws to put a halt to cronyism. I'm Louisiana's JFK."

"Well, the picture itself will be in black and white, not color," Tippy said by way of reassuring herself. She knew by now that an argument with Lana over her appearance was the most futile argument that one could attempt with the people's fresh candidate of new ideas.

"Have you written the literature to go with the brochure?" Lana asked Souchecki.

"Um . . . yes," he replied nervously. He handed her the text.

Lana read it twice and then clapped him on the shoulder. "Not bad, David, not bad. I'll just punch it up a little and then we can send all this to your friend to be printed. Then we'll have one big headache out of the way." Lana rummaged around on her desk. "Wait till you see my next idea. Remember Burma Shave?"

Twenty-one

The Judge raised his head from his desk with a start.

"Catching a few zees, Louis?"

"Stanley. I didn't hear you come in." His damn clerk. He'd told him not to let anyone in his chambers. Since hearing about the Hebert murders, the Judge had been tossing and turning at night, wracked with guilt. During the day, he was trying to rest up whenever he could. Now he eyed his visitor warily. Did the sociopath have a gun? For not the first time, it occurred to the Judge that Stanley might want *him* dead, too.

"What can I do for you?" he asked with false bravura. "I hate to tell you this, but I won't be out on the links for a few more weeks. Still recovering from the heart attack and all." Would the clerk be able to hear him if he screamed?

"Louis, I wish I were here about golf." Leighton closed the door to the Judge's chambers behind him. "I don't know any way to make this pleasant, so I'll just cut to the chase. I hate to tell you this, but the district attorney's office is going to be looking into the Acadian Developing deal."

The Judge sank into his chair. "But I got them to drop that years ago. How did they find out? Are they going to be able to tie this to the Heberts?"

"No, no. They'll never put that together. This is just a political move. The elections are coming up and not only have they got bribery here, they can put an environmental spin on it, too. Those are political trump cards. Using your connections to get the D.A.'s office to close the case was intentional concealment. And you know better than I do that the statute of limitations won't apply where there has been intentional concealment by a public official."

"Prescription," mumbled the Judge unhappily. "We call it prescription in Louisiana, not the statute of limitations."

"We can call it whatever damn thing we want. The effect is that the whole Consolidated thing might as well have happened last week."

The Judge slid down in his chair. He was feeling dizzy. "What should we do about this?"

"Let's just lay low for now. Wait to see if anything big develops. But if I were you, I would start looking for some representation. Quietly, of course."

"Of course."

What good was growing old if he couldn't look back with nostalgia on his crimes as a young man?

Twenty-two

This couldn't be the place. Scarlett peered through the windshield of the Lincoln, mulling over the possibility that she taken a wrong turn somewhere upon arriving in New Orleans. She'd left Shady Oaks in the Lincoln almost two hours before, following River Road east, then crossing the Mississippi on the terrifyingly narrow and lofty Huey P. Long Bridge. From there, she'd driven along the levy to Magazine Street, past the lush, moss-laden oaks in Audubon Park, the coffee shops and trendy boutiques of Uptown, and then through steadily declining blocks of dilapidated shotgun shacks and shabby storefronts to arrive at this address. Scarlett rechecked the back cover of the New Orleans phone book, which she had torn off to take with her on the trip. Not only did it have a full-color picture of Lana, posed in front of a wall of law books and wearing a pursed, Mona Lisa smile on her pudgy (and uncharacteristically muted) face, but it had the address of her office—including a bus map. Scarlett looked back and forth between the ad and the decaying building in front of her. Yes, this was it.

Scarlett had decided that she needed to confront Lana about

the marriage. The woman had to know that she had no intention of giving up her inheritance. She was nervous, though. Lana was an intimidating adversary. Scarlett put the key back in the Lincoln's ignition. Maybe this wasn't such a good idea. She'd just forget it and go home. But in her mind, Scarlett saw little winged twenty-dollar bills. They were flapping like butterflies across a cotton candy sky and landing atop one of Lana's pudgy index fingers. She turned the car off again, took a deep breath, and stepped out onto the sidewalk. She strode toward the building, conscious that her feet were far more confident than her brain.

The reception room smelled like a seedy roadside motel. Scarlett wrinkled her nose. This was worse than living next to Consolidated. She heard someone tunelessly whistling and swung around.

There was a man with a banana-yellow crew cut behind the receptionist's desk. He had a large emerald stud in one ear and was wearing a black T-shirt. He cocked one eyebrow at Scarlett. "May I help you? We're closed indefinitely while Miss Pulaski is running for A.G."

"Um, is she here?" Scarlett asked uncertainly. Had she come all this way and worked up all this courage for nothing? She could feel her bravado evaporating with every passing millisecond.

"I'll check. What's your name?"

"Scarlett L'Enfant."

The man slammed his palm on his desk. "Get outta here, girlfriend. Scarlett? Really? No one's named Scarlett."

Scarlett felt her face grow red. "I am," she countered, a bit angrily.

"Well, that's cool," the man conceded, repentant. "Hold on." Scarlett saw him push a button and whisper into a little intercom on the desk. "Miss Pulaski is here. Go on back." The man motioned toward a peeling brown door.

Scarlett walked back and knocked softly, but there was no response from within. She tapped a little harder, then quite loudly. Suddenly, the door swung open. Scarlett leapt back, startled. Lana stood filling the doorframe, more impenetrable than the door itself. She was dressed in what Scarlett took to be casual wear—a knit shirt and pants outfit that was encrusted in rhinestones and glitter paint. There was a pause that was awkward to Scarlett, but, she sensed, intentional on Lana's part. To break the silence, Scarlett whispered, "Hi. There's something that—"

Lana boomed out on top of Scarlett's words. "What can I do for you, Scarlett? I'm fairly busy. I need to drive to Thibodaux today. The police have someone in custody with information about the Hebert murders, and he's going to give a statement this afternoon."

"That's good. This won't take long. Um . . . Can we go inside? It's kind of private."

"All right." Lana moved a bit to the side, her arm resting against the doorframe. Scarlett waited, then realized that Lana wasn't going anywhere. She scooted in under Lana's outstretched arm, barely having to stoop at all. There was a straight-backed chair across from Lana's desk. Scarlett sat down and wiggled a bit—one would need razor-backed posture to be comfortable in the chair.

Lana walked around to her side of the desk and stood looking down at Scarlett, her arms crossed over her chest. Scarlett wiggled a bit more. "So what's the problem, Scarlett?" Lana finally asked.

"It's not a problem, exactly."

"Good. Did you want to talk about the wedding? If you're interested, you can be one of my bridesmaids. I'm sorry, but I already have a maid of honor."

"Well . . ." Scarlett paused, more afraid than ever to bring up the inheritance now that she had told Lana that there was nothing wrong. It didn't seem like a proper negotiating strategy. She felt at a critical disadvantage. On the other hand, she would rather be tied naked and honey-covered to an anthill than be a bridesmaid to Lana. The thought of the bridesmaid's dress alone caused her to shudder. "Now that you mention it"—she'd just let the bridesmaid thing slide for now—"there is a bit of a problem."

"Aha," nodded Lana, as if she now understood everything. "Why don't you tell me about it?"

Scarlett could feel herself retreating again. "I don't know actually if you would call it a 'problem,' but . . ."

"First it's not, then it is, then it's not again. Why don't you just tell me what's on your mind?"

What was on her mind was that all her life, she'd had no money. The Judge gave her an allowance, fifty dollars a week, and out of that she had to buy all her clothes, her paint, her canvases—it could be a tough stretch. She'd tried working to earn more money. When she was seventeen, there had been a disastrous two weeks at a Burger King in Thibodaux. Her coworkers had seemed to Scarlett to be barely literate. They certainly weren't interested in art. After a couple of days at the job, she decided that the best thing was to avoid any social interaction and just make it through her shift. At night when she went home, the smell of grease clung tenaciously to her hair and skin. She finally quit in tears one busy Saturday when one of the boys at the fryer squirted what seemed like a quart of ketchup down the back of her uniform while she was wrapping cheeseburgers. The other employees had laughed as if the fry boy were a teenaged, acned Lenny Bruce. Scarlett had run out the door, dropping cheeseburgers on the floor, ketchup dripping out from under her shirt and down the legs of her blue polyester pants. This memory gave her the strength to persevere with Lana.

"There's something I think you should know, is all. The Judge's money is going to be mine someday."

Lana threw her head back and laughed. "You think I'm after your grandfather's money? That's very funny."

"I'm not stupid, Lana."

"I could buy your grandfather five times over. The law has been very good to me."

"I need the money to get away," Scarlett blurted out.

"Away where?" Lana asked, her curiosity obviously engaged.

"Away from Shady Oaks. Away from St. James Parish. I'm a painter and I need to see the world. Like Gauguin."

"And the money is stopping you?"

Scarlett looked at her lap and nodded, feeling very much the errant child.

"Maybe a little advance on your inheritance can be arranged. I can talk about it to the Judge. After all," Lana said cockily, "I do have some influence with him."

"That would be very kind." Scarlett was relieved, but wary.

"However, it won't be until after the election."

"What does the election have to do with it?"

"Have you seen my opponent, Bobby Taylor? He's started to run a lot of ads on TV. They show him playing ball with his kids, hugging his wife, walking the dog, you know, the whole 'family values' thing."

"So?"

"So the Judge, as much as I love him—" Scarlett was surprised that there wasn't a hint of sarcasm in Lana's voice"—isn't much of a family by himself. But you, my dear, make three."

"You want me to campaign for you?"

"You won't have to hand out buttons on the street. Not yet, anyway. Right now I just need you available for rallies, ads, photos, that sort of thing. After it's all over, we'll talk about your advance. The first thing I'll want you to do is attend the official announcement of my campaign. There will be a pirogue parade on Bayou Boeuf the day after the wedding."

Oh God, thought Scarlett.

"And I'll want you to be in my wedding, of course." Lana picked up a Post-It and pen and scrawled an address. "Here." She leaned over the desk and stuck it on Scarlett's forehead. "That's the address of the bridal store. I hope you like magenta."

"Not particularly."

"Even better."

*   *   *

The little bitch. Lana was amazed at Scarlett's forwardness. Oh well, at least the girl had some fire under that wan façade. After the election, she'd give Scarlett some of her *own* money if she had to, just to get rid of her. But not until November, when Scarlett had outlived her usefulness. Better to keep her scared in the meantime. Scarlett reminded Lana of nothing so much as a dry leaf blowing in circles in the wind. Not a worthy adversary by any stretch of the imagination.

And to think, she had been jealous of Scarlett when she'd first seen Shady Oaks.

Jealousy was not something that Lana admitted to herself easily, but in this case, since the jealousy wasn't her fault, she could entertain it.

The problem was that Lana had grown up poor. The bar had been competently run by Joe, but a grimy waterfront place like that, even if it had been managed by Lee Iacocca, could never have been highly profitable. Their apartment above the bar was five small dark rooms, made smaller and darker by the thick coats of paint and wallpaper on the walls and smoke from the kitchen below. In some places the skin of the wall had been broken (by the shifting of furniture or by a violent outburst from Mrs. Pulaski), and Lana could see the layers of wall coverings as distinctly as a cutaway picture of flesh in an anatomy book.

Even worse, the apartment had always smelled. Not unpleasantly—for the scent was a sharp, ethnic one of cooked meat, spices, and spirits—but the sheer force of the odor drew the walls in even closer.

Shady Oaks, with its light, airy rooms, floor-to-ceiling windows, and antique furniture had seemed to Lana the quintessence of old money. And she had wanted to choke the scrawny girl who had grown up with the security that money had brought. As a child, Lana had been forced to supply her own security. And though the

152

experience only enhanced her image of herself as extraordinarily capable, she would have preferred a little smooth sailing.

Finding out that the helpless Scarlett was also penniless was an unexpected bright spot in Lana's week. It just gave her one more advantage over the girl. Lana no longer felt any pangs of jealousy. She just felt her usual superiority. Cheered, Lana picked up her purse, said goodbye to Carl, and headed out for Thibodaux.

On the drive home, Scarlett's breathing echoed in her ears. It came in ragged pants, a mix of anger and frustration being expelled by her shocked lungs. She'd never had an enemy before, especially one so much larger than she, literally and figuratively. Scarlett didn't trust Lana a bit to ensure her pre-inheritance funds. She was going to have to look out for herself. She pressed harder on the accelerator and sped down River Road, passing tractors, tourists, and all manner of slower vehicles. She almost plowed into a family crawfishing in the borrow pits on the side of the road. Finally, she screeched the Lincoln to a halt in the driveway. It dieseled weakly like an exhausted, sputtering horse at the end of a hard ride.

Scarlett ran in the front door, tripping over a little antique table covered in unopened mail. "Shit!" She gave the table a little kick for good measure, then looked at it more closely. It was in pretty good shape. An idea began to germinate. She walked quickly through the house, peering into the rooms. All were crowded with antiques. Chairs, dishes, mirrors, vases, knickknacks. Shady Oaks must have a fortune in furniture. Incredible that she had never thought about it before. She returned to the front hall and stood smack in the middle, rubbing her chin and thinking. Surely the Judge would not notice a few things missing. A little table here, some silverware there—God, there must be at least three sets of silver.

She scooped the mail off the little table in the hall, tossing it onto the coffeetable in the sitting room. She went into the dining room and searched through the huge china cabinet, coming up with a heavy box of tarnished, unused silver from the back of one of the drawers. She ran back into the hall and laid the silver on the table. Then she hurried up the stairs and began looking through the spare bedrooms.

Lana peered through the one-way mirror into the interrogation room. The dealer was a young guy, about twenty-five. He had long silky dark hair pulled back in a ponytail and arms covered with navy tattoos. He looked bored and mean. He'd cut a deal with the D.A. that morning. Now the D.A. entered the room. He glanced at the one-way mirror and gave a little nod.

"Okay, Neville. Tell us about the gun."

" 'Bout a month ago, I get a new customer. Skinny blond dude . . ."

"What was his name?"

"Hmm. Jimmy, I think. Yeah, Jimmy."

"What was his last name?"

"Fuck if I know. You goin' to ask for his social security number next? 'Cause I didn't get that either."

"Chill out, Neville. Just tell me the story."

"Whatever. So Jimmy tells me he's just beat some big rap. First he tells me bank robbery, then it's murder one. He wants me to think he's bad. I don't give a shit, just pay me. Anyway, the guy tells me he has a deal going down, a hit. So I sell him a .22. Next day, he tells me he did the hit. He scores off me. A few hours later, he comes back wanting another gun. I say, 'What about the .22?' He tells me he threw it away after the hit, but now he has an even bigger job, and he needs a bigger gun. The crackhead's out of money, though. But I'm a businessman. He's one of my better customers. I decide I'll lend him my shotgun so that he can make some money and buy more product from me."

"You're a regular Harvard M.B.A., aren't you, Neville?"

"I like to think out of the box."

"What did he do with the gun?"

"I guess he did his hit. The next morning he returns the shotgun. I smell the barrel, it's been fired. He buys forty bucks of rock off me, and that's the last I see of him for a day or two. Then he comes back with a wad of dough and buys two hundred dollars of crank. So my business gamble paid off. After that, though, he disappeared. I haven't seen him since."

"Okay, Neville. You're going to sit down and look at mug shots now, and you're not getting up until you find us Jimmy."

As Lana watched Neville flip through the mug shots, she ran the story over in her head. Who would have sent a hit man to kill the Heberts? One of the Boudreauxs, still angry about Thierry's death? That was possible. She tried to think who else might be a suspect. Maybe the person who really murdered Thierry was afraid that Dennis Hebert knew his identity. But why wait so long?

She was going to have to step up her efforts if she was going to find out what really happened.

Twenty-three

The Judge puffed on his cigar and watched in meditation as the smoke rings ascended toward the ceiling in his office. A nice stogie had always helped him forget his troubles, and these Cubans were good enough to temporarily cloud over the Hebert situation. The clerk reclined across the desk from him. He, too, was blowing smoke rings at the ceiling. They had been sitting together like this, quietly, for some time. "Can't wait for the honeymoon," the Judge finally said to the clerk, rocking back and forth in his cracked leather chair in anticipation. The clerk snickered conspiratorially. There was a knock at the door. "What's that?" asked the Judge. Was Leighton back?

"It's the door," answered the clerk, who did not move.

"I guess you'd better answer it," muttered the Judge. Who was coming in to destroy their reverie?

The clerk sighed, laid his cigar butt in an old ceramic ashtray that Scarlett had made for the Judge in the third grade, rose, and opened the door.

A heavyset man stood on the other side. He stepped into the

room tentatively, blinking his eyes against the haze and stench of the cigar smoke, and gave a little cough. "Judge L'Enfant? I'm Harry Carter. I'm from the district attorney's office."

"What do you want?" the Judge snapped curtly.

"I'm here to ask you a few questions about Acadian Developing."

The Judge motioned to the clerk. "You'd better leave us alone." The clerk nodded and softly closed the door behind him. Carter sat with a thud in the chair formerly occupied by the clerk. The Judge smiled a wicked, denture-baring smile, picked up the clerk's spittle-damp, smoldering butt, and held it out to Carter.

"Cigar?"

The clerk had to bring the Judge home early. He'd had nothing on his docket and the talk with Carter had tired him inordinately. Besides, he had to look through that lockbox. It had been years since he'd seen it, and he couldn't remember exactly what form the paper trail took. He hobbled through the front door, took off his hat, and absently tossed it toward the hall table. It fell to the floor. His eyesight must be getting worse. The Judge picked up the hat and turned around several times, looking in vain for the table. Odd. He hung the fedora over the newel post at the end of the banister.

He went into the sitting room and pulled out the bottom drawer of the rolltop desk. Empty. He looked in the other drawers. Nothing there either. Where else could it be? Shady Oaks had no closets, because the French had originally levied extra property taxes on them as if they were rooms. But there were two huge armoires in the front hall. The Judge searched through the tangle of boots and seldom-used coats that littered the floor of the wardrobe. No box. Maybe it was in his room. Grasping the banister with white-knuckled intensity, the Judge started up the stairs, then heard the front door open below. "Scarlett?" he called, peering down.

She looked up, startled. She had a small wad of bills in her right hand.

"Have you seen that metal box that was in the desk?"

"I haven't touched it," Scarlett answered quickly.

"Hmm." He was about to ask her about the hall table, but that could wait until later. He had to find that box. "I'll just look upstairs. Tell me if you come across it." He squinted at her. She appeared to be wearing some of Odile's old jewelry. "You know, you look more like your grandmother every day. You need to gain some weight. And get out in the sun." The Judge started back up the steps.

Scarlett scooted into the kitchen and shut the door behind her. She quickly counted through the money in her hand. Eight hundred dollars. At this rate, she would have to empty the entire house before she would have enough to get away. She fingered Odile's earrings and bracelets. They were white gold, and the earrings were even set with small rubies, but the antique dealer had not offered her more than fifty dollars for any of the pieces. He had said the market for antique jewelry was soft, and had then implied that the items were stolen.

Why did everything have to be so difficult? She opened the refrigerator and took out a soda, then sat down at the kitchen table. The Judge's newspaper was lying on the place mat. He insisted on getting the *New Orleans Times-Picayune* delivered. He didn't put any stock in the *Star*, especially since Hultgrew had been on the warpath. Scarlett picked up the paper and gave it a quick glance. She noted with minor interest a small column at the bottom of the page headlined CONSOLIDATED SPOKESMAN DENIES BRIBERY ALLEGA-TIONS. Maybe they'd finally shut that place down. She flipped through the comics and horoscope, then rolled up the paper and got up to toss it in the trashcan.

As she stood, she caught her reflection in the chrome of the toaster. God, she did look almost exactly like Odile, especially with the jewelry. Just like the old picture from the trunk. Odile had died just before Scarlett was born. It was almost as if she was her reincarnation or something. If she put any credibility in that sort of thing. Not that she *didn't* believe it. Scarlett had no strong convictions on any topic, which allowed her to adapt her beliefs with the least pain possible to any situation. Now that she thought about it, she remembered a movie she saw once on late night TV. A woman moved into a scary old house, and there was a picture on the wall that looked just like her. It soon became obvious that the heroine was a direct descendant of a witch who had lived in the house. By the end of the movie, the woman was a witch, too.

Scarlett slammed the can of soda down on the kitchen table and hurried into the living room. No one really used the living room, which was uncomfortably warm in the summer. The sitting room was much more breezy and inviting. It was also unencumbered by the small altar that had been set up in the living room years ago by the maid (in accordance with Cajun tradition) as a postmortem shrine to Odile. The Judge had never really visited the altar, and Scarlett had been taking care of it for years without really noticing it. There was a large picture of Odile taken about a year before her death, surrounded by holy cards, an obituary, and some of Odile's favorite knickknacks. Scarlett stared at the picture. Then she ran up the stairs to her room. From under the bed, she pulled out the old alligator purse and dumped its contents onto the floor. The photograph of young Odile—the image of Scarlett—stared out from underneath the teeth and the voodoo doll. Of course. It was Odile speaking to her from beyond the grave. Scarlett heard a mental thunderclap. Odile wanted Scarlett to use voodoo to stop Lana.

Jesus. How would she begin? Scarlett had never met anyone who did voodoo. There was a shop in the French Quarter in New Orleans, but that was just for tourists. Maybe there were books on the subject. There was no time to waste.

On her way out of the house, Scarlett passed the Judge, who was in the sitting room on the floor. His bony rear protruded from underneath the loveseat. He heard her footsteps and called out about the lockbox, but Scarlett was out the door, down the drive, and into the Lincoln.

Twenty minutes later, she was standing before the desk in Thibodaux Public Library. The woman in front of her in line had a stack of romance novels a foot and a half high. Impatiently, Scarlett shifted her weight from one leg to another and noisily flicked her library card, stiff with nonuse, between her fingers. After an interminable length of time, the librarian turned to Scarlett.

"You're all flushed, honey," she scolded Scarlett in a motherly voice. The librarian had used the same tone when Scarlett was seven and had tried to check out *Where Do Babies Come From?*

"Where are the books on voodoo?" The best tactic, really, was to ignore the woman.

"Voodoo? I don't know that we have any. Why are you interested in that?"

Scarlett could feel herself about to burst with frustration. Why was it, whenever she wanted to do something quietly, the world conspired to draw attention to her actions? Like the time in high school when she had bought cellulite cream—just as a precautionary measure—and the salesgirl in the K&B screamed across the store for a price on the "cellulite stuff," in front of the junior class president, for whom Scarlett had carried a torch since the seventh grade.

Predictably, the librarian called, at a very un-librarian level of volume, across the stacks to a woman deep within nonfiction. "Hey, Marie, do we have any books on voodoo?"

"I think there's one. It's with the books on witchcraft."

"It's over there." The librarian pointed to a corner, remote and dimly lit. Or maybe Scarlett only perceived it that way. "On the second shelf against the wall."

"Thank you." Scarlett began to turn away.

"You know," the librarian announced to Scarlett and the small line that had formed behind her, "I read in *Reader's Digest* that a lot of young people are getting into witchcraft and satanic worship."

She looked at Scarlett suspiciously. "Have you heard anything about that?"

Scarlett let out a nervous burst of laughter. "Well, I'm Catholic, you know. I wouldn't really know anything about it. I just need the book for a paper that I'm writing for school. On the history of the area,"

"Ah. I understand. A lot of the slaves practiced voodoo."

"I think that's part of the reason we lost the war," said a woman standing behind Scarlett.

"Now, Margaret, you can't believe everything you hear," the librarian scolded.

Smiling, Scarlett slowly backed away from the counter, then turned and hurried into the stacks. Breathlessly, she ran her finger along the second shelf. The book wasn't there. Scarlett went back to the left and started over again. She reached the end of the shelf without flushing her quarry and was about to swallow her pride and go back to the librarian. Then she caught a glimpse of a book that had fallen behind the others. Scarlett saw a large "VO" on its spine, peeking from between several more mundane volumes on folklore and fables. She pulled out a handful of the books lined up in front, reached in and grabbed the elusive volume. It was covered with an opaque layer of dust and smelled as if it had been sitting in a basement for the past twenty years. Scarlett directed a puff of breath at the cover, but the dust held firmly to the book. She sighed and wiped the book on the knee of her jeans. In gold script appeared the words *The Compleat Guide to Voodoo: Magik and Spells*. Scarlett sank to the floor and started to read.

She quickly realized that to succeed at this project, she was going to need specialized equipment.

"What kind of snake do you want?" The skinny, red-haired kid behind the counter at Pet Paradise looked excited. Selling someone a snake was obviously more interesting than scooping goldfish out of a tank.

"I don't know." Did the type of snake matter? It seemed to Scarlett that it might. God, hopefully it didn't need to be a poisonous one. By virtue of its snake-ness, a snake was scary enough. "What kind do you have?"

"We got a nice python, but he's five hundred dollars, a couple little snakes from South America, and, oh, let me show you this one." The kid led Scarlett back toward a row of aquariums. He pointed to one containing a muscular but distinctly unanimated snake about two feet long. "This one is a boa."

"Does he always just lie there?"

"Yeah, pretty much. They have a slow metabolism. The good thing is, you don't have to feed them as often." The kid rapped a knuckle against the aquarium, but the snake remained in a quiescent state. "He's on sale. Seventy-five bucks."

"I'll take him."

"Cool. You into snakes?"

The question sounded vaguely sexual to Scarlett. She looked at the kid. He was grinning. "No, it's for a biology project," she answered.

"You're not going to dissect him, are you?" The kid looked alarmed.

"No, no," Scarlett comforted him. "I'm just going to observe him. You know, take notes and measurements and things."

"Oh good." The kid reached in barehanded, pulled out the somnambulant snake, and placed it in a box. "Do you have food for him?"

"Do you have snakechow or something?"

"Yeah, we have snakechow. But we call it mice."

"Mice?" Scarlett felt her stomach churn.

"Yeah, he eats mice. One or two a month. And they have to be alive. He won't eat dead ones." The kid showed none of the concern for the welfare of the mice that he had toward the boa. "You live near here?"

"Why?"

"If not, I can sell you a pair. That way you can raise his food at your house, or wherever you're keeping him, and you'll always have a fresh supply. You don't have to keep running here every time he gets hungry."

Scarlett swallowed. "That seems like a good idea. I guess."

"Yeah. I'll get it all ready to go, then. I'll even throw in a snake book, no charge, so you know what you're doing."

"Great."

The kid helped her carry her purchases out to the car. Scarlett put the snake in the backseat, and the little box containing the pair of white mice in the front seat next to her. On the lid of the box of mice was a drawing of a goldfish, a guinea pig, and a canary and in pink curlicue letters, intertwined with hearts, the words "I'm Going Home."

Twenty-four

Lana watched from a chair several yards away as the tuxedo was pinned and tucked on the Judge. There had been some discussion of fitting him with a tux from the boys' department, but the Judge had bridled at that suggestion, showing a sartorial awareness that Lana had never dreamed existed. "You see, dear," the Judge called over his shoulder, "it's beginning to fit quite well. The L'Enfants have always been of a finer build. But it's quality, not quantity, eh?"

"That's right, hon." Though Lana knew that in her case, both were amply represented. But everyone couldn't be that way. She had wanted to wear heels with her dress, but it was clear that she would loom almost a foot above the Judge in anything other than flats. That might look odd in the wedding pictures. Lana sighed. Even with the fabric of the tuxedo nipped in, the Judge looked like an assortment of bones in a black wool bag. Why couldn't he be just a little taller—say, tall enough to get on the rides at Disneyland? Still, there was something endearing about his small stature. Lana realized that she was beginning to feel protective toward him.

Lana wrinkled her brow. This maternal instinct was both new and worrisome.

Her cell phone rang. Lana pulled it out of her purse. "Hello?"

"Officer Aucoin here."

Lana had given a nice contribution to the Police Athletic League to ensure Aucoin's continued helpfulness. It was encouraging to see that she was getting a return on her investment.

"It's good to hear from you, Officer. Has Neville identified the shooter?"

"He has. A loser named Jimmy Crouton. We're all familiar with Crouton here. He's a regular guest. I'm kind of surprised about the murder allegations, though. Jimmy has always been small-time."

"Do you think Neville's telling the truth?"

"Yeah, I do. There's a connection. Crouton was Hebert's cellmate. We figure that Hebert let on that he had some dough, and Crouton decided to get himself a piece of it."

"What about this Crouton's claim that he was doing a hit?"

"I'm sure that was bullshit. His dealer even said that Jimmy told stories about how bad he was. We'll look into the murder-for-hire aspect, but I doubt we'll find anything."

"I still think that there's something to that story," she pressed. "It doesn't make sense that he would do a burglary but take so little."

"He's an incompetent burglar, that's all. Crouton had priors for B&E. This job fits his M.O. He's never been so violent before, but crack can make these guys violent, too."

It seemed like a logical explanation for the killings. Still, Lana was more sure than ever that the murders were connected to Boudreaux's death. But she knew that there was no way of convincing Aucoin of that. He just wanted to haul in Crouton and close the case.

"Would you mind if I went down to the jail and asked around a little? See if anyone knows what Crouton and Hebert might have discussed?"

"If it will set your mind at ease."

Lana signed off. She'd go to the jail tomorrow. Right now, there were other matters that she needed to deal with. She couldn't let her campaign fall by the wayside because of her obsession with finding the truth about what had happened to the Heberts.

"Louis, I wanted to talk to you about the guest list."

"I'll only be asking a few people, darling. Judge McAllister will be my best man. There will be Scarlett, my clerk, just a couple more. You invite whomever you wish."

It seemed to have escaped the Judge that the whole point of a big wedding was to allow the festivities to double as a business—or in this case, political—opportunity. Lana would have to approach the subject as tactfully as possible. "I'd feel much better if you invited whoever you wanted to, Louis. As many people as you would like. Maybe the parish president. What's his name? Guidry? And how about all of the other judges? Not just in Thibodaux, but all over the area." Lana looked down at the list she had made of possible guests. It was quite long and so heavy with local influence that the piece of paper it was written on practically caused her hand to tremble. "What about the men on the police jury?"

"What about them? I don't even know who they are anymore."

"Well, we don't want anyone's feelings hurt, do we, hon?"

"If you think so," the Judge replied doubtfully. "But let's make plans for the honeymoon."

"And maybe some members of the local press."

"Whomever you'd like."

It was obvious to Lana that the Judge had stopped listening. He was gazing at himself in the mirror, squaring what was left of his shoulders and puffing out his chest.

"Now," he said happily, "let's talk about the honeymoon."

The fitting took almost another half hour, after which Lana dropped the exhausted and somewhat perforated Judge (there had been so many pins in the tux that minor injuries were inevitable) back at Shady Oaks. Lana headed for the caterers, with some misgivings gnawing at her brain.

The Judge appeared to be less in touch with the local powers-that-be than she had hoped. But he was well known and respected. She had run a computer search and found a good number of opinions published under his name. And she had checked through the microfiche in the library in New Orleans. There were plenty of articles about the Judge. Well, not many within the last ten years, but he had been a very influential man. She reassured herself. He didn't have to be involved with the politicos on a daily basis to remain influential. And he added that touch of class, that "old family" *je ne sais quois*.

She'd even begun to feel some affection toward him. He was reasonably sophisticated, quite sweet, and obviously taken with her. Lana usually eschewed any signs of devotion from her male companions, but the Judge's attentions sprung from his loyalty and respect, not from any need to possess or control her. No, the marriage was a good idea. She wouldn't have come this far with the plan if it weren't an effective one. Suddenly, Lana had another stroke of genius. Perhaps the wedding could be even more effective, publicity-wise.

The caterer had given Lana a large photo album filled with pictures of place settings, wedding cakes, and various foodstuffs. Lana entered the shop and slammed the album onto the counter to catch the attention of the caterer's assistant, who was sitting at her desk watching Jerry Springer on a miniature TV. The assistant drew herself away reluctantly and walked over to Lana.

"May I help you?"

"Yes. I've picked out the food I want for the wedding. What's your name?"

"Darla."

"Darla, I told your boss I'd need food for about a hundred and fifty, but now I'm thinking closer to a thousand."

Darla looked at Lana skeptically. "Are you sure you've counted right, ma'm? That's an awfully large reception."

"I've counted correctly. I'm inviting the whole town." Lana smiled, pleased with this new idea. "Literally."

Twenty-five

The snake had barely moved since it'd been at Shady Oaks. Scarlett peered down into its aquarium. Was it breathing? She inched her finger in, ever so slowly, and carefully prodded the snake. It moved a little. Scarlett snatched her finger out and leapt back. She didn't want it crushing any bones, though right now it looked incapable of anything more violent than a snore. The mice, on the other hand, were a whirlwind of activity. Squeaking happily, they ran in their wheel, they chased each other, they chewed the newspaper in their cage into adorable little nests. One of the mice even let Scarlett pick it up, and would sit contentedly on her shoulder. Scarlett had grown rather fond of the little rodents. The salesclerk at the pet store had assured her that the snake was fed for the month, so the mice were safe for now.

Scarlett left the menagerie in her room and went back out onto the gallery, where she'd been sitting on the ancient porch swing and taking notes from the voodoo book. The ceiling fan beat lazily overhead. It was midafternoon, and quite hot. Scarlett drank large gulps of iced tea as she studied. Soon she grew tired in the heat. She stretched herself out on the porch swing, and stared up at the underside of the roof over the gallery. It was painted a pale aqua, the color of a Caribbean sea, although the paint was peeling in spots and smudged with black mildew. Scarlett swung slowly in the slight breeze. It was almost as if she were rocking in a boat. Within minutes, she was asleep.

She was in Haiti. She'd never been there, but she recognized it immediately. There was a grouping of small, brightly painted shacks, raised above the ground on posts. Chickens ran in the dirt, around and under the houses. It was night, and a fire burned in the center of the cluster of shacks. Lucie danced before the fire, a slow, swaying dance. Scarlett could hear drums in the distance. Suddenly, Odile appeared next to Lucie. She was young, Scarlett's age, and dressed in nothing but a pareo. The boa was wound around her neck. It was no longer asleep, but coiled and uncoiled to the beat of the drums. Odile held something in her hands. It was the voodoo doll. And it looked exactly like Lana. Odile smiled broadly, picked up a pin, and stuck it through the doll. The doll turned into Scarlett.

Scarlett awoke with a start. It was another message from Odile. She had better get going. The wedding was less than a week away.

Cami Gooch dropped a week-old copy of the *New Orleans Times-Picayune* on Hultgrew's desk. "Did you see this?"

"See what?" Hultgrew never read the *Times-Picayune*. Or the *Star*, for that matter. It was depressing enough to write for it without having to read it, too.

"This article about Consolidated Chemical."

"Did they dump something again? I thought my tap water tasted funny."

"Jesus, Hultgrew, you drink that stuff? No wonder you're so slow on the uptake—you're poisoned. I don't know why I give you any leads, but I guess it's my charitable nature. And I'm so busy covering the elections, I don't have time to pursue this."

Hultgrew knew that Gooch would have to rub that last one in.

"If you're so on the ball, how come this article is from last Tuesday?"

"If I had known that I would have to do your job as well as mine, I would have gotten it to you sooner. God, you're ungrateful. I came across it while doing some research of my own."

"I still don't see what Consolidated has to do with anything I'm doing."

"Read the article, Hultgrew, you stupid bastard."

Hultgrew wouldn't give her the satisfaction. He tossed it to the back of the desk and continued typing up his article on Mamie Breaux, who had recently retired after fifty years of service in the local elementary school cafeteria. Cami shook her head and stalked off. As soon as she was out of sight, Hultgrew picked up the newspaper and perused the article.

CONSOLIDATED SPOKESMAN DENIES
BRIBERY ALLEGATIONS

ST. JAMES PARISH—The chairman and chief financial officer of Consolidated Chemical, Gerald Smith, today denied allegations made by the district attorney's office that Consolidated Chemical obtained its zoning variances and license to operate in Vacherie through bribery and fraudulent maneuvers involving "shell" corporations. "These dealings occurred over twenty years ago, and were all above board," said Smith. "If there had been any improper negotiations, which there were not, these allegations would have arisen long ago." Consolidated Chemical manufactures paints, solvents, and base chemicals, and employs over 350 workers at its facility west of Vacherie. It is the largest employer in the parish.

Jesus. L'Enfant was in it up to his skinny neck. Hultgrew had him now. Gleefully, his feet beat out a little dance under the desk.

He pulled the Breaux article out of the typewriter, crumpled it up, and threw it in the trash. He put in a clean sheet of paper. He needed the documents in the lockbox, then he would call the district attorney's office. It would be an exclusive, tying the Judge to Consolidated. Not only would he get his picture above his column, they'd put it on the front page over the masthead just to sell papers. He'd be bumping Dear Abby.

Hultgrew opened his drawer, and was hit in the face with Fang's stench. Ugh. He pulled out the lockbox and opened the lid.

The aged papers inside had fused together into a smelly mass. Ink had run all over. At Hultgrew's slightest touch, the documents crumbled. He was afraid to even pull them out of the box. He put his head down on the desk and started to cry.

Surely this was not normal behavior.

Scarlett was all set up in front of Odile's altar. She had her lemons, salt, gunpowder, voodoo doll, she had the snake.

And the nagging worry that she was losing her mind.

Growing up out in the parishes, Scarlett had always felt out of step with the rest of her peers. She wasn't quite sure how a normal twenty-four year old was supposed to act. But she was willing to wager that none of her former fellow LSU students were in their living room with a snake and a heart full of bad intent. How come her hold on reality wasn't as strong as everyone else's? This was insane. She was probably certifiable. But she didn't know what else to do. Oh hell. They said that if you thought you were crazy, you probably weren't.

Scarlett steeled herself, reached into the aquarium, and pulled out the snake.

He was surprisingly heavy. His skin was dry and smooth, not at all slimy. As she lifted him toward the altar, she was amazed at how self-supporting he was. She had expected him to be limp, but he was like a huge stiff muscle. He cantilevered himself toward the altar, flicking his tongue in and out. Scarlett laid him down gently. The snake was supposed to be her conduit to the other world. According to the voodoo book, he would speak or even sing to her and tell her what he knew.

Scarlett took a pen and a piece of paper and wrote the names of the Judge and Lana on it nine times. Then she cut a hole in the stem end of the lemon and poured some of the gunpowder in the hole. She rolled the paper up tight and shoved it in the lemon, then leaned in toward the snake. "Talk to me." She waited, but there was nothing to hear but the whirring of the ceiling fan above. Scarlett took the snake's silence as a tacit sign that she was to continue. She now had to drive to Lana's office, bury the lemon, and spread out the salt. First, though, she picked up the doll.

She had stuck bright orange yarn on its head, and drawn on matching lips and electric-blue eye shadow. It looked amazingly like Lana, what with its overstuffed contours. Scarlett held the doll in front of her face. "Leave the man alone," she intoned nine times in her best Caribbean accent. Might as well be as authentic as possible. She felt a rush of adrenaline. She was taking charge, she was helping herself and the Judge. Scarlett laughed and tossed the doll into the air, higher and higher. She gave the doll one last victory toss, right into the ceiling fan. The blade caught the doll below the head, cleaving it neatly in two.

"Ouch!" Lana rubbed at her neck. "I've got pain right above my shoulders from standing still so long."

"Mmmphhm mmrph," said the woman on her knees at the pedestal under Lana's feet.

"What? I can't understand a word you're saying."

The seamstress pulled several pins from her mouth and stuck them in the hem of the lace-and-satin-rosette-encrusted, princess-necked, puffed-sleeved, thirty-pounds-of-bugle-beads-and-taffeta wedding gown that was being altered to fit tightly about Lana's curves.

"I said 'I'm sorry,' because some of the pins seem to be poking you."

"Oh. Well, get them out, then." Didn't this woman know how to do her job?

The seamstress stood and pulled several pins from the neck of the dress. "Your maid of honor came in yesterday, Miss Pulaski. I got her all fitted. A difficult body, that one."

"Yeah, I can imagine. What about my bridesmaid?"

"She came in yesterday, too. She has a very nice figure."

"A little scrawny, isn't she?"

"Yes," said the woman diplomatically. "She could use a few pounds. But that's how they look these days."

Lana turned on the pedestal, catching views of herself from the three-way mirror. "Very bridal, don't you think?"

The seamstress suddenly became intent on the dress, tugging at one cuff. "Well, the way we have it fitted . . . If you'd like, I can make the dress just a bit more . . . demure. I can let it out a little in the bust and the hips."

"I don't want to look like I'm wearing a sack."

The seamstress stepped back from the figure on the pedestal. "Of course not," she answered, chastened. "Let's try out the veil."

She lifted the lace headpiece from atop a Styrofoam head near the mirrors. On the display, it had hung in graceful, fluid pleats. On Lana's head, the stiff lace stuck out almost horizontally, propped up by the bright orange flip. The lace appeared to be held out by centrifugal force, as if Lana's head were spinning so fast that it looked as if it were standing still. Lana patted at the veil, smoothing it into verticality, but as soon as she removed her hands, it sprung back.

"Jesus," she mused, "this could take a little work."

After leaving the seamstress, Lana drove to the LaFourche Parish Prison, a long, squat cinder-block building in the middle of a huge cane field. Several of the guards remembered her from when she'd come to talk to Dennis Hebert (people tended to remember Lana). The guards reminded Lana of the type of men who frequented Joe's bar—blue-collar, no-nonsense, and disillusioned. They recognized her as one of their own, and she was accorded more civility and assistance than the average defense attorney. She asked around, and eventually found a guard who had been on duty in Hebert and Crouton's section.

"Did you hear them discussing anything?" Lana asked him.

"You tend to tune these guys out.'It's always 'I'm innocent, I'm innocent,' or 'I'm a badder motherfucker than you.' It's never 'Gosh, I'm a loser. Maybe I should make some changes.' " As he spoke, the guard scratched idly at the ample belly spilling over the pants of his shiny polyester uniform. "I'm really sick of listening to these assholes. I'm sorry, but I don't remember anything that was said between those two prisoners."

Lana asked him a few more questions, but he had nothing helpful to tell her. Then, as she was leaving the prison, he jogged out and caught her in the parking lot.

"There is something kinda strange that happened," he told her, panting with exertion. "I don't know if it means anything."

"Any information that you have would be helpful."

"Well, some guy came to see Crouton. He wasn't an attorney, and he sure wasn't a relative. He was a rich-looking guy, an old guy. That was weird enough. The other strange part was that they let him right into the section. He didn't have to see Crouton in the visiting room like everyone else."

"Who let him in?"

"I don't know. I can ask around."

"I'd appreciate it." Lana gave the guard her card. "If you ever need any legal work done, give me a call. I'll give you a special deal."

"Thanks," said the guard. "I'll check it out."

Scarlett parked the Lincoln around the corner from the Offices. She had with her the lemon, the bowl of salt, and a trowel hidden in a large shoulder bag. She walked around the block and into the alley behind the building looking for Lana's car, but Lana appeared to be gone. Good. The lemon had to be buried in a spot where the setting sun would shine on it. Unfortunately, that spot was right outside the Offices' front door. Scarlett went back around to look for a place to dig. She hadn't taken into account that this was the city and that there was a dearth of earth, so to speak. But several yards from Lana's front door a chunk was missing from the pavement, and there was enough dirt to bury the lemon. Scarlett stood in front of the Offices as nonchalantly as she could, and waited for the bus to come and pick up several people standing at the bus stop in front of the building. As soon as they were gone, she whipped the trowel from the shoulder bag, dug a small hole, and planted the lemon, bloom-end down. Several pedestrians stepped over her while she was accomplishing her task, but they took little notice. This was New Orleans. Strange behavior was not only approved of, but cultivated.

When she was done, Scarlett stood, wiped her hands on her pants, and turned around. She was looking right into the face of Lana's secretary.

"Why, Miss Scarlett, whatever are you doing?"

Scarlett was surprised at how easily the lie came, but then again, the Judge had always told her that the L'Enfants were talented liars. "I'm planting this lemon in front of Lana's office. It's a Creole custom. You put the sour into the ground, and that leaves only the sweet for the newlyweds."

"That's very charming. I've never heard that before."

"Oh yes. It's a very old custom. Uh . . . to finish up, I have to spread this salt around inside." Scarlett lifted the bowl out of her bag and smiled at the secretary. "Do you mind?"

"No, come on in. I'll watch. It'll be like the Discovery Channel."

"By the way, don't mention this to Lana. It's a surprise. I'll tell her at the wedding."

"Don't worry. I'm very good with secrets."

God, Scarlett thought. What happens if I start believing myself?

Mission accomplished, Scarlett drove back to Shady Oaks. As she pulled into the drive, she realized that she had forgotten to pick the Judge up from work. He was going to be angry. She ran inside to call him and tell him that she was on her way.

The Judge was standing in the living room, peering at the altar, where the snake was fast asleep. "Grandfather!" Scarlett shrieked, alarmed. "How did you get here?"

"Judge McAllister's clerk brought me home. What is this fellow doing here?"

"He's my new pet."

"He's quite handsome. I've always been rather fond of snakes, myself. They keep to themselves, don't jump on the table like cats. Interesting creatures." The Judge pointed at the altar. "I see you've found Odile's voodoo doll."

Scarlett swallowed hard. "Yes. In the attic."

"I remember when she dressed up like a voodoo princess for that Halloween party. I think it was right after the war. She had on a grass skirt, and this bracelet made of alligator teeth that she bought in some tourist trap in New Orleans. She looked quite exotic. Of course she had her knickers on under the skirt." The Judge shook his head. "Odile was never that daring."

Scarlett felt her stomach drop. "It was a Halloween costume?"

"Well, it wasn't her Easter frock."

"But I thought Lucie taught her, you know, voodoo. I mean, she was from Haiti and all."

"Lucie?" the Judge scoffed. "She was one of the most Catholic women I've ever met. Could have been a nun. Even if she did know voodoo, she never would have taught a white woman. Those hoodoo people keep to themselves. By the way, have you seen that lockbox? I've been looking for it for weeks."

"No, Grandfather. I don't have any idea what you're talking about." Scarlett picked up the snake, hung him over one shoulder, and started up the stairs. It looked like she was going to be one of Lana's bridesmaids after all. Clearly, her only option was revenge. It shouldn't be too hard to get hold of Bobby Taylor. He'd probably be very interested to hear about Lana's campaign plans. Maybe he'd even pay her.

Twenty-six

The Judge woke early this Saturday morning. As he opened his eyes, he knew that something exciting was happening that day, but he was still groggy from the handful of sleeping pills he'd taken the night before. The Heberts' murders weighed heavily on his mind, and slumber eluded him without narcotic assistance. He sat up in bed and willed himself into consciousness, then it came to him. Today was his wedding to the radiant Lana.

You just never knew. Here he had been a judge for almost four decades. He hadn't thought anything new would ever happen to him. He would just go on living at Shady Oaks and being a judge until he died. Not a bad life by anyone's standards, but not so thrill-packed, either. He'd been just *existing*, waiting to die, really. But now . . . to be his age and embark on a new adventure! It was just grand. The Heberts momentarily forgotten, the Judge nearly jumped out from under the covers. He was filled with piss and vinegar today. Literally. He ran to the bathroom and relieved himself. At eighty-four, one had to heed nature's call without delay.

He went to the window and yanked back the heavy draperies.

There was no light. Was it that early? Then he realized that the shutters were still shut. With some difficulty he pulled up the peeling sash and threw open the shutters. From now on, they would stay open. He would let light flood the room, flood the whole house! Just like Lana's light was flooding his life. Then he caught sight of Consolidated belching opaque smoke less than a quarter mile away and quickly pulled the sash back down. No sense in stinking up the place.

The Judge pressed his long nose against the glass and tried to peer around to the front yard. He could just make out the corner of the tent that the caterer had set up the day before for the wedding. It was a pink and yellow stripe. He wasn't too thrilled with the color scheme, but it was more important that Lana be happy.

This wedding, he was sure, was going to be nothing like his wedding to Odile, which had taken place in St. Patrick's Church in New Orleans, where Odile's cousin was a priest. St. Patrick's was old, even back then, with frescoes on the ceilings and a huge, carved mahogany clamshell that served as a pulpit. An odd but effective blending of the Vatican and the Gulf Coast. Although Odile stood by his side throughout the ceremony, the Judge had had the distinct impression that she was rising out of the clamshell like a Botticelli maiden. As the Judge put the ring on her finger—her hands were tiny, almost childlike—he'd looked into her eyes, expecting to see azure, renaissance depths. Instead, he saw only his own reflection, as if her pupils were backed with opaque silver, like a mirror. There had been no Botticelli, no Odile even, just a young girl who wanted a fancy wedding, a proper husband, a big house. The Judge had felt the first of the sometimes acute pangs of disappointment that were to punctuate his marriage. But he had swept the foreboding out of his mind, kissed her, smiled as they walked down the aisle, and laughed merrily at the reception after. When he looked back on the wedding, though, he remembered it as a funeral. Odile was dressed in heavy black robes, and instead of her rising from the clamshell pulpit, the wooden mollusk clamped down, trapping the Judge himself inside.

But today's ceremony, well, it was going to be a party. Lana had told him that she wanted to invite the whole town. He'd been all for it. After all, he reasoned, he was a bit like the town's father. Revered, respected, someone they idolized. It was only proper to invite his "children" to the wedding. Lana had mailed an invitation to every household. She'd also tacked up notices on the telephone poles, she'd told him, so no one would get left out inadvertently. What a thoughtful girl. Where Odile was closed and small, Lana was open and expansive. He couldn't wait to show her off.

The bridesmaid's dress hung on the door of the armoire. The fluorescent magenta of the taffeta glowed so brightly that it leaked in under the bedspread that covered Scarlett's face, pried open her tightly clenched eyelids, and stabbed into her pupils like a knife. There would be no more sleep this morning. She rolled onto her stomach, groaned, and covered her head with the pillow. Maybe she could suffocate herself before the ceremony.

When a half hour passed and she hadn't managed to asphyxiate herself, Scarlett realized that there was no putting it off any longer. She got out of bed and took the dress off the hanger. It crinkled and crackled as she pulled it on and zipped it up. She stood before the full-length mirror. There were more ruffles on this one dress than on the rental tuxes of an entire junior prom. The humiliation of the wedding rose like bile into her throat.

She could hear the caterers setting up the buffet under the tent on the lawn. It might be time for a drink. Scarlett wandered out onto the lawn, the dress creaking and cracking so with every step that the caterers jolted their heads up and watched her approach from a good fifty yards away. She was very self-conscious of the noise that she was making and tried to take small, mincing steps to minimize the clamor, but it was futile. By the time she'd reached the table that had been set up as a bar, she was red-faced with effort and embarrassment.

"May I have a vodka on the rocks, please?" she asked the bartender. His bow tie was on crooked, and Scarlett could see where it was clipped on to his stained shirt.

"The ceremony doesn't start for another forty-five minutes. It's a little early, isn't it?"

"Not if you have to wear this dress."

"I see what you mean. Is Taaka okay? She didn't order any top shelf. I can make it a vodka tonic and hide the taste a little."

"Okay."

The bartender put some ice into a plastic cup and started pouring. "Are you her daughter or her little sister? You kind of look like her, at least in that dress."

The horror. The horror. "No!" Scarlett grabbed the drink and stomped off to a lawn chair under the chinaberry tree. From this perspective, she could see a sign on the roof of the tent: LANA PULASKI FOR ATTORNEY GENERAL. Jesus.

Scarlett wasn't even halfway through her drink—not far enough to have gotten any beneficial effect from the vodka—when Lana pulled into the driveway behind the caterer's trucks. She stepped heavily from the car. An enormous garment bag hung over her right arm, causing her to tilt dangerously in her stilettos. She caught sight of Scarlett underneath the tree and trundled over, her pointy heels sinking almost an inch into the soft earth with every step.

"That's a new look for you," she said, perusing the dress. "I like it. You look alive. Here." She rummaged through her bag with her free hand and pulled out a small package wrapped in iridescent pink paper. "This is my gift to my bridesmaid, i.e., you."

Scarlett took the box gingerly. "Thank you."

"Open it."

"Now?"

"No time like the present."

Scarlett picked at the paper with her sore, bitten fingertips. She couldn't get the tape off the seams.

"Let me." Lana snatched the package away and neatly sliced through the tape with the switchbladelike edge of one hot pink acrylic nail. She handed the package back.

Scarlett tore off the paper and opened the little pink velvet box inside. She lifted out a gold chain. On the end was a nugget pendant. Engraved on the smooth side of the pendant was "Louis L'Enfant and Lana Pulaski—June 17, 1998." Scarlett felt a fist close around her stomach and twist. "Ungh," she winced.

"Put it on."

"I'm wearing silver earrings today. It would clash in the wedding photos."

"Nonsense. I don't mind," Lana said, too sweetly. "I think it will look lovely with the dress."

Defeated, Scarlett hung the chain around her neck. It felt inordinately heavy—the exact weight, in fact, of a dead albatross. The chain immediately tangled in her hair, pulling out a clump the thickness of a shoelace.

Lana made a clucking sound. "Better watch that hair." She walked off, picking her way through the yard. "Beauty," she called behind her, pausing for effect, "is a dangerous thing."

Hultgrew could not believe his good fortune when the invitation had arrived on his desk at the *Star*. He had chased down the mailgirl, sure that it was a hoax perpetrated on him by Cami. But the invitation was real! Obviously it had been a slip-up on someone's part— after all, there was no love lost between the Judge and Hultgrew. It wasn't like he was going to be asked to be best man. But why question providence?

Hultgrew had always known he was destined for greatness. Destiny was the only way he could possibly achieve it—he was far too lazy to earn it on his own. But at least he was honest enough with himself to realize his limitations. That was why he had chosen journalism as a major in college. It didn't require that much research, at least not the book kind, which had always been difficult for Hultgrew. The mere sight of a library book had always acted upon him as a strong soporific. Nor did journalism necessitate a facility with math or the sciences. Hultgrew wasn't good with anything he couldn't touch or see. With journalism, you could read *Playboy* and call it homework. There was nothing to memorize for a final. Instead of spending college locked in a library or a lab, Hultgrew had four years of touch football with his fraternity brothers, got quite good at pool, and typed up his assignments in between keg parties. He wasn't exactly Phi Beta Kappa, but he'd graduated. And his father, president of a chain of hardware stores and a big advertiser in the *Star*, had talked to the owner of the paper and Hultgrew had a job. Hultgrew had never worked too hard as a reporter; he'd just waited for fate to catch up with him, and here it was. A little late, but still welcome.

Hultgrew stepped carefully amidst the papers from the lockbox. He had brought the brick of sodden pulp home and put it in the oven to dry out. Hell, he never cooked anyway. Fang's scent had filled the house, but it had been worth it. The papers had reknit themselves, for the most part. Hultgrew had spent hours the night before painstakingly prying the sheets apart, and had then strewn them about the living room carpet to finish drying. Unfortunately, it seemed that the carpet had absorbed the remaining moisture—it was now acrid and stiff—but he hadn't expected to get his security deposit back anyway.

Hultgrew picked up the counter letters, straightened his tie, and stepped out the door.

The crowd was thickening. Lana watched out the window as yet another car pulled in and parked by the side of the long gravel drive. It looked like at least five hundred people, and she was sure more would show for the reception. She turned from the window and spun in front of the mirror. The dress was exquisite, the fanciest she had ever seen. Despite herself, Lana felt a prickle of excitement more appropriate to a twenty-year-old girl. She was getting married! It was her day. She allowed herself to thrill for several more seconds, then snapped to attention. Enough of that. She had to stay level-headed, calm. Frivolity was no excuse for not maximizing the opportunities of this occasion.

She sat down on the bed, careful not to crush any of the rosettes or snag any bugle beads, and bounced up and down a little. It seemed like a firm mattress. She would be comfortable enough in this guest room. It didn't have its own bath, much less a Jacuzzi like her plush condominium, but what could one expect out here in the parishes? Anyway, it was only a matter of months until the election, and after that she could move to Baton Rouge.

There was a knock at the door. "Is that you, Louis?" Lana called.

"It's your matron of honor, sweetie."

Lana opened the door a crack and peeked out. Madam of honor would be more appropriate: On the other side of the door stood Lana's Aunt Flo, wearing her towering jet-black curls, a matching beauty mark on one cheek, and red lipstick so shiny that Lana could see her face reflected in the gloss on Flo's lips. Though almost thirty years her senior, Flo's cleavage was still remarkable— spectacular, really, forming a shelf of flesh under the bridesmaid's dress so sturdy and perfectly cantilevered that one could rest a carpenter's level on the mounds of breast and watch the bubble line up perfectly on center. Flo had supplied the girls that lingered among the sailors in Joe Pulaski's bar. She had helped raise Lana from a little girl, and had a soft spot for her niece.

"The dress fits good. I think magenta is my color."

Lana looked Flo up and down with a critical eye. "Yeah, she did a pretty good job on the alterations."

"I'm so excited for you, honey. I never thought I'd see this day.

Men are such rats. I'm glad you finally found one worthwhile. I feel proud enough to be your mother myself." Tears welled up in Flo's eyes. Lana hurried over to the dressing table, grabbed some Kleenex and smacked it over Flo's eyeballs before the tears rushed through her lashes, washing goopy mascara down her cheeks like mud and silt in streaming floodwaters. "Ya' just look beautiful, honey," Flo sniffled, dabbing at her eyes with the blackened tissue.

"Here," said Lana, pinning a "Pulaski—Attorney General" button to Flo's ruffled cleavage.

Fate was a strange thing. Crouton would not have even been in Thibodaux to find out about the wedding had it not been for the beating he'd taken in New Orleans.

Once his attacker was safely away from the scene, Crouton had pulled himself out of the gutter and started down the street toward his flophouse. He was immediately stopped by a cop.

"How did your face get so fucked up?" the pig asked.

"I tripped," Crouton answered. "I'm clumsy that way."

At that point, Crouton realized how very *obvious* he was and decided that it would be a good idea to clear out off the Crescent City and regroup in the familiar environs of Thibodaux. He had no money for a bus ticket, and he knew that no one would pick him up hitchhiking with the ever-worsening condition of his face. So he stole another car. This time he made sure it had automatic transmission.

Upon his arrival in Thibodaux, Crouton had gone straight to his mama's. He needed to lay low and nurse his injuries. Unfortunately, Mrs. Crouton had not been very sympathetic to her prodigal son's condition. She'd opened the front door, taken one look at his filthy clothes and bruised, distorted, snot-smeared face, and refused to allow him into the house. She wouldn't even let him sleep in the tool shed until Crouton agreed to let her spray him down with the garden hose and burn his T-shirt and jeans.

Crouton had spent several weeks out back. Once the shakes and nausea of his withdrawal ceased, Crouton realized that he needed to disguise himself if he was going to get near enough to take out the scary lawyer. He used the garden shears hanging on the shed wall to cut his hair close to his skull. It wasn't the most professional job; spots of bare scalp alternated with patches of blond fuzz, but Crouton wasn't concerned with looking pretty. He wheedled his mother for some of the shoe-polish-black haircolor she used on her coif. After the dye job, his head looked like a checkerboard of pink skin and jet fur. Crouton was rather pleased with the effect. He looked tough. When the swelling had receded in his face, and his features (although not his scalp) had assumed a somewhat normal aspect, Crouton drove the Chevette to the local drugstore and shoplifted a pair of large, dark, Jackie O sunglasses that covered a good half of his face.

On the way home from the drugstore, he had caught sight of the lawyer's name on a large, hot pink sign tacked to a telephone pole. Crouton pulled over to the side of the road and read: "Share our joy! Lana Pulaski and Judge Louis L'Enfant are pleased to invite you to their wedding, to take place on June 22nd at noon at Shady Oaks Plantation. To be followed by a reception with OPEN BAR!"

Now, Crouton watched from the fringes of the crowd as the wedding party approached the tent. He noticed several of the people near him sidling away. They undoubtedly sensed the menace that exuded from the assassin.

"Weirdo," said a middle-aged woman behind him.

Then again, maybe it was his two-tone head and bug-eyed, women's sunglasses. No matter—Crouton was busy multitasking. While he cased Shady Oaks through his oversized shades, he picked the pockets of several of the more inebriated guests. He was going to need a bankroll to arm himself against the lawyer. As the wedding march began, Crouton raised his plastic cupful of Jack and Coke in a salute to the bride and groom.

*　*　*

Two attendants unrolled a long pink carpet up to the altar, like foot-
men for Marie Antoinette. The large woman in front of Scarlett
began to step down the aisle. Right foot, pause, left foot, pause. She
was surprisingly light on her feet. Scarlett looked around the tent at
the wedding guests. They were arranged in fifteen rows of white
folding chairs. Each chair had a ribboned floral arrangement stuck
to the back of it. All the guests had craned their necks to watch the
ascent up the aisle. Scarlett thought that she recognized several of
the people from the town. There was Millie, the woman who ran the
small grocery store, in the third row. And several of the local
policemen were sitting in the last row. What were they all doing
here? The Judge had invited almost no one; they must be guests of
Lana's. How did she know all these people?

The matron of honor was halfway up the aisle. Scarlett
stepped tentatively onto the carpet. It was warm and humid this
afternoon, even for June, and the magenta dress had started to
cling and stick to Scarlett's skin. She paused and took another
step. All the faces watching her made Scarlett fiercely uncomfortable. As she walked, she kept her eyes on the bouquet in her
hands, comforted by the childish illusion that if she couldn't see
someone, they couldn't see her either. The flowers were starting to
wilt in the heat. Scarlett, feeling a trickle of sweat roll down the
back of her neck and into the dress, empathized. There was a murmur from the crowd. Lana must be starting up the aisle. Feeling a
little lightheaded, Scarlett reached the front of the tent and turned
to face the bride. Lana stepped daintily on the carpet, a Cheshire
smile on her face. Surprisingly, she looked cool and comfortable,
even in the tight, heavy dress. Scarlett realized that Lana was at
her best with an audience. Lana took several more steps, and then
she was next to the Judge. She was so much larger than the Judge.
She looked, Scarlett thought, like she was from some other species
of human, a giant, dominant breed. A conquering race. With this

thought, patches of black appeared before Scarlett's eyes. Her skin suddenly felt cold and clammy. Her knees buckled underneath her. Scarlett and the bridesmaid's dress crinkled noisily to the floor.

When she woke, she was on her bed. The dress had been removed, and Flo's large, heavily powdered face peered down at her. Scarlett was struck that it was the kind of face that should have had a wart or two, and seemed incomplete without one.

"How are ya' feeling, sweetie?"

"Kind of weird."

"Ya' fainted. Ya' probably haven't been eatin' right. A girl like you needs some meat on her bones. Poor thing. Ya' missed the whole ceremony."

"It's over?"

"Yeah. You were dead to the world for about fifteen minutes. The doctor looked at you while you was out. He said you just needed to rest."

"It's over." Scarlett sat up and placed her feet on the floor. There was a little residual dizziness, and she waited until it passed. She looked out the window. Below, under the tent, some of the chairs had been cleared away and a Cajun band was playing. People were milling about with pink plastic plates of jambalaya and bread pudding. A number of guests were dancing, and in the middle of the dancers stood the Judge and Lana, swaying slowly to the music. Lana had her meaty arms wrapped around the Judge—he was virtually engulfed by flesh and tulle. Scarlett rubbed her face. Her eyes were bleary and her tongue seemed to be twice its normal size. "I'm going to brush my teeth," she told Flo. "I'm fine, you can go back down now. I wouldn't want you to miss Lana's wedding."

"Ya' sure, sweetie?"

"Yeah, it's okay." As she was turning from the window, Scarlett caught a glimpse of someone familiar out of the corner of her eye. Standing alone next to the band, holding a Coke and watching the dancers, was the Bugman. Scarlett felt a frisson of excitement. Her frailty forgotten, she raced to her room, changed into a sundress, then hurried from the house into the crowd of wedding guests.

When Scarlett had crumpled at her feet, Lana's first instinct was to pick her up by her skinny neck and shake her until she stood erect. Unfortunately, the voters were watching, and she could not indulge the impulse. Though she took for granted that Scarlett was faking, Lana knelt over her, the embodiment of maternal concern. "Scarlett," she hissed at the girl, quietly enough so that no one else would hear, but with enough force to send a glob of spittle sliding down Scarlett's ear canal, "get up, now!" There had been no response. Lana pushed back one of Scarlett's eyelids with the tip of her frosted pink fingernail. The pupil was rolled back into the top of Scarlett's head. Lana considered the possibility that the girl really was sick. After all, she seemed far too afraid of Lana to intentionally try and pull something like this off. Lana placed her fingers on Scarlett's wrist. There was still a pulse. Lana sighed in defeat. "Is there a doctor here?" she had called out to the wedding guests.

Now Lana turned to see the invalid walking slowly through the dancers. She groaned and released the Judge from her viselike clasp. No longer pressurized, he began to reinflate, his clothing and stature expanding like an inner tube being blown up at the beach. Lana smiled sweetly at Scarlett. "All better?" she called across the heads in the crowd.

"Um . . . yeah, I guess." Scarlett's head bobbed like a bird's as she searched through the crowd. "Congratulations," she said absently, then wandered off toward the band.

Lana grabbed the Judge by the elbow and tapped the shoulder of a man dancing next to her. "Hello, I'm Lana Pulaski. We're so glad you could come today. I'm running for attorney general this fall, and I value this opportunity to meet my future constituency."

The man seemed puzzled. "But I ain't never been arrested."

Lana raised one eyebrow. "Of course not."

The man vigorously pumped the Judge's hand several times. "Congratulations, Judge. Nice party."

Lana reached into the layers of tulle, pulled out a campaign button, and pinned it to the man's lapel. "Party favors." She smiled at him.

The man looked down at the button and shrugged. "Thanks."

As he danced off, Lana called after him. "I would appreciate your support in November!"

The Judge clenched and unclenched his fingers painfully. "That Tee-Bob has a firm grip."

Carl wandered over to her, drink in hand. "Quite a catch. You've outdone yourself this time," he whispered in her ear.

"You should try to catch one just like him. Then you wouldn't have to work for me."

"And lose my main form of entertainment? Besides, I've already found a friend." Carl raised his glass in the direction of the bartender, who smiled and waved back.

"Just make sure you give him a button and some campaign literature."

Scarlett sidled up to the Bugman, who was dancing alone in front of the speakers and oblivious to her approach. She leaned over and brought her face under his. "Hi," she shouted over the music.

"Hey."

She pointed at the soda bottle in his hand. "Can I get you a beer, or some champagne or something?"

"Can't drink today." The Bugman continued to dance as he spoke. "I'm flyin' the banner in a few minutes."

"Flying the banner?"

"Behind my uncle's Cessna 182."

"What banner?"

"You haven't seen the banner?"

"No."

"It's, like, pink."

"Does it say anything?"

"Yeah. It says . . . um . . . 'Pulaski for something.' "

"Attorney general."

"Yeah. It's pretty wild 'n' wacky. I'm supposed to fly over as they're cutting the cake." The Bugman grabbed one of Scarlett's hands and pulled her up against him. He shook his hair out of his eyes. "May I have this dance?"

Scarlett felt pangs shoot from her heart into her extremities. She was numb in her fingers and toes and couldn't seem to coordinate her movements to the beat of the music. God, how embarrassing. As the song ended, Scarlett stumbled. She tried to cover it up with a little bow in the Bugman's direction.

"Gotta bolt. Have you ever been up in a Cessna?"

"No," Scarlett answered, hopefully.

"I'd ask you to come up, but since you're in the wedding and all, I guess you have to stay here, huh?"

"I don't have to stay," Scarlett answered quickly.

"Cool. The plane's at the airport in Geismar."

"I don't know where that is."

"You can ride with me."

"Thanks." Scarlett mused happily, picturing herself on the Harley, arms wrapped tightly around the Bugman's waist.

"I'll take the insecticide tanks out. You can ride in the sidecar."

On the way to the airport, they passed a series of signs just outside of Burnside. Scarlett read them with incredulity as they whizzed past.

"Honesty and . . ."

"Integrity . . ."

"Should not be . . ."

"A fantasy . . ."

"If you want . . ."

"To find the key . . ."

"On November 2nd,"

"Vote Pulaski!"

"Burma Shave," the Bugman yelled over the sound of the wind.

Hultgrew gulped from his drink and smiled. The Judge had finally broken away from his new wife and was standing alone by the buffet table, eating heartily from a bowl of mixed nuts. He could hear the old bastard's dentures clacking like castanets as they pulverized a cashew. Hultgrew felt a little unsteady on his feet. Perhaps he shouldn't have had those bourbons. But it was against his creed to pass up free liquor. Maybe, he reassured himself, it was just a newshound's natural excitement at being so close to a big story. He drained the glass, pulled the counter letters from his pocket, and began to weave through the crowd. He projected the confrontation on the movie screen in his head. "Is it not true," he cornered the Judge in this mental film, "that you and Acadian Developing are one and the same, and that you accepted bribes from Consolidated Chemical to persuade the zoning board to vote for a variance on the Vacherie property that you sold to Consolidated at a premium?" Hultgrew saw himself thrusting the evidence at the Judge, who crumpled in terror before him.

A large hand clapped down on Hultgrew's shoulder and a voice hissed, "Just what do you think you're doing here?"

Hultgrew wheeled around, and took a step back in shock. The hand was attached to the bride, whom, he instantaneously realized, he had bedded at the Hilton in Baton Rouge. "Heh, heh," he gulped, stalling for time, "good to see you again."

The bride's face was frightening in its intensity. "What are you doing at my wedding? It was just one night. You may have imagined some big love affair between us, but it meant nothing!" Her fingernails squeezed into his shoulder.

"Ouch," Hultgrew whined. "Jesus." He tried to pull her hand away.

"Is this man botherin' you, darlin'?"

Hultgrew thought he was seeing double, or maybe it was just the bourbon again. In any event, a second woman now stood alongside the bride, her glare affixed on his face.

"Help me get him out of here, Flo. I'll explain later," the bride said to the woman.

The second woman grasped his other shoulder. "I've got him, honey. Don't trouble yourself. This is your day, and I want it to be perfect."

"Thanks, Flo." The bride stalked off.

The other woman dragged him by his shoulder. "Where's your car, buddy? Shame on you, botherin' a bride at her wedding."

Hultgrew, still tongue-tied, stumbled along behind her. Gathering his courage, he dug his heels into the turf, coming to a halt. "Just how well do you know the bridegroom?" he queried, in his best Mike Wallace voice.

"Well enough to know that he loves that girl and doesn't want you hasslin' her." With that, the woman adeptly kneed him in the crotch.

Hultgrew folded over in pain. "I'm parked right over there," he managed to grunt through clenched teeth.

The woman shoved him into the car. She shut the door, and then leaned into the open window. "No hard feelin's, honey." She reached into her handbag, pulled out a card, and dropped it in his lap. "Give us a call if you're ever in New Orleans."

Hultgrew started the engine and pulled out as quickly as he could. Once he had left the wedding a safe distance behind, he looked down at the card. Above the phone, mobile phone, fax number, and E-mail address, it read, "Crescent City Escorts."

"It's not very big, is it?" Scarlett scanned the plane worriedly. She reached out and grabbed one of the wings. It wiggled slightly in her grasp, as if it was not firmly attached to the fuselage of the plane. "Um . . . Are you sure this is screwed together right?"

"Guess we'll find out." The Bugman grinned. He stuck a small plastic tube into the bottom of one of the wings and extracted a little fuel. "Got a little water. It's humid as hell." He emptied the tube out onto the ground and repeated the procedure several times, before nodding happily. "Cool."

"What happens if there's water in the fuel?"

The Bugman held his hand out, palm down, above his head. "Hmmmmmmmmmmmm," he hummed, his hand slicing through the air. Then he made a sputtering noise. Then, in a less-than-convincing Scottish accent, "I can't hold her, Captain, she's breaking up!" His hand took a precipitous dive toward earth. He made an exploding sound. Then he shrugged and smiled at Scarlett.

"It crashes?" she squeaked.

"Well, maybe not. It's like a bird. It wants to fly. It would probably be okay. Here." He opened the door for her. "Hop in."

And then they were in the air. It wasn't anything like being in a commercial jet. There was almost nothing between her and the ground below—just the thin wall of the cabin. And the plane didn't have that standing-still feeling of a jet, either. It dipped and lolled from side to side. The movement, coupled with the buzzing engine, made Scarlett feel like a giant bee aloft. As if she, herself, were flying through the air. "This is great," she screamed over the noise.

"Yeah, it's a total rush. Look out your window. We're above your house." The Bugman tilted the plane so that her window faced almost straight down toward the earth. Scarlett willfully overcame the feeling that she was about to fall out her door and hurtle downward. The wedding guests didn't look nearly as small as she expected. In fact, she could pick Lana out—a large white circle topped with a slightly smaller red circle of hair. Hearing the noise of the Cessna, the guests began to look toward the sky. Lana and the Judge were now over by the cake.

"Let's buzz them," Scarlett laughed, giddy with the sensation that she'd been cut loose not only from gravity, but from all her problems below.

"Awesome."

Suddenly the Bugman pushed in on the yoke of the plane and twirled a dial between the seats. The plane dipped precipitously. Scarlett felt herself float up toward the ceiling, but her seat belt held her in. He took his right hand from the dial and placed it on her knee.

"Look out the window."

Scarlett looked, conscious of his fingers on her leg. Alarmed, she saw that the plane was zooming directly toward the buffet table. They cleared it by what seemed like only a matter of yards, before he pulled back on the yoke and the plane rose again. Scarlett fell back against the seat. "Oh my God," she panted, "I didn't really think you'd do it."

"It's a rush, huh?"

Scarlett, the adrenaline causing her hands to shake, pushed her hair back from her face and looked outside once more. The plane was back up in the blue, far above the madding crowd. The Bugman's hand had moved a bit farther up her thigh. She turned to him. "That *was* a rush. Let's do it one more time."

Cake knife in hand, Lana and the Judge hit the ground at the Cessna's approach. Rather, the Judge hit the ground. Lana landed squarely on the Judge. The Judge found it difficult to breathe, pinned facedown in the dirt by pounds of bride. Several of the guests screamed. Others, having imbibed liberally from the fountain of champagne, just laughed and clapped as the Cessna's wheels skimmed over their heads. The banner behind the plane whisked across the table holding the wedding cake, clearing it of cups, plates, and napkins and taking a chunk out of the side of the cake.

"Stay calm," the Judge gasped from under Lana, though he doubted anyone could hear him over the sounds of the crowd and the propeller. If this were the end, he comforted himself, at least he was meeting it under Lana. Then the plane passed. The Judge took a deep breath as Lana lifted herself from him.

"Good God," she bellowed, "I'm reporting this to the FAA right away."

"It's only Joey Edwards's nephew," called one of the guests. "He's a stunt pilot. He buzzes all the football games at the high school."

"I didn't ask him to buzz my wedding," Lana snapped.

"Now, dear," consoled the Judge, patting her ankle from his position under the buffet table, "I'm sure he was just trying to make our day even more memorable." He waved one bony hand from under the tablecloth. "Darling, could you help me up?"

Extracted from under the table, the Judge held the beribboned cake knife up to the crowd. "Let's cut the cake," he called as loudly as he could. A cheer rose from the guests as another escalating roar approached from the heavens.

This time, she knew not to duck. Lana shook her fist at the plane. As she did, she caught sight of Scarlett's face through the window. The little bitch, trying to kill her at her own wedding. This behavior would not go unpunished. The thought of paybacks cheered Lana considerably. Laughing, she grabbed the cake knife clenched in the Judge's fist and brought it down on the pink-iced layers with a swift chop and a flourish. "Let's eat," she commanded, brandishing the knife over her head.

As she was finishing the last bite of her third piece of cake (what the hell, it was her wedding), a small woman approached her shyly. "Harry and I wish you the best of luck, Mrs. L'Enfant," the woman said. Then she reached out and pinned a ten-dollar bill to one of the ruffles on the dress. "My, that is some gown!"

Lana was still staring after the woman, incredulous, when yet another woman (this one a grandmotherly type in a yellow hat), patted her on the arm and pinned three fives next to the other bill. "What a joyous wedding," the grandmother cooed. "I especially enjoyed the air show." This time, Lana had the presence of mind to provide her with a campaign button.

Within the hour, Lana was covered from head to foot in a variety of currency. She realized happily that it had to be quite a bit of money to so thoroughly encrust the massive gown. She saw the Judge toddle toward her from between the guests. He, too, was papered with bills, giving him the look of a millionaire's rag doll. "Louis," she breathed as he drew near, "what is all this for?"

"It's a custom in this area. The money is our wedding gift."

Maybe the parishes weren't so bad after all. "I have to make an announcement." Lana sashayed over to the band, careful not to dislodge any bills as she moved. She motioned to the singer, who was in the midst of "Jolie Blond." "Hand me that mike." The singer looked surprised, but handed down the microphone. One by one, the band members stopped playing. "Quiet, please. I'd like to make an announcement." She waited for the angry murmurs of the thwarted dancers to die down. "Judge L'Enfant and I would like to thank you for being with us on this joyous occasion, and for your thoughtful and generous gifts. I feel like you have opened your hearts to us today." Off the cuff, but it sounded sincere, she thought, sincere and in touch with the people. "I would like to assure you that all your gifts will be applied toward my campaign for—" Lana increased the pitch and volume of her voice for the big finish, "—attorney general of the State of Louisiana!" More noise from the crowd. They were impressed with her dedication. "If you want to volunteer to help with the campaign, there are sign-up cards on the buffet table." Pleased with herself, Lana squelched the impulse to make a campaign speech then and there—she didn't want to seem opportunistic—and handed the mike back to the singer. He stared after her as she stepped down from the stage. After a moment, the washboard player began to scrape away, and the rest of the band joined in.

As the evening wore on, Lana noticed the Judge was getting more and more antsy, following her with his eyes through the crowd, occasionally licking his lips. She tried to stay as far away as possible. Finally, while the band was on break, he approached her, a glass of champagne in each hand. "Don't you think it's time for us to go upstairs, dear?"

"We still have a yard full of guests, Louis. It would be rude to leave."

"They won't even notice, as long as the free liquor is flowing and the band is playing."

Lana looked at the crowd, which had grown more loose and boisterous with each passing song. Several of the men had removed their shirts in the heat, and a number of the dancers, male and female, were in bare feet. She had to concede that even a great litigator like herself could not come up with a credible rebuttal to the Judge's statement. "All right. You must be getting tired," she said hopefully, patting him on his hairless head with her hand. The engagement ring clanked painfully against his skull, but he didn't seem to notice.

"Never felt better."

She began to grow alarmed. "Don't forget that we have to start active campaigning right away. It's going to be tough. Exhausting, even."

The Judge wrapped his thin arm around her waist, and with surprising strength, ushered her toward the house. "I know. So we'd better get some fun in before it starts." He winked salaciously. "After all, I'm not as young as I used to be."

"Are you almost done in there?" the Judge called down the hall to Lana. She had been in the bathroom for a good half an hour. She must be nervous, the Judge thought. Poor girl. He settled back into the bed to wait, but the phone started ringing. He tried to ignore it, but whoever was on the other end refused to give up. "Lana?" he called again. There was no reply. He sighed and picked up the receiver. "Hello?"

"Louis, you got some 'splainin' to do," sang a mocking Ricky Ricardo voice.

"Stanley," the Judge said with a sinking heart.

Leighton dropped the accent. "I'm on a nice three-week vacation at Pebble Beach, when I get a call. And what do I hear? My oldest friend is marrying Hebert's attorney."

"You can congratulate me, Stanley. The ceremony is over."

"Congratulations, Louis. Congratulations on setting me up to take the fall."

"What?" the Judge squeaked.

"So blackmail is your game."

"I don't know what you're talking about."

"Come on, Louis. I know that senile old man thing is just an act. But I didn't realize that you were this calculating."

"I'm not planning anything, Stanley, I swear it. Oh, maybe I've been hoping that she could help with the Acadian Developing problem, but that's all. The fact of the matter is that I love her."

"That's very touching. I'll be back in town next week. I'll be by to see you then. I hope that we can work this out." Leighton hung up.

The Judge fumbled frantically in the drawer of the bedside table, and located a bottle of Valium. He swallowed five. Several minutes later, Lana entered wearing a ruffled flannel nightgown buttoned up to her throat. The Judge sank into the bedclothes, disappointed. He thought she had more fashion sense than that. He had been imagining something sheer and red, or at least black. Instead she looked like his Aunt Genevieve, *after* the family had sent her to the Acadian Villa Nursing Home. "Isn't it a little hot for that?" he asked tactfully.

"I get cold at night," Lana answered him. She was carrying a champagne bucket in one hand and two glasses in the other. "I took the liberty of getting some Cristal for the occasion." She set the bucket on the bedside table, withdrew the bottle, and expertly extracted the cork. She poured them each a glass. "Here, drink up," she said, handing it to him.

"Let's have a toast," he said, raising his glass. "To our first night together." He smiled as debonairly as he could, under the circumstances, and clinked his glass against hers. Then he tossed back the champagne in one gulp. He gazed at Lana and was conscious of a stirring he hadn't felt in years. He set down his empty glass and took hers from her hand. As he unfastened the small pearl buttons on her nightgown, he noticed that she was shivering. He'd thought that she would be more bold. He'd have to be very gentle. Suddenly, he began to feel a little woozy. He shouldn't have drained his glass so quickly; together with the Valium, the champagne had dealt him a knockout punch. The ample mounds of Lana's chest looked like two big, fluffy, down pillows calling out in concert with gravity to his head. The Judge's face, led by his beaky nose, fell in between them. "Mmmph," he said happily.

A great crashing sounded from outside the window. "What's that?" Lana said, startled.

"Mmm," the Judge mumbled, barely willing or able to speak. To be polite, he partially extracted his face from Lana's breasts. "It's another tradition. The guests bang on plates outside, and we're supposed to go feed them. Just ignore them, they'll go away soon enough."

Lana jumped up, knocking him back into the bed pillows. "We can't do that. It wouldn't be right. You stay here, Louis. I'll go down and find them something to eat."

"That's a good idea," he answered. His eyelids were growing very heavy. The need to close them was overpowering—even stronger than his need for Lana. He'd let his lids drop, just for a second or two.

Lana let out a breath of relief as the Judge began to snore. Just in the nick of time. It had never occurred to her that the Judge would actually want or be able to consummate the marriage—God, what if he'd gotten a hold of some Viagra? She had grown fond of the old man, but not *that* fond. Lana tugged the bedclothes over the Judge. His snores, regular and wheezy, continued uninterrupted. She pulled on her robe and went downstairs to try and shut up the guests. No sense in taking a chance of waking him.

Twenty-seven

Jesus, what a hangover. The Judge sat up carefully in the bed and groaned. He'd obviously aged about twenty years since yesterday, and a man of that age had no right to be alive, no right at all. He massaged his throbbing temples with his bony fingers and smacked his lips. His dentures were coated with a sour bacterial paste and his breath tasted like something belched from the smokestacks at Consolidated.

Which seemed fitting. After all, if he hadn't taken that money, that gift of green twenties stacked in surprisingly solid bricklike blocks (there had been enough of the bricks to construct a small doghouse), Consolidated would never have gotten the approval to locate next door. On land he'd sold them at a premium price, land worn out and useless for anything. Which made him part of Consolidated, as much as the pipes, storage tanks, and smokestacks. In a gesture of unity, the Judge burped some fetid air from his gut. He lay back into the pillows, jaw sagging, and started to sink back into sleep.

"Louis!" He peeled open his eyes and looked up, right into

Lana's face looming above him and glowing like an orange helium balloon in the dim light of the room. "Did you know that the average person swallows six spiders over a lifetime from sleeping with his mouth open?"

At his age, he must already be in double digits. Well, that would explain the state of his stomach. "Good morning, dear," he offered weakly.

"Morning? It's already noon, Louis." She frowned. "Time to get up. I'm launching my campaign today."

"Do I need to be there?"

"Of course. I need your support. These people respect you. And you are my husband, after all."

Hmm. The Judge couldn't remember the relationship actually being consummated. How could he forget something like that? Jesus, how many pills had he taken? He glanced over at Lana's side of the bed. The covers were not even mussed. "Darling, where did you sleep last night?"

"In the guest room." Lana tugged the covers off him. "You passed out. I didn't want to disturb you."

If he'd passed out, it was pretty obvious that he couldn't be disturbed, wasn't it? Well, she was just being thoughtful. That was so like her. "I'll just take a quick shower," he said, repentant. As he stood to get out of bed, he felt a wave of dizziness. Lana steadied him by gripping him firmly by the shoulders and led him to the bathroom. "Would you care to join me?" he asked, hopefully.

"As I hope you can see, I've already done my hair and makeup."

He'd obviously put his foot in it. "And you look quite lovely," he finished, lamely.

"I took the liberty of getting you a few new suits," she said, holding out a seersucker. "I hope you don't mind."

"No, no. You obviously have the fashion sense in the family, my love."

He emerged from the bathroom a half-hour later, scrubbed pink as a new baby, dressed, and with his few remaining hairs tidily slicked back over his skull. Lana was standing waiting, annoyed at something. What could he have done? He hadn't even been in the same room. Poor thing, she was probably just tense about the speech. He remembered the first time he had sat on the bench. How frightened he'd been! The Judge smiled inwardly at the memory. He patted her hand, but she brushed his fingers aside.

"There's a friend of yours downstairs, Louis. I wish you wouldn't invite people over when we have plans."

"I'm sorry, dear. I wasn't expecting anyone." Good God, what if it were Leighton? "I'll get rid of him as soon as possible," he said, more to assure himself than her.

Still a little queasy, the Judge started down the stairs. A pair of brown, gum-soled shoes stared up at him from the hallway below. His eyes moved up legs draped in gray, double-knit polyester, to the matching tie cinching a meaty neck, to the myopic eyes of Harry Carter, staring boldly from behind black, two-pair-for-$39 frames.

"Ack!" the Judge crowed in alarm and dismay. "What are you doing here?"

"I just came to congratulate you on your wedding, and to let you know that I've been thinking about you."

"I appreciate your concern. It's been nice to see you again, Mr. Carter, but my wife and I have to go somewhere."

"I know. She's throwing her hat into the ring today. Lotta press should be there. I bet they'd be real interested in hearing about your colorful past."

"I told you before, I don't know what you're talking about."

"We'll see."

Just then, Lana appeared at the top of the steps. The Judge felt a bolt of fear shoot through his bowels. He was going to have to come clean to her, but he didn't want it to be until after the day's festivities. How would he find the courage to broach the subject? Well, you see, dear, I did some things I maybe shouldn't have, illegal things, and now two innocent people are dead. The Judge grimaced. The story needed work. With the enhanced strength of a desperate man, he pushed Carter toward the door. "You'll understand if we have to be going now."

"I understand a lot of things. You'd be surprised." Carter smiled sourly and stepped out onto the gallery. The Judge quickly slammed the door behind him, and peeped anxiously from behind the curtains until Carter got into his beige Chrysler and started down the drive.

"Who was that?" Lana asked.

"Oh, just an old friend."

"You should have introduced me."

"He doesn't vote."

"Oh."

She seemed satisfied.

Scarlett pushed open the door to Millie's Grocery. The little brass bell attached to the torn screen door tinkled softly as she entered.

"You look nice, baby," Millie called from behind the counter.

"Thanks," said Scarlett, glum. Lana had woken her up at eight and tossed a frou-frou flowered dress at her head, commanding that she wear it at the bayou that day. Scarlett shifted uncomfortably. The dress was made of some kind of cheap starched fabric that scratched like burlap. Oh well, it was all worth it. She'd called Taylor several days ago and told him about the event, and he'd sent her two hundred dollars for the information.

"That was some weddin', Scarlett," Millie said. She was an elderly black woman with the taut skin of someone half her age and a thick Cajun accent.

"Ain't seen a party like that since I don't know when," said a woman waiting at the register.

"It was something, all right," Scarlett admitted.

"Whattaya need, honey?"

"Just a bottle of Tylenol."

Millie let out a peal of amusement. "I think someone had a little too much to drink last night." She rummaged through a pile of assorted boxes behind the counter. "Here 'dey is. Hey." She leaned over the counter and whispered in Scarlett's ear. "You know how much we all love 'de Judge."

"I know."

"He's been there for us, and you know we'll all be behind him in 'dis thing."

"Uh . . . thanks." Though she was grateful, the statement struck her as uncharacteristically tactless of Millie.

"I'm sure it'll all get straightened out in 'de end." Millie dropped the Tylenol into a small bag. "Here, babe."

"How much is it?"

"It's on me, sweetie. It's 'de least I can do."

Scarlett looked at Millie, a little puzzled. She tried to remember if the Judge had ever done anything really nice for Millie or her family, which would account for her empathy in the Lana situation. Maybe he had gotten her grandson his job at Consolidated.

Millie interrupted her thoughts. "Saw you dancin' with Joey Edwards's nephew last night. He's a good-lookin' boy."

Scarlett felt her cheeks go bright red. "I guess he is. I didn't notice."

"Yeah, you didn't notice. Okay, sweetie, if you say so."

How could she help but notice? Last night, last night. It had simultaneously been the best and worst night of her life. The wedding—God, just the memory of it caused a cramp in her abdomen. But then the Bugman had appeared, and everything had changed. She was above the wedding, high in the sky. Then she was back on the ground, but still above the crowd, aloft in the arms of the Bugman. She could spend her whole life there.

She drifted out of the store—since yesterday she felt like she drifted, wafted, flowed liquidly instead of walking—leaving the Tylenol bottle on the counter next to Millie. Sheepishly (and in solid form), she plodded back into the store, picked up the bottle without meeting Millie's eyes, and, gossamer once again, she floated back out to the Judge's Lincoln. As she wove down River Road toward Shady Oaks, noting every curve she'd taken with the Bugman on the motorcycle (she'd been breathing in as they passed *that* tree, she'd shifted her arms down toward his hips as they flew around *that* bend), she realized that she didn't know when she would see him again. She felt a fist tighten around her stomach.

She pulled into the driveway, where she'd first met the Bugman. Scarlett wandered slowly up the steps and into the house. He'd walked on those steps. What was he doing now? The knowledge that he was *somewhere*, doing *something*, was unexpectedly thrilling. She closed her eyes and tried to picture what it was. Was he eating? She could see his Adam's apple bobbing up and down in his tan throat as he swallowed. Was he working? The muscles in his arms flexed as he lifted the tanks of insecticide out of the sidecar. Was he thinking about her? She sighed. It seemed unlikely. Last night they'd made love under the chinaberry tree. Afterward, he'd merely grinned and gunned the throttle of the motorcycle. "You're something," he said, then roared off. He didn't even put forth the effort to say he'd call.

Devastating. She threw herself onto her bed and rolled from side to side with the quilt wadded in each fist. When she'd worked the bedclothes into knots, she kicked her feet a few times, whining, then collapsed onto her back. For almost ten minutes she lay still with her eyes squeezed shut. How would she ever get him to come back? Finally, distracted by the squeaking of the mice in their cage next to the bed, she opened her eyes. Time to be proactive.

Scarlett picked the cage up, carried it out into the hall, and opened the little trapdoor. It took the mice a minute or two, but they soon realized they were free, and rushed out into the hall, disappearing behind furniture and under closed doors. She went back in and removed the snake from his cage. Might as well give him a chance to hunt for himself. She released him in the hall, too, then left for Lana's pirogue parade.

Lana and the Judge pulled up at the bayou. The Judge felt about the inside of the car door. After Carter's departure, he'd run into the bathroom and tossed back a couple more Valium. Now the door handle was somehow eluding his detection. He rapped against the windshield. "I'm stuck!" he mouthed to Lana. He saw her shake her head in exasperation as she strode over to free him from the Buick. "I'm sorry, dear. I guess I'm a little bushed after the wedding yesterday." He placed both feet on the ground and, grasping the door pillar, pulled himself to within several degrees of verticality. "My goodness." There was quite a crowd milling about in the soupy noon heat of the Bayou Boeuf. "Mad dogs and Englishmen," mumbled the Judge, before realizing that he was among them.

Scarlett was waiting for them, leaning morosely against the Lincoln. "Why do I have to wear this dress?" she asked plaintively.

"You can't campaign for me dressed like some punk." Lana opened the trunk and took out a paper grocery bag.

"Why not? You're dressed like a—"

"You look quite lovely, Scarlett," the Judge rushed in. Actually, she did look a damn sight better than usual. The starched, flowered dress hid her thin frame, and her hair, brushed back from her face for once, spread gracefully over the lace collar.

"Let's go." Lana kick-started the Judge by snagging his elbow and pulling him toward the crowd. Scarlett shuffled slowly behind them. Some of the people in the crowd began to take note of their approach.

"Wave," Lana whispered in his ear.

"Who are all these people?" The pills were really doing a number on him. He couldn't seem to focus on the events at hand.

Lana stopped in her tracks and turned to him. "Louis, what's wrong with you?"

"Nothing, nothing. Just tired."

"This is the pirogue procession. To kick off the campaign. Carl put up posters around town. There's going to be free jambalaya and lemonade at the dock."

"Of course. Of course."

When they drew closer, he could see that the crowd contained several video cameras and at least one anchorwoman from Baton Rouge. Lana had spotted her, too.

"Fantastic," she breathed.

Then the sound of a small prop plane roared next to his right ear. Visions of the dive-bombing at the wedding filled his brain. Alarmed, he flung his arms across his head for protection. The noise ceased and he felt something wet against the skin of his forearm. Holding it out, he saw the blood and mangled legs of a mosquito that must have been a good inch long in life. There was more buzzing. He began to swat frantically at the mosquitoes that swarmed about him in the thick heat. Angered, Lana pushed him behind her with a swish of her hips and began motioning to the TV crew. The video-toting men rushed over, the anchorwoman walking slowly so as to avoid breaking a sweat visible to the TV cameras.

"Jesus," the anchorwoman mumbled, slapping at her neck. Her hand left a blood spot the size of a quarter where she had crushed a particularly large mosquito against her jugular. "These fuckers are vampires."

Lana waved her hands about her face, warding off the insects. "I wonder if they're registered to vote?" she said with a forced laugh.

"Makes you wish for the good old days of DDT," said one of the cameramen.

"Okay," the anchorwoman said to Lana. "I'm just going to ask you a few questions like where in God's name you got this idea . . ."—she scratched viciously at her upper arm—". . . if you will be doing any more armadas, that sort of thing. Who's that?" She nodded toward the glum Scarlett, who stood silently, chewing on a lock of hair.

"This is my granddaughter, Scarlett." Lana reached out and

grasped her by the shoulder. Scarlett twisted away with a percepti-
ble wince. "By the way, I'm calling it a procession, not an armada.
That's got a slightly negative connotation, don't you think?

"Whatever."

From behind Lana's stern, the Judge cleared his throat softly.
The anchorwoman craned her neck around Lana to find the source
of the phlegm.

"Judge L'Enfant," she said in a pleasant voice. "I haven't seen
you for too long. Since my little brother's eighth grade graduation
from St. James. That was a great speech you gave."

The Judge smiled and patted her hand. "Always glad to help
out at the old alma mater."

"Maybe we could get some tape of you pushing off in the
pirogue."

"Certainly," he assured her.

The anchorwoman motioned to the cameraman and they started
off toward the water's edge. Lana and the Judge followed behind,
trailed by Scarlett. The Judge leaned over to Lana. "What
pirogue?"

"Good Lord, Louis!" The cameraman turned around to look.
"Listen carefully," she said more quietly. "I am having a pirogue
procession through Cajun Country to officially start the campaign.
Banners, P.A., the works. It is an event. That is why the press is
here. Help me out here, Louis. Stay focused."

"Don't worry, sweetheart. I've got it now." He scratched at a
bony knuckle where a large, itchy pink bump was rising.

They drew up alongside the bank. Five pirogues floated at a
rickety dock under the cypress branches. The pilots wore Styrofoam
boaters with red, white, and blue ribbons emblazoned with Lana's
name. They looked like gondoliers who'd somehow taken a wrong
turn at the Piazza San Marco and gotten terribly lost.

"We'll be getting in the lead boat," Lana called out. "But first I
have some things for the people who were so kind to come and see
us 'launch' the campaign!" She reached into the bag she'd been

carrying and pulled out a handful of buttons, which she tossed in the air to the crowd. Then she threw out stacks of bumper stickers. Several of the children scrambled for them; most of the adults, the Judge noted, were too busy scratching to grab for the booty.

"Here." Lana handed the bag to Scarlett. "Distribute the rest of this." Scarlett stood silent, staring at Lana. "Remember our agreement," Lana whispered, though not so quietly that the Judge couldn't hear.

"What agreement?" he asked, as Scarlett halfheartedly flung buttons and bumper stickers in the direction of the crowd.

"Don't worry about it." Lana turned to the anchorwoman. "Okay, we're ready to go."

The cameramen clicked on their video cameras.

"We're here," the anchorwoman said, "at Bayou Boeuf, where Lana Pulaski and her husband, Judge Louis L'Enfant, are about to board these pirogues you see behind me, to float her campaign for attorney general to the people of Louisiana." She drew her finger across her throat. "Okay, Gary, let's get a picture of the Judge getting into the boat."

"My fifteen minutes of fame." The Judge smiled. His orthopedic shoes clunked softly across the uneven boards of the dock. He stopped at the end of the dock, the tips of his toes hanging over the water, and looked down. The boat was a good two or three feet below. He turned to the anchorwoman. "How am I going to get down there?"

"I'll help ya' out, Judge," the pilot called up.

"Darling," he called to Lana, "maybe this isn't such a good idea. I tend to get seasick."

"Are those things on?" Lana nodded toward the video cameras.

"Yes," said the anchorwoman.

"Here, Louis," Lana said sweetly, "I'll help you down." She lifted the Judge under the armpits and dangled him over the water like a prize bass. The Judge heard laughter in the background and several cameras clicking.

"I got him." The pilot reached for the Judge's waist. The Judge felt Lana's hands slide away. But instead of feeling the pilot grasping him, the Judge heard him exclaim "son of a bitch," and slap at his arm. Then the Judge was falling through the steamy air. With a splash, he hit the murky water of the bayou.

"Oh, this is good," said the anchorwoman.

"Grandfather!" Scarlett was running down the deck toward him.

"I got it, I got it!" exclaimed the cameraman.

Through sheer muscle memory, and without any consciousness of what he was doing, the Judge picked himself off the bottom of the bayou and came to a standing position. He was relieved to find that the water was only waist-deep. Actually, the temperature was quite pleasant. "Ahh." He splashed it about his face and neck. The crowd cheered. Assuming they were expressing their enthusiasm for his swimming prowess, the Judge reached up and waved. "Thank you, thank you."

The pilot had climbed out of the pirogue and was standing next to him in the water. Unceremoniously, he picked the Judge up and set him on the dock. "They're not cheerin' for you, Judge, they're cheerin' for the bug spray."

The Judge looked toward the whooping crowd. The cameramen jockeyed for position. Bobby Taylor stood in the thick of the observers, tossing small aerosol cans into the air. The scent of citronella wafted toward the Judge. One of the cans rolled to a stop at his feet. He picked it up.

DON'T GET STUNG. VOTE FOR BOBBY TAYLOR FOR ATTORNEY GENERAL was written in bold red letters on the can. The Judge looked toward Lana. He could practically see the steam coming out of her ears. Fortunately, her attention was riveted on Taylor. With a sigh of relief, the Judge took the lid off the can and sprayed himself liberally.

Twenty-eight

Crouton drove as far as he could into the woods, but the path grew wetter with every twist. Afraid he'd get the stolen Chevette stuck and have to walk back to the road, he got out, took off his shoes, rolled up his jeans, and proceeded squishily on foot.

Henri lived way back in the bayou without electricity or running water. His one nod to modern technology was a portable digital phone (they can't scan it, he'd told a worried Crouton), with which he conducted his thriving business in illegal arms. Any criminal who was anyone on the Gulf Coast depended on Henri, who could supply them with a .38, a semi-automatic—he could even special order C-4 or anti-tank weapons.

A month ago, Henri would not have returned Crouton's call. But the word was out that Crouton had graduated from petty crime and was now a force to be reckoned with. Crouton attributed part of this newfound respect to his makeover. The other lowlifes figured that anyone with the guts to go around in a pair of women's sunglasses and a haircut that looked like the result of electroshock therapy *had* to be a heavy. Little did they know he was just scared of being recognized by the lawyer.

The path had turned into swamp. Birds and insects trilled as Crouton slogged along in the twilight created by the heavy foliage. He hoped that there were no alligators around. Henri had told him to just keep walking straight ahead. After fifteen or twenty minutes he came to a clearing, and there was the shack in the sunlight. Unpainted, covered in tar paper and the occasional flapping shingle, it sat on stilts five feet above the water. A brand-new aluminum boat with a Mercury outboard was tied to one of the stilts. Crouton could see no way to get up to the warped boards of the front porch.

"Hey!" he called. "Henri!"

"What 'de fuck!" A muscular black man appeared in the door to the cabin. He was holding a Kalashnikov, which he pointed at Crouton.

Crouton shot his arms up in the air. "Don't shoot. It's me, Jimmy."

Henri lowered the gun. "Yeah, I see 'dat." He squinted and peered down at Crouton. "Some hairdo you got 'dere, my friend."

Crouton ran his palm over the irregular patches of black fuzz. "Thanks."

Henri bent down and tossed a rope ladder over the side. "Come on up, 'den."

Crouton waded over to the ladder, climbed up, and threw himself onto the porch. "Man, this is bumfuck Egypt."

"Yeah, it's a sacrifice I make to 'de business. Too easy to get caught in town. But it's okay. I got me a nice house in Provence. I live 'dere in 'de spring and fall."

"Where's Provence? Is that in Plaquemines Parish?"

Henri laughed. "No, man. It's in 'de south of France. Nice place. Good wine country."

"I'm a beer man, myself," said Crouton.

"Yeah, I figured 'dat. So, what can I do for you?"

"I need some powerful firepower, man. Something that can

bring down a fuckin' rabid elephant. But it's gotta be light and easy to carry. And a silencer would be really cool."

"I got just 'de thing for you. But it ain't cheap."

"That's no problem." Crouton patted his pocket. He had over three hundred dollars from the wedding. He'd also burglarized his mama. She didn't trust the banks, and had several hundred dollars stuffed in a shoe in her closet. She would kill him if she found the money missing, but Crouton intended to replace it when Stanley paid him. She'd never be the wiser. "Let me see what you've got."

Henri went into the shack and returned a minute later carrying a matte aluminum case the size of a woman's handbag. He stroked the expensive-looking metal lovingly, then clicked open the clasps and pulled out a small, stubby gun.

"That's an ugly piece of shit," said Crouton, disappointed.

"You gonna fuck it or shoot it? 'Dis gun is a James Bond gun. I got it from someone in Kazakistan. He got it off a dead CIA agent."

"Yeah? Why would he sell it to you?"

"Business been bad since 'dat fall of communism thing."

"Maybe I'll just get me another shotgun."

"Let me show you what 'dis gun can do. First off, feel it." Henri handed Crouton the gun. Crouton bounced it up and down in his palm. It was very light.

"It feels like a toy gun. It's plastic!"

"It may be plastic, but it's no toy, my friend. 'Dis is a space-age polymer. Look." Henri pointed to a tree about twenty yards away. "Shoot 'dat cypress."

Crouton lifted his Jackie O glasses. "Yeah, okay." He closed one eye, looked through the sights, and placed his finger against the trigger. He squeezed. The trigger yielded smoothly. The hammer released with precision. The noise of the shot tore through the bayou. The cypress, at least two feet in diameter, cleaved in two and the top dropped into the bayou with a splash.

Wow.

"Not bad, eh?"

"It got a silencer?" asked Crouton.

Henri reached into the case and handed him a small cylinder. "Put it on. Give it a try."

This time Crouton aimed at an old refrigerator rusting in the water. With the silencer, the gun made only a muffled pop. Still, it blew a hole the size of a basketball in the refrigerator door.

"Nice. How is it at distance?"

"No good at distance. It's for close up. You want distance, I can sell you a rocket launcher. Gulf War surplus."

Although Crouton could not deny the visceral appeal of blasting the lawyer with a rocket, he knew that the logistics of transporting the launcher in his stolen Chevette would be difficult.

"Nah, this should do." As an afterthought, he asked, "How do you think this would work on 'gators?"

Twenty-nine

The Rotarians met in a prefab corrugated steel building near the edge of town, which was negligibly farther than the center of town. After the morning's debacle at the Bayou, Lana was just relieved that this speech was indoors and away from Louisiana's robust insect population.

She pulled into the gravel lot between the pickup trucks and Chevys, parked, and peered at herself in the rearview mirror. She looked great, no question about it. She smoothed the jacket of her peacock blue linen suit (she had felt, when she changed out of the sweat-soaked outfit she'd worn to the Bayou, that this was a conservative gig), smacked her lips a couple of times to evenly distribute her Poppy Splash lipstick (conservative didn't mean you couldn't have a little color in your face), and shook the Judge's angular shoulder.

"Unnh," he said.

"Louis, get up. We're here."

"Where?" His eyes were still shut.

"At the Rotarian's hall." Actually, it looked more like a pole barn.

"But I'm not a Rotarian."

Though he was showing subtle signs of being awake, she shook him again out of aggravation. "I know that. I have a speech to give."

"Oh my." He looked puzzled. "I didn't think those boys would ever accept women."

"I'm not a Rotarian either. I'm running for attorney general." When had he become so vague? It was worrisome. Perhaps he had suffered some type of stroke. Lana made a mental note to hustle him off to the doctor as soon as she had some free time.

"Yes, yes, I know that."

Lana got out of the car, walked over to the Judge's side, and pulled him out. She patted at him, straightening him out, adjusting his tie. She licked her fingers and slicked back his hairs, which had come unglued when she'd hit a particularly bad pothole a couple of miles back. "There."

"Do I look all right?" he asked.

"You look very handsome."

He patted at his jacket. "Now, where did I put that speech?"

"Louis, it's *my speech.*"

"Oh yes," he chuckled warmly, as if they were sharing a little joke. "You told me that."

The interior of the hall swirled with thick gray smoke from the kind of cheap cigars that a middle-aged man's wife would not let him smoke near the house, much less in it. Through the haze, a pudgy pink hand was thrust at her.

"Ah, Mrs. L'Enfant." The hand's owner broke through the gloom. "I'm Pongo de Witt. I'm the fearless leader of these boys." He chortled merrily. "We're glad to have you here today. Bobby Taylor was here last week, you know. He's an old friend of ours." Peering around Lana, Pongo zeroed in on the Judge, who was happily inhaling the sour, tobacco-filled air. "Your honor. We're so glad to see you again." He clasped the Judge's hand between both of his and gave several vigorous shakes that traveled up the Judge's arm to his neck and head, which bobbed rhythmically like a toy dog in the back window of a '72 Impala.

"Yes, yes . . . When was that?"

"Why, you dedicated this facility almost ten years ago." Pongo laughed indulgently, slapping the Judge on the arm. "Here." He reached into the inside of his jacket and pulled out a cigar. "If I recall, you are a stogie man."

"Quite right." The Judge fumbled with the cellophane wrapper, finally extracting the cigar and sticking it between his thin purple lips. The cellophane now clung to the back of his hand. He gave it several small shakes, but the static was like epoxy. Resignedly, he leaned toward Pongo for a light.

"You don't mind, do you, Mrs. Candidate?" asked Pongo.

"No," Lana lied, "not at all."

"Don't worry, dear, this is an infrequent indulgence," the Judge assured her.

Lana plucked the wrapper from his hand, dropping it on the cement floor of the hall. "Well, Mr. de Witt, let's get started. There's no time like the present."

From the stage, the last few rows of Rotarians were lost in the thick cigar smoke. Lana blinked against the lights shining at her, then tapped the microphone in front of her with her fingernails. The staccato clicking echoed against the corrugated walls. "Ahem." The room continued to buzz with basso laughter. "*Ahem*. Gentlemen." The buzz diminished somewhat. It was time to dive in. "Good afternoon. I'm Lana Pulaski, and this," she indicated the diminutive figure of the Judge, seated on the stage behind her and engulfed in his own small atmospheric system of cigar smog, "is my husband, the Honorable Louis L'Enfant."

"Hey, how's it goin', Judge?" one of the men in the third row called out.

The Judge perked up. "Is that you, Sam?"

"Nah, it's Artie Parker. We're behind you, Judge."

There was a rumble of agreement from the rest of the crowd.

What was that about? Lana wondered. She was the candidate, not the Judge. Better make that clear. She turned back to her future constituency.

"We're very pleased to be invited to talk to you today. . . ." Actually, Lana had been forced to invite herself. She had put David Souchecki to work compiling a list of Taylor's speaking engagements, and then had him call all the associations, churches, businesses, and schools where Taylor had given his dog-and-pony show. Souchecki had pointed out that equal time was the cornerstone of democracy. Probably because Lana was free, most of the organizations had agreed to let her speak. Following Taylor by a week to ten days allowed her to clear up any of the lies and misconceptions that she was sure Taylor was scattering ahead of her like manure.

"As you may or may not know, I have been practicing law in the city of New Orleans for the last twenty-two years. I never imagined, when I started out, that I would want—or should I say be forced— to run for public office. But when I saw that my opponent was not only running, but gathering support in his bid for attorney general, I could be silent no longer. And neither should you. You must be vocal in your opposition to the election of Bobby Taylor, a man who has openly aided the corrupt opportunists who have brought gambling to this state solely to line their pockets with money taken from hard-working Louisianans like yourselves!"

There was an angry murmur form the crowd. Lana paused to catch her breath, pleased. These men were behind her in trying to change things. They were outraged at Taylor's brazen support of his crooked cronies. She turned to smile in victory at the Judge, but noticed that he had sunk into his chair with his hand over his eyes. Turning back to the audience, she saw several of the men in the first few rows shaking their heads and whispering angrily among themselves. Suddenly, it occurred to her that their anger might not be directed at Taylor after all. What had Pongo said about Taylor being an old friend? At the time she had dismissed it as hyperbole. How could these men support someone who was little better than a felon? "I stand before you today as a candidate for change," she continued. She had expected this line to receive some applause, but instead there was silence. "My goal is to take this state away from the special interests and give it back to the people of Louisiana." She was beginning to feel a little uneasy. "As your attorney general, I will make sure that the office is a respected warrior in our fight for the future instead of a private club handing out gambling licenses like party favors to the corrupt!"

From the back of the room came a hiss, the heckler anonymous in the smoke.

Thirty

The migraine would not go away. It was behind Lana's eyes, boomeranging around her skull, suctioned around her brain like the arms of an octopus. Not the deep-fried Italian restaurant type octopus, but the enormous creatures featured on *The Undersea World of Jacques Cousteau.* The effect was enhanced by the stale cigar stench that she could not seem to wash from her hair. Lana groaned and rubbed an ice pack about her temples. She was going to have to be more careful—if she had given it any thought, she would have surmised that Taylor was a Rotarian. He was probably also a Mason, a Kiwanis, a Shriner, a fucking Boy Scout leader. He probably belonged to every damn club, country club, order, and organization to be found within the borders of the State of Louisiana. He was a hand-shaker, that Taylor, a real back-slapping, behind-the-scenes, hail-fellow-well-met type of guy. A people kind of person. Whereas she, and no amount of self-deception could mask the truth, was not.

She was more a "herself" kind of person. She had to be. No one had ever cared about her, with the exception of Flo and her father.

One hand still on the icepack, Lana reached for the telephone and punched out Flo's number with the tip of her fingernail.

"Decatur Escorts." The thick voice on the other end of the line belonged to Tommy, Flo's longtime boyfriend. A fireplug of a man, not over five and a half feet tall and sporting body hair in places lesser men never even dreamed of bearing fur, Tommy had once been in the seminary. That was before "the trouble" (what that trouble was, Lana could imagine with enough ease that she avoided thinking about it at all). Still, Tommy's old life stayed with him like a hangover. He still went to Latin mass at St. Peter's every Sunday at nine, and had taken a fatherly interest in Flo's girls; he sometimes heard confessions or even dragged them to mass with him. Flo was always angry when she found out, telling Tommy it was bad for employee morale, but he would only reply that Jesus had plenty of mercy for fallen women. The two had gone round and round about the issue for years. So far none of the girls had left Decatur Escorts for the convent.

"Hey, Tommy."

"Lana!" he answered happily, in his most pious voice. "Where y'at, my child?"

"I'm doing all right."

"How's politics treatin' ya'? Don't let those crooks get ya' down."

"Well, that's what I'm calling about. I was hoping that you and Flo could help me out." There was nothing that Father Tommy liked better than a lamb from his flock bleating with need.

"Hey, sweetie." Flo had picked up the extension.

"Hi, Flo."

"What d'ya' need, babe?"

"Some help with my campaign, actually."

"You know I'd do anything ta' help ya' out. And so would Tommy. Wouldn't ya', Tommy? Tell Lana how we want to help."

"She already knows I'd do anything for her."

"Whatta ya' want, Lana? Tommy and me can hang up signs, or go door to door."

"Hey, how about bumper stickers?" Tommy suggested. "I know where you can get a deal."

"The signs and bumper stickers are a good idea"—Lana doubted that anyone with the sense enough to register to vote would actually open their door to Flo and Tommy—"but what I need right now is dirt."

"You've come to the right place for that, hasn't she, Tommy?"

"What kinda dirt, child?" Tommy asked.

"On my opponent. Taylor. There must be something."

"You heard anything, Tommy?" Flo asked. "I don't think I have."

"I don't think so. I mean, he hasn't been *here*."

"Yeah, we woulda told ya' something like that already," Flo agreed.

"But I'll ask around," Tommy offered. "The girls can help me out."

"Be low-key about it, okay, Tommy?"

"That goes without sayin', my child. You know that."

"Thanks. I really appreciate this. One other thing. Do you know where I could hire myself some professional telephone operators? I need them to find volunteers to canvass their neighborhoods."

"We got some operators here. For the phone line. How many we got now, Tommy?"

"Five. No, wait, four. Shelley quit to go back to broadcasting school."

"I really need . . . business-type operators, Flo."

"These girls know their business. 'Boss and secretary' is one of the most popular calls. They'd do a good job for you. You'll save a lot of money using my operators insteada hiring a new crew."

"I'll think about it. Thanks." Lana wondered if Taylor's operators could fake orgasms over the phone lines.

"Hey, sweetie, how's the married life treatin' you?"

"You know. The old ball and chain."

"Are we goin' to see ya' around soon?"

That was all she needed. The press connecting her with Decatur Escorts.

"Probably not until after the election. Things are really hectic."

"Hon, the doorbell's ringin'. We're gonna have to sign off."

She had just hung up the phone when the Judge wandered into the room. He was wearing his limp terry bathrobe and a pair of vinyl orthopedic slippers. Lana pressed the ice harder to her head.

"Louis. I was just wondering what happened to you. Here." She picked up a mug from the table. "I made you some herbal tea." Hopefully, it would clear his head.

"Ginseng, I hope?" The Judge took the mug in his claws and slurped noisily. He settled into the bed next to her.

He'd only taken several sips when his eyes fluttered shut and he was snoring softly. She lifted his waxy skull from its face-down position on her chest, and, dragging her pillow with her, went down the hall to the guest room.

Thirty-one

The Judge was still in the arms of Morpheus when Lana left the
house the next morning. The wedding and the launch of her campaign had distracted her from the Boudreauxs' Cadillac, but now
the puzzle was weighing on her mind. Preoccupied, she failed to
notice the scraggly-haired figure parked on the levy across the road
from Shady Oaks. Lana pulled out of the gates and down the road.
The car followed, a quarter mile behind.

The rusting hulks had not moved from the Boudreauxs' lawn.
This time, however, Lana knocked on the door without advance
warning. From her last visit she was convinced that Estelle had
been hiding something, and Lana was hoping that the element of
surprise would loosen Mrs. Boudreaux's tongue. She heard the chorus of dogs, and then Estelle opened the door.

"Miss Pulaski! Or should I say Mrs. L'Enfant?"

"I'm keeping my name."

"Good for you. What can I do for you, honey?"

Lana noted that Estelle had not invited her in. So be it, she
could interrogate from the porch at least as well as she could by

shouting over the big screen TV. "I have a couple more questions for you about your brother-in-law's death."

"I figured that's why you were here."

"Do you remember the night he disappeared?"

"Oh yeah. We were at a dance down at the church."

"What year was that again?"

"It was 1977."

"And Thierry left the dance early, right?"

"Yeah, he left about nine. He was pretty drunk."

"Did he leave with anyone?"

"No, he was alone. Pretty rare for Thierry. He had a lot of money, so the girls were all over him."

"What did you think when he disappeared?"

Estelle Boudreaux shifted her weight to her other foot. Sensing her discomfort, the German shepherds milled apprehensively behind her. "What do you mean?"

"Well, after you hadn't heard from Thierry for a few days, what did you think?"

"I don't think we thought too much about it. He was always goin' off with some girl or another."

"Okay, what about after several weeks had passed? What did you think then?"

"We just figured he'd found someone. Anyone can fall in love, even someone like Thierry."

"Did you report his disappearance to the police?"

"There didn't seem to be any need to. Truth is, no one really missed him."

"Here's what I'm curious about, Mrs. Boudreaux. Your husband and his sisters got all of Thierry's money in his succession. What year was that?" The brand-new Cadillac was a seventy-eight. Estelle and her husband must have gotten the money pretty quickly after Thierry's disappearance.

"Hmm . . . I guess it was around 1977."

"Well, if no one suspected that Thierry was dead, how is it that you inherited the money?"

"Thierry was declared dead in 1978."

Just as she'd suspected. God, she was good. "That's odd. As I understand Civil Code Article 54, a person has to be absent five years before he can be declared dead. No one even reported Thierry missing."

"Ms. Pulaski, I don't know about no law. . . ."

"Was an attorney appointed to represent Thierry's interest? Due process requires that an absent person be represented."

"Look, I'm sure it's not news to you that things aren't always done by the book around here. I'm thinkin' maybe I shouldn't be talking to you anymore. I'm really sorry—Hey, who's that?" Estelle pointed at the end of her driveway, where a car sat parked. "He with you?"

"I have no idea who that is." Lana squinted, trying to make out the driver of the car, but he started the engine and peeled out of the driveway.

"Huh. Probably casin' the house. If he comes near here again, I'll sic the dogs on him. Look, I can't help you." With that, Estelle Boudreaux shut the door.

Back at the clerk's office in the courthouse, the younger Boudreaux seemed a little reluctant to hand over the file on Thierry. Lana was pretty sure that Estelle had called ahead. But once Lana lifted her brow against the girl, she was back in two minutes with the papers. Somehow, Lana wasn't at all surprised when she saw the signature on Thierry Boudreaux's death certificate—Louis L'Enfant. She was likewise prepared when she spoke with the guard at the jail to find out who had called the warden and given the mysterious man access to the prison to talk to the Hebert's murder suspect. Her husband.

*   *   *

231

Crouton had a clear view of the courthouse door in the rearview mirror of his stolen Chevette. He was living in the car now. While he was at Henri's, the local pigs had visited his mama, told her about the Hebert murders, and turned the place over looking for him. Although Crouton had denied everything, Mrs. Crouton knew her boy. In tears, she had whacked him with a rolled-up copy of the *National Enquirer* and told him never to return.

Trailing the lawyer was boring, but Crouton didn't have anything else to do. Besides, the experience in New Orleans had taught him the virtue of knowing your prey. He would study the lawyer's habits, her comings and goings. Remove the element of surprise. A nighttime assault had worked well with the Heberts, and he intended to use the same method on the lawyer. She would be much safer asleep than awake.

To help the time pass, Crouton had found a new dealer (he realized that Neville must have been the one who ratted on him to the pigs) and purchased himself some methamphetamine with the money he had left over after buying the gun. Now he opened the vial and poured some of the white powder onto the aluminum gun case. He took a razor out of his pocket, made two lines, and, bending over the case, sucked them up his nose. Ouch, ouch, ouch, ahhhhh . . .

Crouton straightened back up. He adjusted his Jackie O sunglasses and saw the lawyer exit the courthouse. He recognized the set of her jaw from when she'd doused him with the pepper spray. She was angry at something. Despite the meth, Crouton felt a little shiver. Someone was going to get it. He was just glad it wasn't him.

Thirty-two

As the Lincoln pulled closer to the house, the Judge could see a figure in a rocking chair on the gallery. With his weak old eyes, he couldn't identify the chair's occupant—he could only make out that the person was rocking slowly, deliberately, almost . . . menacingly. Was it actually possible to rock menacingly? Then Lana's face came into focus, and the Judge knew that it was.

"Scarlett," she said as the two of them started up the steps, "would you go on inside? I need to talk to your grandfather alone." Scarlett paused a moment. She sensed Lana's hostility, too. But the Judge waved her in. It was time for him to atone. When the door had shut behind the girl, Lana turned to him.

"What is your connection to Thierry Boudreaux's death?"

The Judge knew that procrastination was useless. He took a deep breath and began.

"I suppose you've noticed Consolidated Chemical next door."

"You mean those acres of smokestacks spewing a toxic cloud the size of Rhode Island? I might have caught it out of the corner of my eye."

This was not going well. The Judge wished that he'd had more time to polish his story, make himself look a little less culpable. Then he realized that he could live another fifty years and not come up with the proper angle to minimize his involvement. Maybe confession was like tearing off a Band-Aid. One had to do it quickly, and thereby minimize the pain. Unfortunately, this Band-Aid was the size of a beach towel and was adhered with industrial strength glue to the most tender areas of his psyche. Feeling tremulous, the Judge stiffly sank to a sitting position on the steps. He spoke quietly, his back to Lana.

"When Consolidated decided to locate here, there was some uproar about pollution. Not from the politicians. At least, not at first. This state didn't have a Department of Environmental Quality until 1984. Consolidated could have dumped arsenic in the river for all they cared." They probably *had*. "But Consolidated's competitors didn't want the plant locating here. So they raised a stink and got some of the powers-that-be in their corner. Consolidated couldn't get the zoning variances and licenses that it needed."

"So you decided to help."

"I'm afraid so. Stanley Leighton, who was the president of Consolidated, came to me. We worked out a deal. This plantation used to be much, much larger. But it wasn't producing any money. Sugar is hard on the land, it sucks out the nutrients. By the seventies, I was sitting on a lot of worthless property. So Consolidated agreed to buy the land at a very nice price, and I called in some favors and got them their licenses and zoning. The way the deal worked was that I transferred the fields to Acadian Developing. Well, I didn't. A shell corporation called LaFourche Land Exploration sold it to Acadian. But Acadian never really bought the land at all. Then Consolidated bought the land from Acadian. But they were really buying it from LaFourche. Stanley got a nice kickback off the deal. Are you following this?"

"Well enough. Basically, you used a lot of phony corporations and counter letters to hide your trail."

"Yes."

"How is Boudreaux's death certificate related to Consolidated Chemical?"

"Unfortunately, the Consolidated deal was not the first time that I'd, uh . . . used my influence."

The Judge explained. Initially, the Boudreaux transaction had nothing to do with Consolidated. The Boudreaux deal was merely one in a series of the everyday graft opportunities of which he'd habitually taken advantage.

Fishing on Mink Bayou one Sunday, Thierry Boudreaux had spotted Dennis Hebert trolling for shrimp (again!) on his oyster leases. The leases were only profitable during Lent, when the fasting faithful were paying top dollar for seafood, but Boudreaux was a possessive man. Boudreaux yelled a profane warning to Hebert, who responded in kind. At this, Boudreaux picked up his hunting rifle (bagging a nutria or two was always a possibility on the Bayou, so Boudreaux was usually armed when he went out on his boat) and discharged a round in the direction of Hebert's boat.

Dennis Hebert did not take kindly to being a target. The next morning, Boudreaux awoke to find Hebert astride his horse, driving fifty head of cattle onto Boudreaux's front lawn.

"Your mangy cows are grazing on my fields," Hebert informed the barefoot, pajama-clad Boudreaux.

"Our cattle have been grazing on those fields since before I was born, you bastard," Boudreaux replied.

"If I find your animals on my land again, I'll shoot them one by one," Hebert called over his shoulder as he rode off.

At first, Boudreaux's only fear was the loss of the grazing lands. Then he started thinking about the oil leases. He and Hebert had both profited greatly from the leases on their respective lands. Why should Hebert be reaping royalties from Boudreaux's fields? Hebert didn't even know what to do with the money, the dumb coon-ass. He stuck it in the bank and continued to live like a trapper on the back bayou. The money would be used to much better effect passing quickly and efficiently through Boudreaux's hands. Boudreaux went into town, found a lawyer, and filed an acquisitive prescription suit that day. The case landed with a thud on the Judge's docket.

When the Judge saw the pleadings, it only took him a few minutes to ascertain that Boudreaux would lose. To prevail in an acquisitive prescription case, Boudreaux would bear the burden of proving uninterrupted possession for thirty years. The Boudreauxs' cattle had been on the land for decades. The family had even fenced in the disputed acreage. Yet here was Hebert's clan regularly renegotiating new oil leases on the land. Their lessees had surely been on the land during that time, which would have interrupted Boudreaux's possession. Of course, there was a way that both Boudreaux and the Judge could win.

"The trick is the jury instructions," the Judge had told Boudreaux. The two had met in the back corner of a strip bar in the French Quarter. Ever cautious, the Judge had refused to meet Boudreaux anywhere near the river parishes. Even in this dark nook of New Orleans, the Judge compulsively shot glances over his shoulder every minute or two. "Your attorney and Hebert's attorney will each submit them. But I choose which instructions go to the jury. The instructions will tell them what the elements of an acquisitive prescription claim are. With the right instructions, you win."

"What if Hebert appeals?"

"Don't worry. I'll talk with the judges. They'll be on your side."

"And how much will this cost me?"

The Judge had been little taken aback. Boudreaux wasn't one to mince words. But he was obviously a man who understood the bottom line, and would be glad to avail himself of the benefits of an arrangement. "A one-fifth interest in the royalties from the disputed land for the next ten years. You can assign the interest to the Bayou Development and Exploration Corporation." Bayou was the shell corporation where the Judge and Leighton put most of their illegally gotten gains.

"I don't know, Judge. That seems pretty high to me. I have a lawyer I have to pay, I have court costs. Where am I gonna get that kind of money?"

"Now, Thierry, you and I both know that you've already got leases with Texaco on five hundred acres. You've got plenty of cash."

"I've got plenty of cash because I don't like to share. I've got a better proposal."

"I'm listening."

"You'll make sure the jury sees things my way because I know some things about Consolidated Chemical."

What could Boudreaux know? Then it had hit the Judge. Boudreaux's sister-in-law was a file clerk in the courthouse. She'd probably seen the notices he'd filed on the counter letters, nosed around, and made some logical conclusions.

"Thierry, I don't know what you're talking about, but I have to tell you. Some important people are involved in the Consolidated deal. I don't think you want to go down that road."

"You threatenin' me, Judge?"

"I'm just telling you the facts."

Several days later, Boudreaux left the *fais-do-do* and was never seen again. A couple of weeks later, Thierry's kin were in the Judge's chambers. Even if they knew nothing about the conversation between Thierry and the Judge, they knew about Consolidated Chemical and were negotiating from a position of strength. Dollar signs in their eyes, they wanted the Judge to declare Thierry dead.

"He's only been gone for a couple of weeks," the Judge had pointed out. "Don't you think that's a little premature? What if he comes waltzing back to town next week with a bimbo on his arm and a smile on his face?"

"Oh, he won't do that, Judge," assured Thierry's brother.

"And how do you know that?"

The Boudreaux kin had glanced back and forth for a moment. Finally, Estelle spoke. "We got a call."

"A call? Like 'Hello, this is Thierry, and I'm never coming home'?"

"A call from the police in Beaumont, Texas. They found his car stickin' out of the swamp, but no Thierry anywhere."

"Maybe he drove into the swamp by accident."

"Swamp was almost a mile from the road, Judge. I don't think so," said Thierry's brother.

"Maybe someone stole the car and ditched it there."

"Then why didn't Thierry report it?"

The Judge called the Beaumont police. They *had* found the car, although there was no evidence of foul play. It was a shaky reason to declare Thierry dead, but by this time, the Judge knew that Thierry really wasn't coming back. To simplify matters, Thierry had no life insurance ("selfish bastard," his brother had commented), so the Judge was sure that no one would be contesting Thierry's judicial demise.

"Did his family kill Thierry Boudreaux?" asked Lana.

"No. They may not be the nicest people in the world, but they wouldn't kill their own brother."

"Was it someone from Consolidated?"

The Judge was silent for a moment. Then he told her how after the meeting in New Orleans, he had called his friend Stanley Leighton and told him that Boudreaux was a loose cannon who knew about everything. It hadn't occurred to him right then that Stanley might want to silence Boudreaux. Leighton had made a rare appearance at the *fais-do-do* several days later. The Judge saw Leighton and Boudreaux having some words off in a corner, which no one heard over the music. Soon after, Thierry left. Leighton did, too, but no one really noticed aside from the Judge—people came and went continually. When Boudreaux was not seen again, the Judge realized what had happened, but the truth was that he hadn't felt very bad about Boudreaux's death. The passage of time had only served to erase any trifling moral quandaries he may have once had. It wasn't like he'd been the one to crush Boudreaux's thick skull. And it wasn't like Thierry's kin were going to raise a fuss from their brand new brick colonial with the red Cadillac out front.

The Heberts were a different matter. They were totally innocent. Their deaths had been torturing his conscience. The Judge told Lana what little he knew—that someone working for Leighton had murdered them.

"I wanted to tell you, but I didn't know how to approach it. I knew you'd be upset with me. And I guess I'm just afraid of going to prison."

There was a long silence from Lana. When she spoke, her voice was firm and resolute. "Louis, you are going to have to come clean about all this. Leighton is going to pay for the Heberts' deaths." Then she said quietly, "This is not going to bring down my campaign."

"I know, dear," said the Judge. "The D.A.'s office is investigating Acadian Developing. They haven't tied it to Boudreaux or the Hebert murders, though. Harry Carter is in charge. I suppose we should go talk to him."

"Not yet. There will be leaks and it will turn into a media circus. Leighton might find out and disappear. And my campaign could be destroyed." Lana rocked slowly. The Judge could practically hear her thinking.

"No, what we'll do is get Leighton to confess. Then I'll call a press conference. That way we can feed the information to the media my way."

"All right, dear." Though he knew the answer, he had to ask. "You *are* very disappointed in me, aren't you?"

"Not only am I disappointed, I'm angry." She got up and went inside, leaving him alone on the gallery.

He could only imagine how angry she would have been if he'd told her *everything*.

Scarlett listened to the entire conversation from the floor of the hall, where she lay with her ear pressed against the door. She heard Lana rise from the rocker, and she scurried up the stairs. Now was not the time to get caught. Once safely in her room, she considered her options.

She had always known that the L'Enfants were good liars. She just wished the Judge had been a really world-class fabricator. Then, maybe he wouldn't be going to jail. Now her chances of getting her inheritance were about as good as the Judge's chances of a Nobel prize. All these years, she'd been counting on the money to pave her escape from Shady Oaks, from the parish, from the State of Louisiana. She'd been picturing herself as an expatriate *artiste* in Tangier. She'd be featured in *Vogue* magazine. They'd speak of her Moroccan period.

Now she'd be lucky to have a St. James Parish period.

Lana's charity was her only remaining hope. Scarlett began to sob. She buried her face in the pillow so that no one would hear. Why had she ever started leaking the campaign strategy to Taylor? Then she wondered if telling him about her exhibit had also been a mistake.

Thirty-three

Lana gave the whole story to Tippy, leaving nothing out.

"I suppose you want to resign now."

"Nonsense, Lana. I look at this as a challenge. Corruption is the lifeblood of our political system. Without it, the voters become complacent. Louis didn't kill anyone, did he?"

"No."

"Then this election is not over yet. Imagine how honest and upstanding you will look when your beloved husband tells the press that he's turning himself in because you have helped him see the light and he understands the importance of your mission to the people of this state. Can't you see it? 'I'm willing to spend the rest of my life in prison if it means Louisiana will reap the benefits of my wife's leadership.' "

It was spin, but it might be effective spin. Lana was beginning to appreciate Tippy.

Together they'd decided that it was best that Souchecki know nothing. "He wouldn't see the opportunities here," Tippy opined. "In the meantime, you should continue full speed ahead. I have a publicity idea for you. It involves one of the charities that I'm involved with."

"Charities are always good," agreed Lana.

In the meantime, she had gone ahead with assembling a group of campaign volunteers. Now she scrutinized the motley crew munching doughnuts in conference room A of the LaPlace Days Inn. They all looked like people who had nothing better to do that day. Or any day.

Beyond the quality of the volunteers, the turnout was not nearly as large as she'd expected. The free coffee and pastries had gotten about thirty-five of the three hundred people that she'd made Scarlett call (the volunteers' names had been culled from the application cards at the wedding). How many would she have gotten with free beer? Maybe fifty, sixty. It wouldn't have been cost effective. For that amount of cash, she could hire people to staple her campaign signs to telephone poles. In fact, she'd wanted to hire them. A paycheck always made even the most unreliable of workers feel at least a little responsibility. A volunteer, on the other hand, was likely to chuck the signs in the trash if his staple gun so much as jammed. But Tippy had insisted that she use volunteers.

"Each one of them is good for a vote, because they feel like they're an integral part of the campaign effort," she'd explained. Lana wasn't so sure. If she spent several hours putting up signs in the rain for free, she would be pretty sure to vote for the other guy.

Within a half hour, the doughnuts were all gone. Volunteers had begun to lick the sugar off their fingers and put down their paper coffee cups. Lana cleared her throat to bring them to attention before starting to speak.

"I'm so glad to see you all again. I know that you're eager to get to work and be a part of a new era in honest government." She paused. "And I'm eager to make you work." She laughed. It was a joke. Several of the volunteers chuckled a little; most of them just stared.

"You will play a very important part in this campaign. It will be your job to get the word out. You will do this by hanging signs, and by distributing campaign literature and these." Lana held up a red, white, and blue bumper sticker.

"Excuse me." A woman up front raised her hand.

"Yes?"

"Do those come off? We went to South of the Border last year, and my son put their bumper stickers all over the back of our Toyota, and I must've spent hours scratching them off with an X-Acto Knife."

Several of the other volunteers nodded in agreement.

"You won't have to worry about these. They're made with a special type of glue." Yeah, it magically releases the morning after election day. It was the first lie of her campaign. But by the time they found out that the stickers could only be burned off with industrial-strength mercuric acid, she would already be elected.

Lana continued. "This is my granddaughter, Scarlett." She motioned at the girl, who was trying to hide her face behind a large cruller. "She has graciously volunteered to be the Visibility Chairman in this campaign." Lana couldn't understand Scarlett's sudden enthusiasm for the campaign, but why look a gift horse in the mouth? "She will assign you to teams."

"Okay," Scarlett croaked hoarsely to the volunteers (she had lost her voice somewhere around the 250th call), "I need ten of you to give out buttons and bumper stickers outside supermarkets, video stores, those kind of places."

"But it's raining," spoke up one of the volunteers. "Can't we do it inside?"

"Despite the importance of our mission," Lana explained, "it's unlikely that we could get permission to do that. It has to be outside."

There were grumbles of discontent among the ranks. Finally, a middle-aged woman spoke up. "I'll do it. A little rain never hurt anybody."

"Anyone else?" Scarlett asked. Lana knew that Scarlett didn't want to be the one standing in the Louisiana rain outside of Blockbuster.

There were no responses.

"Okay," Scarlett said, walking over to the woman and handing her a box of supplies. "Would you mind covering several locations?"

"I guess not," the woman replied.

The woman was obviously sorry that she'd spoken up. Scarlett circled three supermarkets on a photocopied list and handed it to the woman.

"Thank you," Lana told the woman. That was probably a vote lost.

By the end of the evening, Scarlett had succeeded in getting seven people assigned to putting up signs, demonstrated the use of the staple guns ("Make sure no one is going to shoot themselves in the eye," Lana had told her. "We don't want to get sued and lose a vote at the same time."), and given the rest of the volunteers instructions on when and where to show up and stuff envelopes with campaign literature.

"Is there anything else that I can do?" Scarlett asked her in the car on the way back to Shady Oaks.

"My, but you're Little Miss Helpful."

Scarlett didn't reply.

"As a matter of fact, there is. Tomorrow we're going to meet Tippy in Lafayette. She has a great photo op for me." Lana couldn't help but chuckle to herself.

Scarlett's legs trembled as she stood in the cherry picker. She looked down through the leaves of the large live oak. At its roots, Lana and Tippy stood safely on terra firma. The candidate was wearing a straw hat, a red-checked shirt shot through with Lurex, matching red cowboy boots, and a pair of voluminous jeans. She was holding up a pitchfork covered in Spanish moss, posing happily for a reporter from the Lafayette paper. She looked like a demented Dale Evans.

Tippy had arranged for Lana and Scarlett to assist her Spanish Moss committee. All day long, the three had been going from house to house, from farm to farm, followed by a hay truck filled with moss and a cherry picker on loan from the local phone company (Tippy's husband was on the company's board of directors). Scarlett had been forced to ride in the phone company truck. "Tippy and I have things to discuss," Lana had informed her. Scarlett knew that they were talking about the Judge and how to save Lana's campaign. That was probably why the Judge had been excluded from this publicity stunt. Or maybe sending an eighty-four-year-old man fifty feet above the ground in a small basket had seemed like a bad idea. But Scarlett didn't attribute that much discretion to Lana.

The middle-aged, leathery-skinned man driving the cherry-picker was hitting on Scarlett without mercy. As the day wore on, Scarlett's hair had become filled with moss, her exposed skin had turned green, and flies buzzed about her sweaty face. This only excited the driver more. Unfortunately, he was not horny enough to offer to go up in the basket of the cherry picker ("I'm union," he'd stated. "I can drive, and that's it."). Thus, Scarlett was assigned the task of being raised into the branches of the trees and actually distributing the moss. Lana and Tippy were serving strictly as ground crew, directing her as if she were hanging Christmas tree lights.

"Lana," she called down from her lofty perch, "I think this tree has enough moss in it now."

"I think the other side looks a little bare," Lana retorted. "George," she said to the driver, "could you swing Scarlett around to that big branch on the other side?"

"I'm out of moss."

"Bring her down instead. She needs to reload."

To Scarlett's temporary relief, the arm of the cherry picker slowly lowered. She wished that she could refuse to go back up, but if she didn't keep Lana happy . . . Scarlett could just see herself, destitute, working the swing shift back at the Thibodaux Burger King. She could visit the Judge in prison on her lunch hour. God, she needed some money.

She reached the ground, and Lana and Tippy began filling the basket with moss.

"How much more do I have to do?" Scarlett whispered. "I'm turning into a druid up there!"

"It's important that the moss is evenly distributed," Tippy chastened her. "Otherwise it ruins the aesthetics of the tree."

"I know a little about aesthetics," Scarlett protested, "and it looks fine to me."

Tippy ignored her, tossing in one last pitchfork of moss. "Take it back up, George." The cherry picker started moving. Scarlett heard Tippy whisper to Lana, "I think that girl is trouble."

I'll show her trouble, thought Scarlett. She gripped the sides of the basket with all her might. It swung up and off to the right, then stopped near a bare branch. Scarlett lifted out an armful of moss. "Oops," she called, watching with pleasure as it rained squarely on Tippy's head. The photographer captured several nice shots. Tippy appeared to suffer the moss with equanimity, but announced several minutes later that they were adding two more properties to their schedule.

It was almost eight P.M. by the time they brought Scarlett down to sea level for good. To her chagrin, Lana informed her that she would be spending the next day putting up posters all over Baton Rouge. "And Scarlett," she warned, "I expect to be as visible as a virgin in a whorehouse."

It was not the metaphor that Scarlett would have chosen.

Thirty-four

Hultgrew rang the bell of the nondescript house on Rampart Street. After a few seconds, the door was opened by a short, stocky man in a stiff collar buttoned tightly around his large neck. "What can I do for you, son?" he asked Hultgrew.

Hultgrew looked again at the card. "Is this Crescent City Escorts?"

"D/b/a Decatur Escorts. You've come to the right place."

"A woman gave me this card." Hultgrew held it before the man's face. "Do I get a discount?"

"We don't give no discounts, son."

Hultgrew mentally added the money in his wallet. He should have enough. Besides, the *Star* surely would compensate him when he broke the story. The Judge running a prostitution ring. Amazing. Well, in Louisiana, maybe not amazing . . . but it was news nevertheless.

"That's okay," Hultgrew told the man. "You get what you pay for."

"Ain't that the truth." The man motioned Hultgrew into the foyer and shut the door behind him. "It's a hundred an hour."

Hultgrew took out his wallet and searched through the rumpled gum wrappers and receipts for some currency. He could just make it. He handed the man a stack of bills that included a large wad of wrinkled singles.

The man counted the money out, turning the bills to face neatly in the same direction, and then secured them in a money clip. "Right this way, son." He led Hultgrew into a dimly lit room off the hall.

As Hultgrew's eyes adjusted he made out the not unpleasant forms of a group of women draped over the couch and red velvet chairs that lined the back wall. The women ignored him. Several were reading dog-eared magazines; one was crocheting. "Choose a date," the man told him.

Hultgrew ruled out the crocheter. Too homey. He rejected two brunettes, a redhead, and a slender Asian woman. His eyes fell on the last girl—a big-haired blond wearing a pink lace teddy. What should he do? Pointing seemed rude. He leaned over to the man. "Ah . . . what's her name?" he asked, inclining his head in the direction of the blond.

"I'm Tiffany," the girl mumbled, without looking up from her magazine.

"Tiffany. C'mere, child."

The blond gave her *Cosmo* a last, lingering glance before rising slowly to her feet, where she teetered in her high-heeled marabou slippers. She wobbled over to Hultgrew and took him by the arm. "C'mon up, babe."

They walked up the stairs and past several identical, closed doors and were soon safely ensconced in Tiffany's room, a depressing cubicle with cracking ecru paint and exposed pipes. Tiffany settled herself on the sagging bed, legs crossed, and looked at him expectantly. "So . . ." Hultgrew started awkwardly. What should he say? "Tiffany. That's a pretty name."

"I'm glad ya' like it, babe. I picked it just for you. You looked like a Tiffany man." She crooked her finger and motioned him to come and sit next to her. When he had, she grasped his thigh. "So, what d'ya' wanna do?"

Hultgrew leaned away from her a bit. "Maybe we should talk a while first."

"Fine." She propped herself against the headboard. "But the price is the same."

"Yeah, okay." The *Star* had better pay him back.

"Whatta ya' wanna talk about?"

He didn't want to dive right into it, tip his hand by bringing up the Judge right away. "What do people usually talk about?"

"Hmm. Not too many talk at all, ta' tell ya' the truth. Uh . . . about their wives, I guess. Seems kinda weird to talk about your wife with an escort, but . . ."

"I'm not married."

"Got a girlfriend?"

"No," said Hultgrew after a pause.

"Why not? A handsome guy like you."

Hultgrew thought about Cami Gooch, and felt the anger rising in his chest. Yeah, why not? It was like she thought he wasn't good enough for her. The anger transmuted into a twinge of insecurity. Maybe he wasn't good enough. Maybe he was destined to be second rate.

". . . 'Cause I'd go out with you."

"You would?"

"Yeah, I would."

She gave him a toothy grin. She seemed sincere. Hultgrew smiled back, noting the glint in her gray eyes. She was actually quite attractive.

"What's your name, handsome?"

"Bolton."

"That's nice. That's my favorite name."

"Really?" What a coincidence. Before he knew what he was doing, Hultgrew was leaning in toward her face.

"No kissing, babe," she told him.

249

* * *

The short man started beating on the door before Hultgrew even had a chance to ask about the Judge. "Time's up."

"Shit." Hultgrew reached over the side of the bed and grabbed his pants off the floor. He searched futilely for more money. All he needed was another fifteen minutes. "Do you take credit cards?" he hollered in the direction of the door.

"Visa, MasterCard, American Express, Discovery, and Diners Club."

Gooch would never let him hear the end of it if he submitted this expense to Accounting.

Cami Gooch looked down the length of her silky legs at the man at the foot of the bed who was neatly painting her toenails fire-engine red. She reached out with her unpainted foot and ruffled Bobby Taylor's hair with her toes. "That Hultgrew is so fucking stupid. I think I'm going to have to type the story for him."

Taylor was actually relieved at Hultgrew's laziness and ineptitude, otherwise he might happen across some things that Taylor *didn't* want found. That was why he'd had Cami delegate the media duties, instead of letting the little firecracker do it herself. Cami was overly thorough and competent. Taylor needed someone sloppy, and he knew that Hultgrew was far too unmotivated to look anywhere that Cami didn't point him.

"Well, make sure he gets on this thing. The granddaughter told me all about these paintings of hers." Taylor smiled. "They sound God-awful. Of course, I don't give a shit about their artistic merit. I only care about their damage potential. I want it in the paper before the indictment comes out and Pulaski has a chance to spin it."

"What about that whorehouse her aunt owns?" Cami asked Taylor. "That would hurt if it got into the papers."

"Yeah, it's embarrassing, but some of my friends are clients there. I wouldn't want any heat coming down on them. We'll just stick with the granddaughter, the aspiring pornographer." Taylor shook his head. "Poor ol' Judge L'Enfant. Ordinarily, I'm a forgiving soul, but politics is an ugly business."

Thirty-five

The bait shop was in an old frame building on stilts at the edge of Bayou Crab. A rickety gangplank led from the small gravel parking lot to the front door. Lana and Carl clattered up the plank and into the dark, unair-conditioned interior of the shop. Even though a ceiling fan turned slowly under the eaves, the shop smelled of earth and stagnant water. Flies buzzed in the dirty windows. An old man stood behind the counter, looking askance at Lana's stiletto pumps and tight clam diggers and Carl's pink hair.

"We need to rent a boat for the day."

"Hundred dollar deposit and driver's license."

Lana handed him the money and I.D., along with a campaign button. The man blinked at the button for a moment, then put it in the cash register drawer with Lana's twenties. He reached under the counter, took out two damp life jackets, and handed them to Carl. He pointed through the back door, which opened onto a dock.

"Boat's out there."

"Be sure to vote for me in November."

"Uh-huh."

He was obviously not an enthusiastic participant in the electoral system. Lana had half a mind to ask for the button back, then decided it wasn't worth it.

She and Carl walked back out into the daylight to the dock. Lana looked down at the boat. It was awfully small, and foreign enough to be a little unsettling. The Pulaskis were not boat people.

"Are you sure you can handle this thing?"

"No problem. Do you know how many weekends I spent driving my father's ski boat on the lake? He thought that sports would straighten me out. Instead, it just made me lust after athletic men." Carl handed her a life jacket. Lana wrinkled her nose at the dirty orange fabric and tossed it aside.

"Why the hell are we going out to some shack on the back bayou anyway?" he asked.

"Sorry. That's on a need-to-know basis."

Lana had realized that if she was going to trap Leighton, she'd need to get his confession on tape. She figured that the best way to do it was to wire the Judge. She'd called around to several Radio Shacks, asking for bugging equipment. Tiny microphones, matchbook-sized tape recorders, that sort of thing. This approach had been unavailing. Then she'd tried a private investigator she'd worked with on several acrimonious divorce cases. He'd recommended a man named Henri out in the bayou. Henri had electronics that no one else could get. The P.I. had contacted this mysterious figure and made telephone introductions. Henri had then given Lana directions to his watery abode.

Carl climbed off the dock and into the boat. "I'd take those shoes off before I got in, boss."

"Here's a lesson for you. There is no job that cannot or should not be done in heels." Lana stepped gracefully into the boat and sat down in the bow.

"Okay, then," said Carl, impressed. He untied the boat, tossed the lines on the dock, and started the engine. As they pulled away, he began to sing. "Goodbye Joe, me gotta go, me oh, my oh—"

"Don't do that."

It was peaceful out on the bayou, despite the whine of the small outboard motor. Lana found that she was actually enjoying the ride. After twenty minutes or so of winding through the cypress, they came to the clearing with Henri's shack. He was waiting for them on the porch, a Glock pistol in one hand.

"You know what I love about my job?" Carl hissed. "The glamour."

"This is probably a good time to keep your smart mouth shut."

"You can tie 'dat boat to 'de pillar 'dere," Henri called down. "I'll trow you down 'de ladder."

He unfurled the rope ladder, which dangled a foot from the boat. Lana reached over, grabbed the ropes, and placed one heel on the first rung.

"I can't wait to see 'dis," said Henri.

Without incident, Lana scaled the rungs. She leaned back to allow her chest to clear the edge of the porch, then placed her palms on the weather-beaten boards and expertly boosted herself on deck.

"I'll be damned," said Henri.

Carl applauded.

"What do you call this look, Henri—'shabby chic'? "

The man threw his head back and laughed. "Come on inside. I got your equipment in 'dere."

The interior of the shack was softly lit by several oil lamps. Lana looked down and saw that the floor was covered in oriental rugs.

Henri followed her glance. "I get 'dem from Afghanistan along wit my other . . . imports. I always sure my man trows one in wit 'de shipment. 'De workmanship is incredible."

"They're lovely." Lana noted a group of large wooden crates stacked against the wall. She could well imagine what they held.

"Now, you told me you don't know where you'll need to be listenin'," Henri confirmed.

"No. We don't know where or when we'll see the suspect."

"So you can't plant anytin' ahead of time. 'Dat narrows your options. You sure you don't just want to carry one of 'dem microcassette recorders?"

"No. Too bulky. Too easily detected."

"Okay, 'den." Henri went to one of the crates, picked through the contents, then placed an expensive-looking pen on the table in front of Lana. "You will not believe 'de sound quality you get from 'dis. It transmits modulated peak power pulses. It has a range of two or three miles."

"And it transmits to the recorder?"

"Yeah. Here 'dat is." The recorder was the size of a shoebox. "Okay, here's how it works." He clicked the cap of the pen, as if to begin writing. The recorder whirred to life. "Remote control. 'Dat way, no one has to tend the recorder. You click twice," Henri demonstrated, "and the recorder turns off."

"How long will it record?"

"A couple of hours before you need to change 'de tape."

"Is there some sort of guarantee?"

"Miz Pulaski, in my business, one has to be a man of his word."

Scarlett was tired of driving from town to town gluing up campaign posters. Lana had been too cheap to get the self-sticking posters, opting instead for the kind that required a pot of wallpaper paste and a brush. Despite Scarlett's attempts at neatness, the paste had gotten everywhere. Her hair was clumped together with globs of the adhesive, her ass stuck to the seat of the Lincoln, and the tip of one ear was pinned back to her skull.

By eleven A.M., she decided to head back to Shady Oaks, bathe the glue off, and finish wrapping up her paintings. Her exhibition was mere days away and Inez was supposed to show up later with her SUV. Then they'd load the paintings inside and be off to the gallery in Baton Rouge.

After a half-hour soak in the tub, Scarlett had removed most of the paste from her body. She got dressed and went down to the barn. She spent a couple of hours carefully wrapping the canvases in blister plastic before she came to her most recent painting. It was a mural largely inspired by the Bugman. It was even braver than the rest of her work. For once, Scarlett was proud of herself. This painting would surely be the focal point of the show. She carefully wound the packaging around the canvas and taped it up with packing tape. She carried it over to the corner where she'd piled the rest of the paintings and set it down softly. Then she stepped back, admiring the sheer size of her artistic output. The wrapping had been a lot of work. More work, almost, than the paintings themselves. Blowing her sweat-damp hair out of her eyes, Scarlett walked outside and shut the barn door behind her.

Thirty-six

Hultgrew intended to leave for New Orleans at five P.M. sharp to visit Decatur Escorts. He had become quite fond of Tiffany. The better he got to know her, the more he realized that she was a woman of depth. She was even interested in politics. Swept away by their burgeoning relationship, he had revealed to her what he did for a living, and the first thing that she had asked was what he knew about Bobby Taylor. Unfortunately, he'd known nothing. Today, he'd decided that as a present for Tiffany, he would do some research.

He took the elevator down to the *Star*'s dank morgue. Before the doors even opened, he could smell the mildewing clippings. Yecch. Research really sucked.

The pimply-faced archivist was nowhere to be found, so Hultgrew had to go through the microfiche all by himself. It took him a while to figure out how things were filed and how to use the machine, but he eventually got the hang of it. He sat at the viewer, slowly turning the dial. Bobby Taylor at a Kiwanis banquet. Bobby Taylor's daughter's high school graduation picture.

Hultgrew wondered if Tiffany really liked him. She *seemed* to, but then again, he was paying her. She acted sincere, though. Yesterday, she'd even let him kiss her. Would she go out on a date with him? A real date? They could go to dinner and the movies. Hultgrew imagined himself taking Tiffany to his parents' suburban home. Mom, Dad, this is Tiffany, the woman I love. She's a whore. He chuckled, imagining his mother's reaction.

Hultgrew plowed through more microfiche. Taylor with his wife and kids at a campaign fund-raiser. Taylor shaking hands with the mayor. There was nothing good here. He made a list of the pictures and articles that he had found and left it for the archivist. "These are useless. Take a look and see if you can find anything good," he wrote across the top.

Hultgrew took the elevator back up to the newsroom. Cami was waiting by his desk.

"Listen, I've got some more info on the L'Enfants. If you don't get moving on this story, it's going to get scooped right out from under you by some hack at the *Times-Picayune*." Cami's aggravation was obvious. But since he'd begun visiting Decatur Escorts every night, Hultgrew's anger at the Judge had waned significantly. In fact, now he just couldn't see where the story was. Christ, it had all happened years ago. Besides, who cared about zoning? It was fucking boring, that's what it was. On top of that, he'd found nothing to link the Judge to Decatur Escorts. When he'd finally asked Tiffany point-blank about the Judge, she'd seemed so genuinely confused by the question that he could only assume he was on the wrong track.

"Cami, why are you so interested in my success all of a sudden?"

"Because, Hultgrew"—she patted him on the shoulder—"we've come up through the ranks together. I feel like we're almost a team."

Hultgrew didn't know whether to believe her or not but it was far more pleasant to assume that she actually was interested in him, so he decided to trust her. "Okay. What's this new information that you have, and where did you get it?"

"I can't tell you where I got it, but let's just say it was a very reliable source."

Hultgrew rummaged through the trash on his desk until he found a pencil, which he held over a slightly grease-stained Chinese take-out menu. "Okay, give it to me."

"I've got information that the Judge's granddaughter is a pornographer, and she's showing her stuff in a Baton Rouge gallery."

"Why would a gallery show pornography?"

"For God's sake, Hultgrew. Remember Mapplethorpe?"

Actually, Hultgrew didn't, though he had more than a passing acquaintance with the names Hefner and Guccione.

"Which gallery?"

"Jesus, Hultgrew." Cami rolled her eyes. "I should make you find out yourself, but for old times' sake, I'll tell you. It's the Fontenot gallery. I'm sure it's listed in the Yellow Pages."

"Hey." Hultgrew suddenly had an idea. "I could call them and tell them I'm doing a story on the show and get the scoop that way. You think that would work?"

"You're giving Carl Bernstein a run for his money, Bolt."

Cami patted him on the shoulder in a way that seemed very suggestive and swiveled off to her desk, leaving a trail of wounded and gaping male *Star* reporters in her wake. Hultgrew watched until her posterior was firmly seated in her chair and out of eye's reach before he picked up the Yellow Pages from the floor and dialed the gallery.

"This is Bolton Hultgrew, the art section editor from the *Star*," he told the voice on the other end of the line. "I'm doing a story on the Baton Rouge art scene, and I hear that you're going to have an exhibition of a local painter's works."

"You must mean Scarlett L'Enfant," came the reply.

"Bingo," said Hultgrew. "That's the one."

"I didn't realize the *Star* had an art section."

"It does now."

Scarlett and Inez had loaded all of the paintings into Inez's Land Rover and driven to the gallery in Baton Rouge. The gallery owner had helped them unload, and they had immediately set to work hanging the canvases. Scarlett held one of her earlier paintings against the wall, while Inez and the gallery owner stood back about fifteen feet, sizing up its location.

"Yes, I think it's better where you've got it now," the owner told her. "I like the idea of arranging everything thematically, so I think that we should have all the breast paintings in one place."

"They're not really breast paintings. . . ."

"Well, you know what I mean. They can definitely be lumped into distinct groups. I'm just calling them the breast paintings for simplicity's sake."

"Of course we understand that there's more to the paintings than just anatomical parts, Scarlett," comforted Inez. "We understand your work perfectly."

"Are you sure?" Scarlett was beginning to feel a little shaky about the exhibition.

"Don't worry about it, sweetie," said the owner. "I think that this show is going to be very well received. In fact, I've already gotten a call from one of the reporters at the *Star*. He's coming over in a few minutes to take a look at your work. He'd like to talk to you. I think it would be a great idea. If the article comes out in the next day or two, it can only help us get people into the gallery."

"How exciting," cooed Inez. "My goddaughter is giving her first interview. Scarlett, I always knew that you were destined for special things."

Just then, a man stumbled in through the door. His eyes swept the paintings already hung on the walls. "Jesus," he breathed through his teeth. He spotted Scarlett. "You must be the artist. I'm Bolton Hultgrew from the *Star*."

* * *

Hultgrew's first impression on entering the gallery was that he was back in Decatur Escorts. Breasts, buttocks, and groins—both male and female—hung everywhere. This was better than he'd ever imagined. Cami *must* be hot for him to give him a tip like this. He felt the newshound hair at the back of his neck prickling with excitement (other parts of his anatomy were prickling simultaneously at the sight of the paintings).

"So," said Hultgrew, "you did all these."

"Um, yeah. I'm just a little nervous, Mr. Hultgrew. I've never given an interview before," the girl said, eyes cast down at the ground.

"We'll leave you two alone so you can get to work," Inez said, steering the gallery owner away by the elbow.

Hultgrew tried to reconcile her with the paintings. She didn't look like a pornographer. For one thing, she was too, well, skinny. Hultgrew had imagined a more zaftig woman. This girl looked like she could be Hultgrew's (very pale) little sister. He began to feel himself getting protective toward the girl. He shook it off. He was a newshound. "Okay, Miss L'Enfant. Let me ask you a few questions about your work. For example, how does Judge L'Enfant feel about your paintings?"

"Oh, he's been very supportive of my work."

"Well," said Hultgrew, "that's good to know."

The interview lasted about a half hour. Hultgrew got some good material, but he realized that the story needed another angle to be of Pulitzer dimensions. After he left the gallery, he decided to call in a professional.

"Hi, Mom? It's Bolt."

"Bolt! It's nice to hear from you, son." Mrs. Hultgrew's voice was very formal and a little too loud. Even on the phone, she liked to maintain the ordered artifice of a Katharine Hepburn movie. In Mrs. Hultgrew's mind, she was speaking to her son from the drawing room in *The Philadelphia Story*. How she could possibly block out the large tract home in the flat, treeless subdivision where she and Hultgrew's father had lived for the past thirty years was truly a mystery.

"Everything going okay, I hope," Hultgrew ventured.

"Oh, just fine. Your father's out playing racquetball with Dr. Burton. Dad always loses, but he says Al cheats. I don't know, I think your dad just stinks, is all. I'm about to leave for my bridge club at the church." Mrs. Hultgrew, a lifelong Catholic, had converted to the Episcopalian church some ten years ago, following the death of her parents. She had brought Mr. Hultgrew with her (he had learned to take the path of least resistance years before). The Episcopalian church was so much more Main Line. The only thing that had stopped Adele Hultgrew from going all the way and becoming a Quaker was the Society of Friends' unfortunate liberal bent.

"I'm glad I caught you," Hultgrew told her. "I've run across something that you might want to work on with the ladies."

"How marvelous!"

Marvelous? "I don't think that you'll like it that much, Mom. It's an art exhibit."

"What do you mean?"

"A woman, her name is Scarlett L'Enfant, is exhibiting her paintings downtown in Baton Rouge. They're pretty pornographic, if I do say so myself." Hultgrew felt a pang of guilt. Poor Scarlett. "I thought you and the ladies might want to protest or something."

"Oh, sweetie, that's more a job for . . ."—Mrs. Hultgrew dropped her voice—". . . the Catholics."

"But the gallery is right down the street from your church."

"Really? The Fontenot gallery? Well, that's just in bad taste."

The ultimate damnation.

"It's even worse than bad taste, Mom." Hultgrew hated to

exaggerate, but she was forcing him to. "In fact, the paintings depict bestiality."

"Good Lord." Mrs. Hultgrew finally seemed moved. "I'll look into it. The children walk by that gallery on the way to church."

"That's why I called you, Mother. I hate to think of those innocent little faces looking up and seeing those pictures on their way to pray for Jesus." Maybe he was laying it on a little thick. It was nothing they hadn't seen before on cable.

"Don't worry, Bolt, I'll get the girls on the job right away."

Ah, thought Hultgrew, you can take the woman out of the Catholic Church, but you can't take the church out of the woman. There was nothing that Mrs. Hultgrew loved more than a good picket.

"It's even worse than you think, Mom. The artist's grandfather is a judge, and his wife is running for attorney general in the next election."

"What kind of family is this?" Mrs. Hultgrew's voice shook with indignation. "The Mansons?"

"Judge L'Enfant and Lana Pulaski." Hultgrew spelled the names twice to make sure that the ladies would get them right on the picket signs.

Thirty-seven

Lana had been gone for several days. She had said that she had some campaign events elsewhere in the state, but the Judge was worried that she was lying. Since confessing to her, he had been terrified that she would leave him. He had passed the time since her departure in a state of high anxiety, and was more than relieved when he finally heard her steps on the gallery.

She didn't greet him, just entered the sitting room and asked, "Have you heard from Leighton yet?"

"No, dear. But I'm sure that I will. I'm so glad that you're back," he added. She didn't reply. "How did everything go?"

"Fine." She was obviously preoccupied. She placed a black box on the coffeetable, then opened her purse and pulled out a pen. "This is a remote control microphone."

The Judge took the pen and examined it. "It looks very authentic. Quite impressive. Uh . . . Is this device legal?"

"In four republics of the former Soviet Union." Lana patted the black box. "This is the recorder. When you meet with Leighton, you'll have the microphone with you. You have to get him to confess to the murders."

"I know that."

"Do you think that you can handle that, Louis?"

"Yes, dear." The Judge was determined to redeem himself in her eyes. He could do that by sacrificing himself and helping her to trap Leighton. As a result, of course, he'd probably spend the rest of his life in the parish prison. Thank God the days of the chain gang were over—Cool Hand Luke he wasn't.

Lana showed him how the microphone worked, and told him to keep it in his shirt pocket to get used to carrying it. "Be careful with it, it was hard to find. We'll go over how it works again before you meet with Leighton. When you go to see him, I'll drive you. I'll have the recorder in the car. In the meantime, I'll keep it upstairs in my armoire."

Lana picked up the recorder and left the room. Seconds later, the Judge heard her scream. Was Leighton here? How would he protect her? The Judge pulled off his shoe to use as a weapon and hurried into the hall at full shuffle. Lana stood on the staircase, looking down at the floor of the hall. At least nine or ten mice scrabbled back and forth. One sat in a corner cleaning its whiskers.

"This dump is uninhabitable!"

"It's only a few mice, dear. They won't hurt you."

Scarlett entered the door and took note of the rodents.

"Call the exterminator!" demanded Lana. "And why are you smiling?"

Thirty-eight

"Where did she see them?" the Bugman asked. He and Scarlett stood out on the gallery. It was an even hotter day than usual, and he had a sheen of sweat across his cheeks that dampened the tips of his hair. Scarlett realized that she would have to exert superhuman control over herself.

"A bunch were scampering around in the hall."

"Wow. Chaos. Have you seen any?"

"A few." Right before I let them loose, she thought.

"Now, you sure there weren't any rats?"

"No, just mice. Definitely just mice." And one yard-long hungry boa, but she felt that mentioning him might make the Bugman suspicious.

"Well, that's cool. I mean, rats are a real drag. They'll come after you. I did one lady's house, she got bit right on the toe by one in the middle of the night." He shook his hair back and forth. "That's one rude wake-up call, y'know? But don't worry. The mice will leave you alone."

"How are you going to get them?"

"I could set some traps, but then you'd have to empty them yourself. Otherwise they begin to smell."

Scarlett imagined a mouse, cute little nose twitching, approaching a delectable piece of cheese. Snap. Oh God. It wasn't too late to forget the whole thing. She wavered with conflict, then caught sight of the Bugman, idly rubbing one bicep with his palm. Fuck the mice.

"On the other hand," he continued, "poison is a good way. That way they die in the walls, usually. House this size, you won't see them or smell them."

"Do you ever feel bad about this?"

"About what?"

"You know, killing the little mice."

"I figure they just have bad karma. Like maybe they were Hitler in a former life or something."

"Oh."

"So how do you want to do it?"

"Poison, I guess."

"Okay. I'll get started. The poison will be in little pellets. I put it in cabinets, behind furniture, on the counters. I don't like to leave it out like that, but the mice like to run on the counters. And it's not like you have any little kids here to get into it."

"No."

"And I'll put some out in your barn. They probably came from out there." He tossed the hair from his eyes. "I'm, like, glad you called."

No one had ever been so happy in the history of mankind as Scarlett was at that moment.

Back at the *Star*, Hultgrew was typing as fast as his index fingers would allow. "This is good, this is good!" he repeated to himself like a mantra. When the girl came up from photography, Hultgrew practically yanked her fingers off snatching the negatives from her hand. "Ohh," Hultgrew moaned happily, holding them up to the light. "Print this one." He indicated a picture of Scarlett standing in front of a large canvas depicting male genitals. "Put this one next to it." He pointed to a picture of a neatly dressed, well-ordered picket line led by Mrs. Hultgrew. Boy, the ladies worked fast. "And hurry up, I want to get it in the morning edition." He flicked the girl a five-dollar bill as a guarantee.

Hultgrew returned to his typing, the words fairly spilling out onto the paper. "The canvases," he wrote, "are unified by a single theme—genatalia." That word didn't look right, but Hultgrew didn't have the time to worry about spelling. "Genetalia"—that looked a little better—"both male and female, and often on the same canvas. It is a bold statement from an artist as young as Miss L'Enfant, the granddaughter of one of our state's most well-known public figures, Judge Louis L'Enfant." Hultgrew smacked his lips and went in for the kill:

> ... Despite subject matter that some might call pornographic, "the Judge is very supportive of my work," says Miss L'Enfant.
> Judge L'Enfant has recently been implicated in a bribery scandal involving Consolidated Chemical. It will be interesting to see if Miss L'Enfant causes as big a scandal with her "body" of work.

Hultgrew had a feeling that he had covered his last school board meeting. Tiffany would be so impressed with his investigative skills! Now if he could just come up with something on Taylor for her.

The return of the Bugman had inspired Scarlett to begin a new canvas. While he mined the barn with mouse poison, Scarlett stood at her easel, painting. She bit into the apple she'd brought out with her and chewed noisily. The apple. That was a good symbol. The fall of the Garden of Eden and all that. She dipped a brush in some red paint and began to rough in an apple in the middle of the canvas. Wait. Who said the apple had to be red? Time for some real innovation. Scarlett dipped the brush into some blue paint, turning the apple an electric purple. As she swabbed happily at the canvas, the Bugman came up behind her.

"That's pretty cool."

"Thanks." She was a little embarrassed that he had seen her painting, but he seemed to like it, so . . .

The Bugman put his hands on her arms and gently pushed her back against the barn wall. He took the brush from her hand and set it down carefully. Smiling, he grabbed the apple and took a bite out of it and then dropped the core onto the ground by their feet. He leaned in and slowly flicked his tongue over the pale down on her upper lip, where several drops of apple juice still glistened. He drew back and brushed his hair out of his face. "You look great when you paint." He put his mouth back against hers, brushing his lips against hers more and more firmly, catching her lower lip with his teeth. His tongue darted between her lips and he slipped a hand inside her shirt. She could feel his fingertips trailing languorously up over her stomach and then the underside of her breast. He grazed the fingers in little circles over her nipple. Scarlett groaned and sagged against the wall. She thought of a game that she had played with her friends as a child. It was called "light as a feather." At her turn, she would lie on the floor with one girl at her head and the others sitting on either side. The girl at her head would rub her temples and repeat over and over "You are light as a feather, light as a feather." The other little girls would slide a finger of each hand under her, and on a signal from the lead girl, would lift her, easily, from the floor. Scarlett felt light as a feather now, as if she might float off, above the Bugman, above the barn, away. She grabbed his waist to anchor herself.

* * *

272

Crouton propped his Jackie O glasses on his head and pressed his eye to the knothole in the barn wall. The girl had almost no chest, but watching this was a lot more interesting (and safer) than tailing the lawyer.

Thirty-nine

The Judge was once again alone in rodent-infested Shady Oaks. Lana had left to meet with Tippy Sheridan, and Scarlett had been back in the barn with the exterminator for over an hour. He wandered into the sitting room and lowered himself onto the loveseat. He didn't know if it was the Valium, or just the events of the last several weeks, but he was beyond exhaustion. He closed his eyes for just a moment.

When he opened them, Leighton was standing before him.

"Jesus!" choked the Judge, startled.

"Hello, Louis. I hope you don't mind, but I let myself in."

"Hello, Stanley. Too bad Lana isn't here to meet you."

"To tell you the truth, I waited until I saw her go. I wanted to talk to you alone."

Now the Judge was more than startled. He was frightened. He wondered if Leighton intended to murder him, lie in wait for Lana, and then kill her, too. It would certainly be easier to handle them one at a time. The Judge examined Stanley's golf shirt and poplin slacks to see if he could detect the outline of a concealed gun, but

Stanley's clothes fit smoothly against his body. He must intend to kill me with his bare hands, thought the Judge. He wants to enjoy it.

"How about getting us a drink, Louis?"

"Of course. What would you like?" Clearly, Leighton did not feel that the Judge's impending death relieved him of his duty to be a good host.

"Vodka and tonic, I think. You don't mind if I come with you to the kitchen, do you?"

Leighton was *definitely* going to kill him.

"No, no, not at all."

Well, the bright side was that he wouldn't be going to prison after all. The Judge wondered if dying would hurt. Stanley would probably try to strangle him. That didn't sound very pleasant. Or maybe he wanted to stab him. That's why he was trying to get the Judge into the kitchen—so he could get his hands on a knife. Death by stabbing might be easier. Probably just the initial pain of the knife going in, then a gradual loss of consciousness as his blood spilled onto the floor. The Judge was hoping for death by stabbing.

"My God, Louis," said Leighton, glancing at the little bowls of pellets scattered around the kitchen. "You have enough rat poison in here to take out half the parish."

"We've been having a problem with vermin." Of which Leighton was the most recent manifestation. The Judge toddled to the refrigerator, cognizant of Leighton's breath on his neck. He opened the freezer and took out the bottle of vodka.

"Ah, you keep it cold. Good man," said Leighton.

"I just hope that we have some tonic," said the Judge, peering in the refrigerator. He couldn't believe how calm he was. Maybe he was relieved to be facing death; having the Hebert murders and prison on his conscience was close to unbearable. Almost worse was the fact that he'd let Lana down.

Or had he?

The Judge reached up to his pocket. He fumbled around with his old, gnarled fingers and pressed the button on the cap of the pen. Was there any way to tell if it was working? He'd just have to assume that it was. Even if Stanley killed him, the recorder would be able to tell the story. Even though he was sure he was about to die, the Judge actually felt good for the first time in weeks. He turned from the refrigerator.

"Sorry, we seem to be out of tonic."

"Gee, that's too bad, Louis. I guess I'll have to kill you."

"That's a bit extreme, isn't it? Of course, it was extreme to have the Heberts killed just because you thought Dennis might know you'd killed Boudreaux."

"I may have gotten a little carried away, but you aren't the picture of innocence, are you?"

"No, no, I'm not. And I regret that. I regret not saying anything when you killed Boudreaux. I regret getting Bobby Taylor fired when the D.A.'s office tried to investigate us twenty years ago." This last bit was what the Judge had held back in his confession to Lana.

"Does your little wife know about that, Louis? Because that boy's still red as hell over that incident."

Well, if she didn't know before, she'd find out soon.

Taylor looked over the draft of Hultgrew's article that Cami had downloaded from the *Star*'s intranet and emailed to him. Hultgrew might be an idiot, Taylor thought, but he'd done a bang-up job on this piece. He especially liked the title: "Family Values the L'Enfant Way: Pornography and Bribery." Catchy. Taylor hit a key on his laptop and forwarded the article to reporters on the New Orleans, Baton Rouge, and Houston papers, and to an old buddy at Reuters.

Crouton lost interest in the couple when they started to get dressed. He crouched next to the barn and did a couple of lines of the methamphetamine. While he was hoovering, the chick's partner came out of the barn and Crouton pressed himself into the wall.

Whew. He hadn't been seen. The stud went around to the front of the house, then Crouton heard a motorcycle being fired up, and the crunch of tires on the gravel. The girl was still alone in the barn. He momentarily considered going in and getting himself a piece, but his crank was more immediately enticing. The more of the happy powder that he did, the more he wanted. He tilted back his head and poured a large quantity of the meth into his nose. "Son of a bitch," he yelled in pain.

"Daniel?" he heard the girl say from inside the barn. Fuck. Crouton pulled the little gun out of his waistband. He hovered against the wall. The girl came out of the barn. "Daniel?" she called again. "Are you okay?"

As she turned the corner, Crouton reached out, clapped a hand over her mouth, and pulled her up against him. "Don't fuckin' move or make a sound," he said, sticking the pistol in her neck. He could feel her quivering under his hand. It was rather satisfying. Then Crouton noticed that he was quivering, too. Perhaps he'd done a little too much meth. He was wound too tight, too tight, too tight. "Where's that fat lawyer?" he hissed.

"Mmphmm," said the girl.

"Where?"

"Mmphmmmmmm!"

Oh. It might help to take his hand off her mouth.

"Inside, I think."

"Okay. We're going to go in real slow. Did you hear me? Real slow." Crouton nudged the back of her leg with his knee, and they walked to the house. He reached out, opened the kitchen door, and shoved the girl inside. He followed after her.

"Good Lord, Mr. Crouton. What happened to your hair?"

"What are you doin' here, man?" squeaked Crouton, shocked to see Stanley standing by the fridge. There was another old geezer with him. He looked frightened. Well, thought Crouton, he should be.

"I've grown impatient waiting for you to do your job."

"Yeah, well, I'm here now. You ain't thinkin' of backin' out of the deal, are you?"

"Frankly, Mr. Crouton, I don't see why I should pay you. I think I'll just take care of this myself and get it done right."

"I'll tell you why you should pay me. I've got the fuckin' gun." Crouton shoved the girl toward the two men. "Y'all put your hands on your heads, and sit down at the table there. Now, now, now!" Gratifyingly, his three captives did as they were told.

"You seem a little nervous, Jimmy," said Stanley.

"Shut up!"

Crouton boosted himself onto the counter, keeping the gun pointed at the three people seated at the kitchen table. "We're just gonna wait for that fat lawyer to come back," he told them. He swung his legs back and forth, kicking his heels into the cabinet under the counter. Crash, crash, crash.

"Jimmy, as long as we're just sitting here, why don't you take these two out now? You're just going to have to do it anyway," Leighton reasoned.

"Shut up!" Was that a good idea? Maybe it was. Or maybe Leighton was just trying to trick him. Crouton tried to mull over the pros and cons of shooting the girl and the other old man, but he couldn't seem to concentrate. He picked up a bottle of vodka sitting on the counter and took a swig. Kill them now, or kill them later? Now or later? "Now or later, now or later, now or later . . ." he intoned. The rhythm was soothing, like a train chugging down the tracks. "Now or later, now or later . . ." Crouton took another gulp of the vodka. There was a little plate of munchies next to him on the counter. Trail mix or something. With all the crank he'd been doing, he hadn't eaten for days. Even now, he wasn't really hungry, but his grinding teeth wanted to chew on something. He picked up a handful of the trail mix and started popping the pieces into his mouth. Crunch, crunch, crunch, crunch.

The girl gasped.

"Shut *up!*" he yelled. Crouton's tennis shoes crashed against the cabinet in time with the movement of his jaw. Crunch, crunch, crunch, crunch.

A few minutes later, Crouton realized that he wasn't feeling very well.

The headlights picked up the signs by the side of the road. The *Times-Picayune* photographer read them to his colleague as they wound their way toward Shady Oaks.

"If you have a lot of gumption . . ."

"And you want to stop corruption . . ."

"Take a step for DEMO—"

"—CRACY . . ."

"Go to the polls . . ."

"and vote PULASKI."

"Burma Shave," replied the reporter.

"Whatever happened to that stuff anyway?" asked the photographer.

"Went out of business years ago."

Lana returned to Shady Oaks from her meeting with Tippy around nine-thirty. The two of them had drafted her speech for the press conference that was going to be held once she had gotten the goods on Leighton and turned them over to the D.A. She was still not entirely comfortable with the tenor of the speech, however. Lana had wanted to take a somewhat equivocal approach to the Judge's crimes. Disapproval tempered with a Tammy Wynette, stand-by-your-man attitude. "I want them to see that I'm loyal," she told the publicist. "How will it look if I hang my husband out to dry?" But Tippy had insisted that the syntax be unambiguous in relation to the Judge. "You've taken a strong stance against corruption. You have to be consistent." Lana couldn't help feeling bad for the Judge. He was so old. To be abandoned by her might kill him. Although she had originally counted on his prompt departure from this world, she had developed affection for him. Finding out about his crimes had angered her, but she still had feelings for him. He was so *devoted*. He was willing to sacrifice himself for her. That was more than she could say for Marshall Hope or anyone else in her life, with the exception of Flo and Joe. She couldn't help but think that they'd disapprove of her tossing the Judge to the sharks. Too bad it couldn't be Scarlett instead.

Lana looked in the sitting room. No Judge. He must have gone to bed. She thought of his gnarled figure, snoring softly. She would temper the speech.

She walked back to the kitchen to get a snack. Still deep in thought, she was startled when she entered. A freakishly coifed man was sitting on the counter. He caught sight of her, began to raise a gun, then promptly tumbled from where he was sitting onto the floor. He retched as he hit the tiles, and a huge quantity of bright red blood spewed from his mouth and nose. The gun that he'd been holding skittled across the room, where Scarlett, Louis, and a man that Lana assumed to be Stanley Leighton were crowded in the corner. Without consciously thinking the situation through, Lana realized what was happening.

"Get the gun!" she barked at Scarlett.

Scarlett hesitated, and in that split-second, Leighton lunged forward and grabbed the pistol. Damn that girl!

"Ms. Pulaski," Leighton said, pointing the gun at her, "it's so nice to finally meet you."

"I wish I could say the same."

"Why don't you get back there in the corner with the rest of your family." Leighton motioned with the gun. "You, too, Jimmy," he said to the man prostrate on the floor. Jimmy failed to follow the instructions, choosing instead to convulse violently and then stiffen and lie still.

"I have to apologize for Mr. Crouton here," said Leighton. "He seems to have eaten something that didn't agree with him."

"Mouse poison," Scarlett whispered to Lana.

"Stanley, why don't you just put down the gun," said Lana. "You've already killed three people. Don't kill any more."

"Actually, Mr. Crouton here killed the Heberts. Although I must admit, I bashed Thierry Boudreaux with a nine iron. At the time, I thought I was rather inspired, stuffing him in the shed on Hebert's farm. Later, it occurred to me that Boudreaux might have told Hebert something, but since no one found the body, Hebert never said anything."

"Hebert never knew anything," mumbled the Judge. "You killed those people for no reason."

"Any last words before you join them?" Leighton asked.

Scarlett was looking up at the ceiling. "I have a question," she said. "How do you feel about boa constrictors?"

The girl must be delirious with fear, thought Lana.

Then she realized what Scarlett was talking about. Dangling from the chandelier above Leighton was a three-foot-long snake. It coiled and uncoiled slowly, sleepily. Where did that thing come from? Lana wondered as she watched the snake let go of the light fixture and drop on Leighton's head.

"Aaaacckkk!" screamed Leighton, arms flailing at the reptile.

Lana saw her opportunity. She lunged at Leighton with all her might and knocked him flat on his back. His hand hit the floor and the pistol discharged as it was jarred from his grasp. The bullet blew a hole in the ceiling the size of a manhole cover, and as plaster rained down on Lana and Leighton, she drew back her fist and delivered an uppercut to his jaw that snapped his head back like the lid of a cigarette lighter. Lana climbed off the now-unconscious man, and turned to Scarlett and the Judge.

"This place is a fucking zoo!"

forty

Inez's large Acadian-style house was so clean that Scarlett often felt tempted to pull the overstuffed couches away from the walls and inspect behind them to see where all the dust had gone. Everything was covered in chintz (even the electrical cords were slipcovered in shirred fabric), the vases were filled with fresh flowers twice a week by Inez's live-in maid, and the rugs on the shiny hardwood floors were so thick that Scarlett's feet disappeared into the pile with every step. The guest room was decorated in peaches and yellows, with a thick down duvet on the canopied bed to protect against the arctic chill of the air conditioning. Piles of decorative pillows were stacked against the headboard. Every drawer in the dresser was lined with Florentine paper and contained a sachet of potpourri. Scarlett stared glumly into the mirror at her white face. "I feel like I'm living inside Victoria's Secret," she said aloud to her reflection.

She had been in exile with Inez and her husband ever since the incident in the kitchen. Lana remained at Shady Oaks, even though the Judge was in the parish prison. As the step-grandmother was furious with her, Scarlett wasn't ready to face her just yet. It occurred to her that an enraged Lana might be dangerous. Especially after watching her flatten Stanley Leighton.

After Lana knocked out the intruder, Scarlett had caught her breath and had a chance to reflect upon being held hostage at gunpoint, watching Crouton hemorrhage to death before her eyes, and having Leighton point a pistol at her. At that point, she had fainted. Again. It was important to have a coping mechanism, and orthostatic hypotension seemed to work for her.

When she came to, the dead man was still on the floor, and flashbulbs were popping through the windows. A candidate for public office standing amidst two unconscious people and one corpse— it wasn't often you got a photo opportunity like that outside of a legislative session, and the reporters on the lawn were taking full advantage. Lana was furious.

"Where did all these reporters come from?" she shot at the Judge.

"I don't know."

"Hey, Lana, hey!" The reporters were jockeying for position at the door.

"We haven't even had a chance to call the police. How could they know about this?"

One of the reporters pressed a copy of the Acadian *Star* against the window. From her prone position on the floor, Scarlett read the headline. FAMILY VALUES THE L'ENFANT WAY: PORNOGRAPHY AND BRIBERY. She'd made the front page! Pleased, Scarlett noted the photo of her newest canvas. Then Lana looked down at her, and she knew she was going to get it.

"How," hissed Lana, "did they know about that?"

Once again, Scarlett regretted having gone to Bobby Taylor.

Soon after, the police showed up. One of the reporters must have called. Right away, the Judge had pulled his fancy pen out of his pocket and displayed it to the policemen. "I got everything on tape," he'd said proudly.

Lana had patted his thin shoulders. "Good try, Louis, but it's too little, too late." Then she'd made a point of glaring at Scarlett, one eyebrow raised.

They were all led out through a gauntlet of reporters to a waiting patrol car and taken to the station. There, the officer in charge had asked just what was on the tape. Over Lana's insistence that they call an attorney, the Judge explained. Lana had become apoplectic upon hearing that the Judge had had Taylor fired.

"Now I know how this all got to the press, Goddammit!"

Scarlett had realized that it wouldn't be long before Lana found how she'd told Taylor about the pirogue parade and her exhibition. She watched as they fingerprinted the Judge and led him away. At least he'd be safely behind bars while Lana cooled off. But Scarlett had known that she needed some protection from Lana's ire. She called Inez and had her *marrain* pick her up at the police station.

Now she was beginning to get cabin fever staying in this plush, climate-controlled refuge. She rested her forehead against the mirror and breathed hard through her nostrils, watching the little circles of condensation form, disappear, and reform beneath her nose. She had not seen nor heard from the Bugman since the day outside the barn. Should she call? The thought of picking up the phone filled her both with elation (she could hear his voice again) and dread (what if he didn't want to talk to her?). Her stomach churned with nerves. God, if she couldn't see him again, she didn't know what she had to live for. Not seeing the Bugman was bothering her more than the arrest of the Judge.

"Honey." Inez was standing in the doorway. "I'm about to go out shopping if you want to come along."

"No, I'm going into town. I have something I want to do." She had to see the Bugman again.

The Bugman's business was in a storefront in a plain, 1950s office building in the center of Thibodaux. Somehow Scarlett had expected something different. How could someone so magical exist within this very normal building? But there was his Harley, parked right out in front. She shivered involuntarily. She had to go in now. She was powerless to stop herself.

Her mouth was dry as dust when she turned the knob to the door, and her hands were shaking visibly. Her first realization on seeing the reception area was that it looked just like Lana's—there was fake wood paneling, worn indoor-outdoor carpeting, and insufficient fluorescent lighting. There was the chemical smell that the Bugman always carried with him. Except now, instead of exciting her, it made her a little queasy. Some of his mystery was gone, and she felt a little more in control when she saw him stand up from behind a desk in a small office.

"Hey, Scarlett. How you doing?"

"Okay, I guess."

"Sorry about your grandfather." He looked down at the desk and dropped his voice. "Karma is a bitch. It's just like those roaches that I exterminate. They have it coming."

This last bit was delivered in a philosophic tone of voice, but Scarlett was offended. The Judge was a person, not a roach—no matter how corrupt he'd been. Scarlett shifted uneasily on her feet, trying to find something to say.

"You're not having another infestation?"

"No. I don't think so. Everything seems to be fine."

"So, what brings you by?"

Scarlett looked over at the secretary, a middle-aged woman working on a crossword puzzle. She didn't seem to be listening, but you never knew.

"Um . . . can we close the door?"

"Mi casa es su casa." The Bugman got up from his desk, walked past Scarlett, and shut the door.

"Listen—" Scarlett touched him on the arm, and noticed that he drew back almost imperceptibly. "I was wondering what is going to happen."

"What happens, happens." This, too, was delivered in a voice reserved for deep revelations.

"Between us, I mean." Scarlett's hands began to tremble again, and her voice seemed cracked and dry. "I'm just, you know, curious. I just like to know where I stand," she finished limply.

"We stand where fate places us."

What the hell did that mean? She needed clarification. "I guess I need to know, do you want to see me again?"

"You're a survivor, Scarlett."

"What?"

"A survivor. When I met you, you were lost. Now you are strong. You've triumphed over adversity. You are in a different plane."

"Can you just tell me what you mean in English?" Scarlett felt a bit of a whine creep into her voice.

"Well, it's that I see my place—my personal place—in the cosmos as helping women. Women who are adrift. Our paths somehow cross. It's destiny, I guess. You needed something and we were brought together by fate. What we did was fate. Now you don't need me, and I wouldn't be true to myself or to my place in the universe if I didn't move on. It's not a choice I make. It's made for me."

For a moment, Scarlett stared at him with wide eyes. Then with more conviction than she had felt about anything in a long while, she said softly, "God, you're such an asshole."

"I'm sorry that you feel like that."

"And it's 'on' a plane, not 'in' a plane. You can't be 'in' a plane, it's two-dimensional!"

"You should try to be less tied to the so-called 'laws' of geometry," the Bugman said to her back as she slipped out the door and hurried down the stairs to the Lincoln. But instead of finding herself back at Inez's house, she ended up in the drive in front of Shady Oaks.

From the gallery, there was absolutely no indication of whether or not Lana was inside the house. It was entirely possible, thought Scarlett, that Lana had returned to New Orleans. She turned her key in the lock and swung open the door.

"Why are you here?"

Lana stood before her in the front hall. Her appearance caused Scarlett's heart to jump with fright. Her hair stuck out wildly from her head, and there was a good half inch of gray at the roots. Without any makeup, her skin was blotchy and coarse, her thin lips a pale liver color. She was wearing a rumpled satin nightgown with a variety of coffee stains on the front, and the toenails of her bare feet were long, thick, and yellow.

"I want to come home," said Scarlett, after she had retreated several inches.

Lana gave a soft laugh. "You missed our happy little family."

Scarlett was surprised. Lana sounded more sad than angry.

"Look, Lana, I'm sorry about Taylor. I was wrong to do that."

"Yes, you were. But it probably didn't make a difference. I was just fooling myself. I don't think that there was anything I could do to counteract what your grandfather did."

"I know this is a hard time. . . . Are you getting along okay? Maybe you'd feel better in New Orleans."

"It's quiet here."

Scarlett looked up at the lofty ceilings. "That's true."

Lana absently smoothed her hair with the palm of her hand. "Are you coming back now? I was hoping for some peace and quiet for awhile."

"I'm sorry, but I can't stay with Inez forever." Scarlett found that she wasn't nearly as frightened of Lana as she used to be. Lana seemed different. Softened. "Um . . ." Scarlett waved vaguely at the stairway behind Lana. "Can I get up there to my room?"

"Be my guest." Lana extended her arm toward the stair. "I'm about to go to the prison to see your grandfather. Would you like to join me?"

"Uh, no. I'll just go see him later." Being alone with Lana in the car did not seem like a good idea.

Scarlett wandered upstairs to her room. It seemed unfamiliar, as if someone else lived there. She idled for a while, looking through her drawers and reading old magazines. Finally, she heard Lana leave. She waited until the Buick had backed out of the driveway, then went downstairs and out on the gallery. She climbed into the porch swing and stared up at the ceiling. It was late afternoon, and she was starting to get sleepy, as she always did around this time. The damp air enveloped her, and she closed her eyes. She was in that state halfway between sleep and wakefulness when she heard the phone ring from inside. At first she wasn't going to answer, but maybe it was the Judge. She pulled herself out of the swing, ran inside, and picked up the receiver.

"Miss L'Enfant?" The voice was female, but hard and northern.

"Who is this?" Scarlett asked.

"My name is Veronica Guest, and I'm looking for Miss L'Enfant. It's rather important."

Scarlett sat stock still for a second or two, then curiosity took over. "This is Scarlett."

"Oh, good. Miss L'Enfant, I'm a features editor at *Playboy* magazine. We are interested in doing a project with you."

"This is a really stupid joke."

"I know it's natural to think that I'm playing some kind of prank. I'll give you my number, and you can check it out with the operator and then call me back, collect. Do you have a pencil?"

"No, but I'll remember it."

"Okay. If I haven't heard from you in ten minutes, I'll try you again." The woman read off a number and repeated her name.

Scarlett hung up the phone, and, barely pausing, called directory assistance. The numbers matched. Scarlett could feel her heart pounding, though she was not yet sure why. "Can you connect me?" she asked the operator.

She heard the faint beeps as the call went through.

"*Playboy* magazine. How may I direct your call?"

"Veronica Guest, please. This is Scarlett L'Enfant."

A short pause. Then a receiver was picked up on the other end of the line. "Miss L'Enfant. I'm so glad you called back. We have a very interesting offer to make to you."

Several minutes later, Scarlett stood, unclothed, in front of the mirror in her bedroom. Really, she was not bad. A little thin, and she definitely did not have centerfold cleavage, but they could do all that with lighting and makeup. And $50,000 and a national forum for her art was nothing to sneeze at. "Women of Scandal," the feature was named. Scarlett liked that. It sounded like an old black and white movie. Maybe not Audrey Hepburn, but definitely Bette Davis or Joan Crawford.

She went downstairs, found the Yellow Pages, and placed a call.

"I need a one-way ticket from Baton Rouge to Tangier. First class."

Fifty thousand dallars would go a long way in Morocco.

The Judge watched through the glass as Lana seated herself in the chair across from him. She picked up the black telephone in her cubicle, and the Judge did the same.

"How are you doing, Louis?"

"I'm fine, darling." It was true. Prison hadn't been as bad as he had feared it would be; although the other prisoners had shaken him down upon arrival, they'd moved on when they found no cigarettes or drugs. Since he no longer had access to Valium, his head had cleared. And so far, no one seemed interested in making him their bitch.

"How are you? Have you changed your mind about going back to your practice?"

"No, I'm staying at Shady Oaks for now. I don't want to go back yet."

On her last visit, Lana had told him that she didn't want to face what she knew waited for her in New Orleans: When she walked down the streets of the CBD, she'd be able to see her peers nudge each other and whisper. When she went to Galatoire's for lunch, the heads of the three-martini-lunch attorneys would swivel to observe her. In court, the judges, the bailiffs—even the juries—would know of her humiliation. Lana told him that, although she had never cared what people thought before, she'd never been *defeated* before. The Judge felt terrible for her.

On the other hand, the campaign debacle seemed to have given honesty and closeness to their relationship. Lana had even confessed to him that she'd married him for his connections. "That's why I'm not mad at you," she'd told him. "I got what I deserved." The Judge was very sad that she didn't love him, but his disappointment was somewhat mitigated by their nascent friendship.

The L'Enfant article had gotten Hultgrew a raise and job feelers from several well-respected newspapers. He should have been basking in the attention, but instead he was depressed. After the article came out, Tiffany refused to see him. He wondered if the article had been worth it. He missed Tiffany. A lot.

When the phone rang, he picked it up on the first ring, hoping to hear her voice. Instead it was the zit-faced archivist from the morgue.

"I got something for you."

"What do you mean?" Hultgrew asked. He'd forgotten about leaving the research request on the kid's desk.

"On Taylor. That politician."

"Oh. Just send it up in an interoffice envelope."

"You might want to come down and check it out now. It's pretty interesting."

For God's sake. "All right," said Hultgrew. "I'll be down in a minute."

The kid was waiting for him in front of the elevator doors. Wordlessly, he handed Taylor a photocopied article and photograph.

"Holy shit."

"Not bad, eh?"

"How come no one has found this before?"

291

"It was only printed in the *Star*, and it's over twenty-five years old. No one looks back through this paper's archives. Even if they did, they probably wouldn't have found it. You didn't. It's like I told you. I'm a professional."

Hultgrew was pretty sure that Tiffany would see him now.

forty-one

To the disappointment of Flo (and a number of local reporters, who had found in Lana a fertile source of material), Lana continued to show no inclination to return to her legal practice. She had Carl empty out the Offices and put them up for rent. She remained at Shady Oaks, visiting the Judge every week, but seeing no one else. Eventually, she even unplugged Shady Oaks' phones. The peace and quiet had become addictive.

Today, she was lolling in bed, well past noon. There were no visiting hours at the jail today, no real reason to get up, except to eat. Lana was debating whether she was hungry enough yet to drag herself downstairs when the doorbell rang. Ordinarily, she wouldn't have bothered answering, but then she heard a familiar voice waft in the window from the gallery. She pulled herself out from under the sheet, put on a robe, and went downstairs to the front door.

Flo and Tommy were standing outside.

" Ya' haven't been answering the phone, baby."

"I unplugged them."

"We were worried about you."

"Nothing to worry about. I'm just not feeling social lately." She was glad to see Flo and Tommy, though. The only human contact that she'd had for a couple of months was during her jailhouse visits to the Judge.

"Come on in," Lana said, motioning them through the door. They all stood awkwardly in the hall. Finally Tommy spoke.

"Would you mind gettin' me a beer, Lana? It was a long ride."

"I'll see if we have any."

"Me, too, babe," said Flo.

When Lana returned, Tommy and Flo were seated on the loveseat. Flo had a magazine and a large manila envelope in her lap. Lana handed them each a bottle of Abita.

"So what brings you out to the parishes?" she asked them.

"A couple of things. Thought you might find this interesting." Flo handed Lana the magazine.

"Playboy?"

"Take a look inside."

Lana began flipping through the pages, marveling at the wonders of depilation. Then she came to the monthly feature in the center of the magazine.

"Oh my God," she whispered.

There was Scarlett, hair teased wildly, with a large paintbrush held modestly (or provocatively, depending on your point of view, Lana supposed) in front of her crotch. In the background were several of her paintings, and on the facing page a short article. Lana turned the page. Here was Scarlett, ostensibly working on a canvas, paint smeared strategically across her body.

"She doesn't look half bad," Lana mused. Who would have thought that Scarlett would have the guts for something like this? Begrudgingly, Lana allowed herself to feel a little more respect for the girl. Couldn't buy that kind of publicity. It was an easy bet that the value of those crappy paintings had doubled. The girl must have found a good P.R. person.

"Thanks," Lana told them. "But this can't be the only reason you came all the way out here."

"Actually, we have some good news for you. We tried to call you, but . . ." Flo shrugged.

"What kind of good news? I don't want any new clients, Flo. I don't feel like taking on any cases right now."

"No, no, it's nothing like that. Remember when you asked us if we knew anything about Bobby Taylor, and we said we hadn't seen him by our place?"

"Yeah."

"Maybe that was because he was busy with other activities." Flo's tone was sarcastic. She handed the envelope to Lana. "Bolton Hultgrew gave this to one of our girls."

Lana opened the envelope, took out the photo, and examined it. It took her a minute to realize what she was looking at. When she did, she didn't know whether to be pleased or horrified.

Although the young man in the photo looked different, he was still recognizable as Bobby Taylor. Lana had always thought there was something a little strange about Taylor's visage, and now she realized that he'd had plastic surgery. His nose had been refined, his cheekbones augmented. In the photo that she held, Taylor's smug, pre-surgical face was visible only because he'd removed his pointy white hood. A cross burned in the background behind him.

Lana decided. She was horrified.

Leaving Flo and Tommy in the sitting room, she got up, went to the kitchen, and plugged in the telephone. She dialed Tippy's number. The publicist didn't even have a chance to say hello before Lana started talking. "Call Souchecki. We're back in business."